THE

HARMONY

PROJECT

I0588701

RANDY V. DANIELS

MENASCUS BOOKS

Cover design by Miblart exclusively for
Menascus Books, Simi Valley, California

Library of Congress, Reg. #
Cataloging-in Publishing Data, ISBN # 978-0-9855252-2-4

Printed in the United States of America

ISBN-10:
EAN-13: 9780985525224

Library of Congress Control Number:

The Harmony Project was previously published as "Shifter: The Legend of Harmony June," 2012

For Dré, De, and Ana,
My Pride and Joy! You inspire me to pursue my dreams!

For Deb,
My Rock! For keeping me on track through it all!

Acknowledgments

The process of writing this novel wasn't finished simply because I reached the end of the story. The task of editing and rewriting began and I couldn't have tackled, much less completed, such an undertaking without the help of those mentioned below. With great appreciation, I thank each of you.

To my parents, Robert and Sadie- for the many years of love and support. You've never given up on me. I love you both very much.

To Gary Tolin- for reading anything and everything I put in front of you. Thank you for all the time, energy and faith that you have given selflessly. I love ya, GT. You're a wonderful friend, father figure and a great man.

To Jim Cole- for the encouragement, honest feedback and your desire to see me succeed.

To Leyvan M. Jones- for all the years of friendship. We've come quite a ways since the days on S. Portland Ave. Thanks for hanging in there and keeping it real with a brotha. This journey isn't over yet. One!

To Jessica Wardell- for reassuring me that I had something worth reading. Now if we could just get off the damn gates.

To Amy Slade- no one picks apart a story like you do. Your contribution to this project was invaluable.

To Donna Palmer-Crowley- for connecting me with Sherma.

To Deb - again, for being my rock through every storm! For putting up with the countless hours in which I would disappear into the office and sit in front of my computer, writing. You have more patience than I gave you credit for! For your love and support, and for keeping our family healthy and strong. I love you.

No man thoroughly understands a truth until he has contended against it.

– Ralph Waldo Emerson

1

20 years ago.
Los Angeles, California

The hardwood floor in the dining room, freshly cleaned and shimmering in the moonlight that crept through the window, creaked slightly. The blood began to pour out in all directions and blanket the shiny oak finish. Dr. Marcus June stood there. He watched as the crimson red liquid drained from the body onto the floor. Strange. He knew that things might come to this. He knew that, no matter what, he needed to be prepared. Yet, the initial thought that entered his mind was, 'That's going to leave a nasty stain.'

A shriek of fear snapped Marcus out of his trance. He turned to the doorway. Serena, his wife, stood there with her hand over her mouth.

"I told you to get out of here," he yelled at her.

"I couldn't leave you," she managed. Her eyes were transfixed by all of the blood.

"Serena. You have to go."

She took a step into the room. Marcus moved towards her, all the while remaining focused on the body that lay on the floor.

"Serena!" He shook her lightly. Her gaze snapped in his direction. Marcus looked into her eyes. "Where's Christopher?"

Reality took hold of her. "He's in the car. I couldn't just leave you."

"You left him alone? Nothing is more important than Christopher. You know that—"

"Of course I know that," she interrupted. "But I was so scared. I didn't know what to do."

A soft rustling noise emanated from the kitchen. Serena froze. "What was that?"

"The other one. I must not have killed him." Marcus turned to her. "We've got to go. Now!"

"What about that?" Serena motioned to the corner of the room. There, a 9mm rested.

Without uttering a sound, Marcus retrieved the weapon. He shoved it in his jacket pocket and ushered his wife out of the room. "Babe, go. I'll be right behind you."

"What are you doing? You have to come."

"I will," he reassured her. "There's one more thing I have to do."

"Marcus."

"Go!" He pushed her towards the front door. He turned and disappeared into the dining room.

஧

Serena June approached the car. She opened the driver's side door and slid in behind the wheel. She turned and looked towards the backseat. Christopher, snug in his child car seat, had fallen back to sleep. 'Good,' she thought. 'He doesn't need to see any of this.' She checked the ignition. The keys were still there.

Seconds passed. Soon, Marcus exited their home and raced towards the car. His dark, brown skin glistened with sweat. His white shirt was stained with blood. Serena could see something clutched tightly in his grasp. As he got closer, Serena saw that it was a large manila envelope. She started the car. The door opened, and Marcus got in.

"Drive."

Within moments, the grey sedan was cruising down Ventura Boulevard at a breakneck speed.

"Slow down," Marcus barked. "The last thing we need is a cop pulling us over."

Serena gestured to the envelope. "Is that what I think it is?"

"No," he answered. "But right now, it's just as important. Serena, please slow down."

Serena applied the brake and slowed the vehicle to a legally compliant, eastbound velocity. She glanced in her rearview mirror quickly. Christopher's sleeping face filled the frame. Serena allowed herself to smile. She looked at Marcus. She could see his wheels turning. Under normal circumstances, his pensive demeanor would calm her. Marcus had a knack for knowing what to do about everything. Unfortunately, this circumstance was anything but normal. She took a deep breath in an effort to quell her anxiety. She placed a hand on his shoulder. "Where are we going?" she asked softly.

Marcus turned to her. Their eyes met. "James. We have to go see James."

જ઼ન

Dr. James Connelly stood under the bleachers behind Taft High School. He was a tall, slender Caucasian with thick, brown hair. A pair of Ralph Lauren eyeglasses adorned his face. His fashion sense was impeccable. James took great steps in making sure his appearance was unblemished. His good looks and attire would lead one to believe that he was a fashion model or an A-list celebrity. An initial scrutiny of James would, in no way, reveal that he was a brilliant geneticist, one who was partially responsible for what could be the biggest medical breakthrough in human history.

James ran his hand through his hair. He stared across the football field, watching a figure approach him. James shook his head. "Eager beaver," he muttered to himself. A moment later, James stood face to face with Jeremy Platt.

Platt was a plain-faced, guy-next-door type of man. His looks were neither disgusting nor spectacular. His thin, white lips and pointy nose made him, in some ways, look a tad bit feminine. However, that image was instantly shattered every time he opened his mouth and his deep, robust voice came booming out. Platt was a reporter for a local newspaper. His reputation for digging up the nasty truth on just about anybody and everybody was legitimately earned. Nothing made Jeremy Platt happier than uncovering an anti-gay senator's homosexual love triangle, interviewing a mass murderer, or exposing a CEO's decade-long embezzlement. It wasn't that Platt was an evil man. He wasn't. He was just good at his job. The only thing that eluded Platt was a platform big enough upon which he could air everyone's dirty laundry. Oh sure, it was nice to get an occasional guest spot on the local nightly news, but Platt wanted his own syndicated program. He wanted the type of exposure that made Geraldo Rivera a household name. Tonight, Platt was hoping that his dream was about to come true.

"You do realize it's two-thirty in the morning?" Platt asked.

"I thought the news never slept," James responded smugly.

"Is that what you have? Something newsworthy?"

"You tell *me*." James pulled out a small envelope and handed it to Platt. Platt opened it and removed several documents and a key. He took a small step to his right into a stream of light from the overhead streetlamp. He read the documents slowly, carefully. Then, he looked up at James.

"Is this for real?"

"I wouldn't be here if it wasn't," James replied.

"This is . . . no way. I don't believe it," Platt said.

"I don't really care if you believe it, Jeremy. The important thing here is that you're the only person I can trust with it in the event that . . ." James trailed off.

"In the event that what?" Platt looked at James more closely. He hadn't realized it when he walked up, but now he could see it clearly. James was afraid. "Dr. Connelly, what's going on?"

"It's all there, Jeremy. These documents explain it all." James looked around the field nervously.

Platt took a step closer. The volume of his voice was lower. "Why are you giving this to me?"

"I thought this type of thing was right up your alley," James answered.

"This type of thing can get me killed."

"True."

The weight of James' response pressed into Platt's chest. He stepped back and began to pace apprehensively.

James continued. "You know what I'm asking you to do."

"What?" Platt asked, distracted.

"With the documents, Jeremy. You *do* know what I'm asking?"

"You're asking me to go public with this crap in case something happens to you."

"And not a moment before," James continued. "Promise me that."

"I don't know, Doc. This. . . this is the type of thing that should be out in public. People should know about this. But there's a reason why it's been kept a secret, isn't there?"

James nodded.

Platt tilted his head as a thought occurred to him. "They're on to you, aren't they?"

"It won't be long before they come for me."

"And your colleague, the black guy?"

"Dr. June. He's in danger as well."

Platt held up the documents. "And this?"

"Leverage."

"What if I say no?"

James smiled. "You won't." James took a step towards Platt. Platt stood fast as James leaned in closer. "You've always wanted to do the right thing, Jeremy. Even if it means digging up the dirt, you like it when dishonest people get what's coming to them. I know it. You know it."

Platt remained silent. James was right.

"What if nothing happens to you?"

"Then you can hold on to it until something does," James replied morbidly.

Platt looked at the documents again. He opened his left hand that held the key.

"That key unlocks a safe that holds all the evidence," James explained. "Don't lose it."

James' cell phone began to ring quietly. He reached into his trouser pocket and pulled it out.

"I hope you know what you're doing," Platt said.

James looked at the phone screen: CALL FROM MARCUS. James glanced at Platt with a grave look in his eyes. "So do I."

With that, James turned and walked away. He answered his cell phone. Platt could only discern two things from what little he heard James say. One, the call was from Dr. Marcus June. Two, the shit had hit the fan.

෨෦ඁ

"What the hell happened?" Marcus demanded to know as soon as James exited his car at Fryman.

"I don't know," James responded. "One minute I'm asleep in my bed, the next minute I'm getting a call from Amanda."

"Dr. Simons? What did she say?"

"Only that our research was being confiscated at that very moment."

"Where is she now?" Marcus asked.

"I don't know that either, Marcus," James answered sharply. "Her phone goes straight to voice-mail now."

Marcus bit his bottom lip. "She's dead."

"You don't know that," James countered dismissively.

"They came to my house, James."

"What?"

"Two men."

"Who? What men?"

"From the Agency, James. They came to my house."

Reflexively, James put a hand to his own neck.

Marcus took a deep breath. "I killed one of them."

James' eyes widened. "What?"

"What was I supposed to do? They came to kill my family. I had to protect them."

"I understand," James said.

"No, James. I don't think you do." Marcus slapped the hood of his grey sedan. Inside, Serena jumped in fear. "When I saw those men, their guns. . . it stopped being about the Harmony Project and the work. . . it was all about protecting my family."

James placed his hands on Marcus' shoulders. "Marcus, I have a son, too. I understand."

"We have to get out of here, James. You, me, Serena, Christopher . . . all of us."

"You're right," James muttered softly. "Of course, you're right."

"What did you do with the key?" Marcus asked.

"I did what we said we would do."

"My family is at stake here," Marcus said earnestly. "Can we trust him?"

"I think we can. Yes."

Marcus knew he had no choice but to believe in his longtime friend and colleague. He nodded his head. Then, his attention was drawn to the entrance of Fryman Canyon as a dark-colored car with its headlights turned off pulled into the lot.

James followed Marcus' gaze. His jaw tightened. Marcus spoke first. "It's him."

"Who?" Fear leapt into James's chest.

"I only killed one. The other must've followed me." Marcus turned towards the car. "Serena, start the car."

The door to the dark vehicle opened. A man holding a gun emerged from the driver's seat. There was a deep gash across his left eyebrow. It was still bleeding.

Marcus pulled the 9mm from his pocket. "Serena. Get out of here." Marcus fired the weapon at the figure. The front windshield of the shadowed vehicle shattered.

The figure pointed his gun at Marcus and fired.

The bullet slammed into Marcus's chest. Blood splattered as the projectile made an exit wound in his back. Marcus stood for a brief moment before falling backwards in the dirt.

Serena began screaming hysterically in the car. The baby, Christopher, began crying in response to his mother's wailing.

James turned and ran for Marcus' car. He dove over the hood as the dark figure fired a shot at him. James landed on the other side of the car next to Marcus. Though it was dark, James could see the whites of Marcus' lifeless eyes.

James could hear Serena screaming inside the vehicle. There was another gunshot, followed almost simultaneously by the sound of breaking glass. Serena's voice was silent. Only the cries of baby Christopher could be heard.

James grabbed the 9mm that lay next to Marcus. He swallowed hard. He stood and fired a shot at the approaching assailant. Blood spurted from the man's right shoulder. The man stumbled back and fell.

James opened the back door to the car. A manila envelope rested on the floor. Christopher, still strapped into his
car seat, was crying uncontrollably. James glanced towards
the front seat quickly. He couldn't see Serena for she was
slumped over. James didn't need to see her body. The splat-
ter of blood and gray matter on the passenger-side window
told the tale.

James unstrapped the child and pulled him from the
car. As he turned, the man whom he'd just shot stood before him. His gun was pointed at James.

"Wait!" James yelled. "You're about to make a big
mistake."

"Wouldn't be my first," the man responded in a raspy
voice.

"Trust me," James said, "if something happens to me,
there will be irreparable damage."

The man didn't flinch. "I was told you might say something like that."

The child in James' arms began to cry louder. James
began to rock him instinctively. "Listen to me," he pleaded
with the man. "Let me talk to him. Call him."

"I don't need to," the man said as he leveled his gun at
James.

"I've put all the evidence somewhere safe. If I am
harmed, the evidence will be sent to the proper authorities."

"Dr. Connelly," The man began as he steadied the
weapon, "who said anything about harming *you*?"

The man's eyes shifted and focused on Christopher.

James' body stiffened. "No. You couldn't possibly. . ."

The man closed his eyes, and then pulled the trigger.

2

Present Day.
Bronx, New York

The clock was taking its time reaching 2:55. Kelli had already looked at the clock seven times in the past two minutes. The preceding thirty seconds seemed like it was taking thirty years to pass. Another normal day in the life of a high school senior, only normal would be an understatement when it came to Kelli Freeman.

Kelli was a fourteen-year-old senior. She was a young, African-American beauty with a promising future ahead of her. It had been five years since her intelligence quotient was rated 'off the chart.' Kelli excelled in every academic medium in which she was placed. Her ability to learn and grasp concepts was unmatched by any of her peers. By the age of ten, Kelli found herself in Advanced Placement. The AP Curriculum turned out to be too slow for Kelli. Within six months, she was placed in a GATE program, but the Gifted and Talented Education program only served to bore Kelli further.

By age eleven, Kelli had been accelerated into her freshman year at the high school level. This, too, failed to compete with Kelli's growing intellectual abilities. It was suggested to her parents that she begin college level courses right away, but Kelli pleaded with her parents to let her remain in high school. In the past, because of her academic advancement, Kelli had to leave many of her friends behind. This was harder on Kelli than anything else. Fortunately, her intellectual gifts were paralleled in the physical arena, as well. Kelli excelled in track and field, basketball, softball, gymnastics and martial arts. Due to all of these extra curricular activities, Kelli had begun to make new friends. Good friends. She didn't want to give them up. Not yet. Though she was thankful for her gifts, Kelli wanted nothing more than to be a normal girl.

Mrs. Randall, the Philosophy teacher, stood at the front of the classroom. She had asked a question and several hands went up into the air in response. Mrs. Randall scanned the room. Her eyes landed on Kelli who, at the moment, seemed completely oblivious.

"Kelli?" Mrs. Randall called her name.

Kelli's attention snapped from the clock to the front of the room. "Yes?"

"Do you know the answer?"

Kelli sighed heavily, more out of boredom than anything else. "Descartes," Kelli responded. "His most famous quote is 'Cogito ergo sum', which means 'I think, therefore I am'."

"Very good," Mrs. Randall said. "Anything else?"

Kelli shrugged. "He's dead." Quiet chuckles were heard around the room.

Mrs. Randall opened her mouth to reply but was interrupted by the bell. "I guess that's all for today. Don't forget your essays are due Friday."

The students gathered their books and began pouring into the bustling hallway. Kelli slung her backpack over her left shoulder and headed for the door. Mrs. Randall sat at her desk. "Miss Freeman," Mrs. Randall said aloud.

Kelli slowed her pace. She stopped in front of the desk and turned to face Mrs. Randall. Before the teacher could utter a sound, Kelli began, "I'm sorry, Mrs. Randall. I wasn't trying to be a smart alec."

Mrs. Randall smiled. "Kelli, I understand that, given your academic accomplishments and progress, this class may be a little slow for you. But you're still being graded on participation."

"I know. I'll try to pay more attention."

"Thank you," the teacher said, and then continued, "you know, it's only going to be a few months before you graduate and head off to college. Hopefully, the college curriculum will be a little more challenging for you."

Kelli's reply was simple and modest. "Yeah." Kelli smiled. "See ya tomorrow, Mrs. Randall." With that, Kelli was out the door.

She made a bee-line for the girls' locker room. Track and Field practice was starting soon, and she didn't want to be late. Punctuality was a trait she picked up from her mother. As far back as she could remember, her mother always said, "If you're on time, there's no danger of missing anything important." Kelli shook her head to herself. She was dying to find a hole in her mother's theory so she'd have an excuse for not living up to that standard. So far, she hadn't found one.

Kelli entered the locker room. She hustled to her locker and applied the combination. It wasn't long before she was dressed and ready to go. She headed towards the door when Jaleesa Crosby, a seventeen-year-old senior and fellow track mate, came racing in.

"Oh crap," Jaleesa exclaimed as she spied Kelli in her gym clothes. "Am I late?"

"Not yet," Kelli assured her, "but you're cutting it close."

Kelli sighed and followed Jaleesa back into the locker room. Jalessa was the first person in high school who befriended Kelli when she arrived three years prior. Kelli wasn't sure if it was because Jaleesa liked her as a friend, or because Jaleesa, at the time, was dating Kelli's older brother, Martin. Martin was eighteen and had just graduated the year before. When he left for college, Jaleesa and Martin's relationship was over. At first, with Martin gone, Kelli was surprised that Jaleesa remained her friend, but Jaleesa felt that Kelli was the little sister she never had and had grown very fond of her. "Not to mention," Jaleesa added, "having a genius for a friend doesn't hurt, girl."

Jaleesa changed clothes quickly. "Guess who's out there today?"

A large grin formed on Kelli's face. "Darius." Darius Jones was a seventeen- year-old senior who, despite their age difference, had a crush on Kelli. Kelli liked him, too, but she knew her parents would never approve.

"Yep," Jaleesa confirmed, "and he's already asking about you."

Kelli slapped Jaleesa on the shoulder. "Why do you keep telling me these things when you're only going to tell me he's too old for me?"

"He *is* too old for you," Jaleesa laughed, "but I thought you'd like to know."

"Don't do me any favors. Okay?"

Jaleesa finished dressing. She placed her hands on her hips and struck a pose. "How do I look?"

"Like Halle Berry," Kelli answered. It was true.

"That's why I love you," Jaleesa joked. "You ready to kick some ass?"

Kelli gestured towards the door. "Lead the way."

འ·ལ

Kelli and Jaleesa sprinted out towards the track. Kelli's eyes darted in every direction in search of Darius. 'Where did he disappear to?' she wondered.

" 'Sup, Shorty?" a young, male voice said from behind her.

Kelli's heart jumped. She turned in anticipation, only to find Bryan Ling standing in front of her. Her heart sank.

Bryan Ling, or "Bling" as he liked to be called, was a fifteen-year-old sophomore. He was a Chinese-African-American who happened to live in Kelli's neighborhood. Bling lived with his mother. His father had been absent from his life for more than ten years. Bling was a bright kid. Unfortunately, he fell in with a local street gang called The East 222's, aka The Triple Deuces, and had more than a few run-ins with New York's Finest. After his latest thirty-day lockup at the Horizon Juvenile Center, Bling was back in school, attempting to straighten up his life. Few people, it seemed, were willing to cut him a break. Bling sported a pair of baggy jeans that hung slightly off of his waist, a black T-shirt with a colorful print of Bob Marley on the front, and a black hooded sweat jacket. A pair of earphones was plugged into his ears.

Jaleesa stepped in front of Kelli. "Her name is not Shorty, Bryan."

Bling shrugged off Jaleesa's comment. Everyone knew he preferred his 'street name'. "Whateva." He looked past Jaleesa at Kelli. "Can I talk to you?"

"What about?"

"Mr. Huntley said you was gonna help me out in English." Mr. Huntley was their English teacher. He was sympathetic to Bling's situation.

"You missed our tutoring session," Kelli said, frustrated. "It was yesterday."

"I know, I know," Bling said. He shifted his weight from his right leg to his left. He was unaccustomed to asking for help. "Somethin' came up."

"Well, now track practice has come up," Jaleesa countered, answering for Kelli.

Bling ignored Jaleesa. "Come on, girl. How am I gonna catch up if—"

"I don't know," Kelli interrupted. "We have to go." Kelli turned and jogged away. Jaleesa shook her head disapprovingly at Bling before turning and following Kelli towards the field.

Bling kicked the dirt. He reached into his jacket pocket and pressed the button on his iPod. Music blasted in his ears. He began reciting Hip-Hop rhymes as he stormed off in the other direction.

∂∞∂

Track practice went by quickly. Kelli's team had fallen behind in the four-by-four relay, but Kelli, running the anchor leg, closed the gap and sailed in for an easy win. The coach was more than pleased. "I swear I've never seen a girl run so fast," he said happily. He was very optimistic about the upcoming meet this weekend.

Shortly after, Kelli and Jaleesa headed for the parking lot. Jaleesa had her driver's license and gave Kelli rides home after every practice. Kelli scanned the lot for Darius' red convertible. It was nowhere in sight.

Twenty-five minutes later, Kelli was walking into her house and Jaleesa was sounding her car horn as she sped away. Kelli entered the kitchen to find her mother, Diane, making dinner.

Diane Freeman was a beautiful woman. At forty-one years old, she had very little need for make-up and chose to use it sparingly to highlight a cheekbone or hide the small laugh lines that were forming around her mouth. Her skin was a deep chocolate brown. Her figure, though not as fit as it was before giving birth to four children, was still full and curvaceous. Diane was the principal at Middle School 101. She was a stern yet respected leader in the academic community. She fought hard to ensure that the students at her school received whatever supplies they needed in order to thrive. Diane loved her job.

Being a school principal, she made certain that each of her children maintained a strong work ethic when it came to their studies. So far, Diane felt she was doing a fairly decent job. Martin, the oldest, was in his first year at Howard University in Washington, D.C. Cassius, her eleven-year-old son, was a sixth grader at Middle School 101. Although Cassius hadn't said as much, Diane was sure having his mother as the principal added extra pressure on him to succeed. Wilma, the five-year-old, was completing her first year in kindergarten. And then, of course, there was Kelli, her fourteen-year-old genius. With the struggles of governing 583 students on a daily basis, it was comforting to know, when it came to academics, Kelli could take care of herself.

"Hey, Ma," Kelli said as she leaned in and kissed her mother on the cheek.

"Hey, Baby," Diane answered in a tired tone. "How was practice?"

"It was great," Kelli said with a smile. "We're gonna kick their butts."

"We're *going* to kick their butts," Diane corrected. "And I'm glad to hear it. You have a lot of homework?"

"Just calculus," Kelli answered. "It's easy."

"Well, go get it out of the way," Diane ordered. "Dinner will be ready soon."

"Okay," Kelli agreed.

"Oh, Francine called a little while ago," Diane yelled as Kelli disappeared from the kitchen. "I told her you'd call her back."

"Thanks, Ma."

Francine Rodriguez was Kelli's best friend. She and Kelli were the same age, but Francine, being a child of normal intellect, was in the eighth grade. She, too, attended Middle School 101. Kelli, because of her rapid acceleration, never did.

Kelli passed through the living room. Her father, Arthur, was sitting in front of the television watching the Yankees take on the Twins. Kelli knew better than to interrupt her father while the Yankees were on so she crept up and gave him a quick kiss on the cheek. "Hey, Daddy."

"Hey, Baby-girl," he said, barely taking his eyes off the screen.

"Who's winning?"

"Twins are up by three in the bottom of the ninth," he said as he stood suddenly in response to the umpire's call. He stomped his foot and yelled at the tube. "What the hell? That was a ball. Are you blind?"

Kelli rolled her eyes. There were two things in the world that Arthur Freeman loved more than anything else. Baseball and being a cop. Arthur had been a member of the NYPD for twenty-two years. He was set to retire in three. His plan was to travel, kick back, and watch baseball for the rest of his days. Kelli knew Ma would definitely have something to say about that.

Kelli turned and scaled the stairs two steps at a time. As she walked past Cassius' room, she could hear him in there playing with Wilma. Cassius loved having a little sister. When he wasn't outside playing with his friends, he was with Wilma. She decided not to disturb them.

Kelli made it to her bedroom. She closed the door, tossed her backpack on the bed and picked up the phone. She dialed Francine's number and, within minutes, she was lying supine on her bed, deeply engaged in conversation.

It wasn't long before Kelli was changing clothes once again and heading out the door to meet Francine. As Kelli passed through the kitchen, she noticed that Cassius and Wilma were playing on the floor. Diane had finished dinner and Arthur was setting the table.

"Where do you think you're going?" Diane asked sternly.

"Francine and I were going to hang out for a bit before dinner," Kelli answered.

"Dinner's ready. You can hang out with Francine after."

"But, Ma," Kelli began to protest.

"But nothing," Arthur intervened. "You heard your mother."

Kelli sighed heavily. She knew there was no point in arguing. The family had dinner together every night, and that wasn't going to change because she wanted to hang out with her friend.

Arthur set down the final place setting. Diane put the food on the table, and everyone sat down. Arthur closed his eyes; everyone at the table did the same. As he did every night at dinner, Arthur said a prayer.

"Dear Lord, thank you for this food with which you have blessed us today. Thank you for keeping us safe throughout our travels so we may come together at this table once again. Amen."

Everyone repeated in unison, "Amen."

Wilma looked at her plate and grimaced. "What's that?"

"Those are sweet potatoes," her mother explained. "Eat them. They're good."

"I don't like sweet potatoes," Wilma announced.

"You'll like them today," Arthur chimed in. "Mommy made them special."

Diane smiled as the phone began to ring. She excused herself from the table as everyone began to dig in. Cassius made a tunnel in the center of his sweet potatoes and dragged his green beans through it before shoving them into his mouth. A moment passed before Diane returned to the table.

"That was Dr. Fallon," she said before glancing over at Kelli. Dr. Fallon was Diane and Kelli's gynecologist. Diane had taken Kelli to see him because a certain life-changing, pubescent event had yet to happen for Kelli.

"Is everything okay?" Arthur asked.

Diane had Kelli's undivided attention. "That's exactly what he called to tell me," Diane said. She placed a hand on Kelli's and squeezed lightly. "He said the tests came back normal. He saw nothing to suggest that anything is wrong."

"How can that be?" Kelli asked. "I'm fourteen. Every other girl my age has gotten it already. Why haven't I?"

"I don't know, Baby. It happens at different times for different girls." Her mother tried to reassure her, but she wasn't sure if Kelli felt any better. "Don't worry. It'll happen."

"What's the rush?" Arthur asked aloud.

"Arthur!" Diane said as her glare transmitted silent disapproval.

"I'm just asking." Arthur shrugged. He winked at Kelli. He knew that this was bothering Kelli, but he wanted her to look at it from the perspective of, 'if it ain't broke, don't fix it'. "Sorry, Baby."

Kelli nodded. She proceeded to stuff her face and respond to her disappointment with food. She knew her father didn't really understand. How could he? Kelli's whole life had been pretty smooth because of her brains. At times, being extra smart made her feel different, as if she didn't really belong. It didn't help that the one event in her life that was supposed to happen naturally and make her feel normal, wasn't happening at all.

෧ඁ෧

Special Agent Donald West remembered the physical abilities testing he had to undergo when he was pursuing a position with the FBI. Since then, there weren't many instances where he had to run at a full sprint and, frankly, he wasn't sure he was up to it.

Unfortunately, he didn't have a choice. He was in pursuit of an armed and dangerous subject, and he was the only one who could catch him.

West and his partner, Special Agent James Towers, after a temporary transfer to the Tri-State area, had been investigating a series of murders that took place in New Jersey, New York, and Connecticut. The murders seemed to be unrelated until recently when new evidence tied them all together. Towers and West followed the trail of evidence to a small brownstone in downtown Brooklyn owned by Keith Waters. Waters owned a small check cashing business in lower Manhattan. He charged a nominal check-cashing fee and came in contact with commuters from the Tri-State area on a daily basis. When it came to light that every victim had cashed their checks through Waters' business, he was placed under surveillance until enough evidence had accumulated to warrant bringing him down. West, having been with the bureau for three years, asked the veteran, Towers, if they should wait for backup. Towers replied confidently, "No. This should be no problem." This was against bureau policy, but West had learned to trust Towers' judgment. When Towers and West approached Waters' home on South Portland Avenue, he was waiting for them.

The front door to his basement-level apartment was opened. As soon as they entered, Waters began firing a weapon. Towers took a blast to the left shoulder and one to the right thigh. West returned fire but hit nothing except stucco. Waters fled through a rear entrance, leaving West with his bleeding partner. Towers insisted that he was okay and ordered West to "catch the son-of-a-bitch". West bolted out of the apartment and the pursuit began.

As he rounded the corner at DeKalb Avenue, West could see Waters up ahead. Waters was heading for the DeKalb subway substation at the end of the block. If Waters made it into the station, things were going to get worse before they got better. Once inside, Waters could escape on a departing train or, heaven forbid, take a hostage. West had a few blocks to gain on Waters and knew he had to close the gap. For three years, West had worked in awe of Agent Towers. Towers was always the first to figure out the case, the first to tackle the 'perp' and the first to go in shooting. West, the sidekick, admired him but wanted the day to come when *he* was the golden boy. Today was that day.

West pushed a little harder and picked up the pace. He could see ahead of him in the distance that Waters was causing a stir among the pedestrians. 'Of course he is,' West thought to himself. 'He's running down the street waving a gun.' People began to cower in fear and take cover as Waters ran by them. Some of them stepped into the street to avoid the crazed gunman.

"No. Not in the street," West yelled aloud. The last thing he needed was some pedestrian getting plowed over by a car. That would make this whole situation go from bad to worse in a hurry.

West cursed to himself as Waters reached Flatbush Avenue. He turned a slight corner and disappeared down the stairs into the DeKalb Avenue train station. It would be another few seconds before West would reach the corner as well. He hoped there wasn't a train arriving or Waters just might get away.

The shocked pedestrians were still reeling from Waters' sudden burst onto the scene. They began to collect themselves, only to be startled again as West came rushing by. "Federal Agent," he yelled. "Get out of the way." The crowd parted once more. West turned the corner at Flatbush and hit the top of the stairs. He skipped several steps on the first small flight and only touched two on the second. The hysterical screams alerted West to the fact that Waters was still on the platform. West still had a chance to catch him.

West waved his badge in the air as he jumped over the turnstile. Another scream drew his attention. He turned to his left with his gun drawn. There stood Keith Waters.

Waters was sweating profusely. He had a female hostage and was using her as a shield. The woman was slightly heavy-set and was spewing out a terrified rant in Spanish. West took a step towards them.

"Don't come any closer," Waters ordered. "I'll do her right here. You know I will."

Based on their investigation, West knew that Waters was very capable of carrying out his threat. Still, the young agent had no intention of letting another person fall victim to the psychopath who stood before him. "Waters! You have nowhere to run. Drop your weapon and let her go."

"How about I just wait for the D train? I'll let her go at the next stop."

West could tell Waters was desperate. Waters knew full well that Agent West had no intention of letting him board a train with more, potential hostages. No. The line was drawn.

"Waters," West began. "I don't want to shoot you—"

"Whatever, Dude," Waters said and spat in his direction. "Take your best shot."

West tried to reason with him one last time. "Waters. Listen to me."

Waters began backing away, dragging his screaming hostage with him. "No way. If you're gonna shoot, then shoot if you think you're that good."

West heard the roar of the oncoming train. He knew it was time to make a move. He thought about Waters' last taunt. '*Am* I that good?' He questioned himself. The train drew closer. West had only seconds in which to figure it out. He saw the light from the front of the train rounding the corner. Time was up. West looked at the frightened hostage, then at Waters. Finally, he made a decision. '*What the hell?*' he thought. West exhaled slowly, took aim, and squeezed the trigger.

The gunshot made everyone in the train station jump in panic. The female hostage was jerked to the ground. The bullet that passed through Waters' skull imbedded itself in the station wall, carrying a stream of blood in its wake. West lowered his weapon. He covered the space between himself and the hostage in one quick movement. She looked up at him, and then looked at the body of the man who, just a moment before, was threatening her very life. Tears of fear cascaded down her face. She continued to rant hysterically.

West turned and looked behind him. He saw two NYPD officers approaching at full speed. West released a sigh of relief. He raised his hands into the air as the two officers un-holstered their side arms and leveled them in his direction.

"I'm a Federal Agent," he yelled to them.

One of the officers stepped forward. He was all business. "Drop your weapon."

West complied immediately. He knew the procedure and was already lowering himself to his knees. As he did, he peered over at the body of Keith Waters. 'I did it,' he thought, surprised and relieved. 'I got him.'

৯০৫

Evening settled in over the Bronx. The streetlights came on, illuminating the sidewalk as Kelli and Francine strolled through the neighborhood. Francine was a petite girl of Puerto Rican descent. Her hair, dark and curly, flowed down her back like a thick mane. Having been raised in the Bronx her whole life, Francine had more of a typical New York accent than a Hispanic one. She and Kelli had been friends since they met in the second grade. They had been through many things together: crushes on the same boy, playing on the same little league softball team, and copying each other's fashion sense. Tonight their experience was somewhat different. Tonight, Kelli was depressed. Francine, who had already begun having her monthly cycle, was doing what she could to cheer up her best friend.

"Maybe your mom is right," Francine began, "maybe it's just not your time."

Kelli scoffed. "Not my time? Look at me, Francine. Less than a year ago I was completely flat, now I'm already in a B-cup. I think it's safe to say that I've reached a certain stage in my development."

"Maybe so," Francine agreed. "But take it from me; it's kind of a drag. And inconvenient. And gross."

Kelli turned to her and giggled.

Francine grabbed her arm. "And those TV commercials about feminine itching and irritation. . . yeah, not funny anymore." Francine laughed. Kelli chuckled as well.

"I guess I should be thankful, huh?"

"No doubt."

They both began to laugh. Kelli felt better already. She knew that Francine would know how to cheer her up. Francine always did.

"So? Did you talk to him?" Francine asked eagerly.

"Darius? No," Kelli answered, and then giggled.

"Why not?"

"I was going to talk to him after practice but he was already gone," Kelli explained. "Besides, if my parents found out I was trying to talk to him, they would kill me."

"Then don't let them find out," Francine advised.

"He really is too old for me," Kelli said, trying to convince herself.

Francine pointed a finger at her. "Damn, girl. You scared."

"No, I'm not."

"Yes, you are," Francine teased.

"What do I have to be afraid of? I already know that he likes me."

"Yeah," Francine said with a smirk. "That's what you're afraid of. He's seventeen. You know what he wants."

Kelli remained silent. Francine had only voiced what Kelli was already thinking. She was already distraught over her body's rebellion. The last thing she needed was a boy trying to have sex with her. For Kelli, sex was 'not on the menu'. Still, she couldn't deny how cute Darius was.

"Okay," Kelli conceded. "I'm scared." They laughed again. "What should I do?"

"He's got a job, right?"

Kelli thought for a moment. "Yeah. Packing groceries."

"Good enough, girl," Francine said. "Flirt with him, string him along a little, get him to buy you something. When he starts acting like he wants to *do* it, cut him loose. Works like a charm."

"You've been hanging around your sister too long," Kelli concluded.

"She taught me everything I know," Francine admitted. "Take their money, but give them no honey."

"But I think I really like him," Kelli confessed.

"Fine. Do it your way," Francine said. "But when you come home pregnant, don't come crying to me."

Kelli grunted. "Like *that's* going to happen."

Francine stopped in her tracks. "I'm sorry, Kell. I wasn't thinking."

"It's all right," Kelli said with a smile. Then, her face became very serious. "Part of me thinks this is all happening to me for a reason."

"Really?"

"Yeah," Kelli said softly. "I can't explain it, but I feel that something is going on with me and. . ." her voice trailed off. Suddenly, her eyes began to well up with tears. "I'm just really scared. What if something is really wrong with me?"

Francine wrapped her arms around Kelli and hugged her close. "Nothing is wrong with you. Everything is going to be all right. I just know it."

"I hope so," Kelli said as tears began to slide down her cheeks. "It's just this feeling. . . it's so strong. You know?"

Francine squeezed her friend tighter and began to cry as well. Kelli had cried on Francine's shoulder on many occasions before. Usually, it was because Kelli was stressed out over all the attention that her 'brains' garnered. Everyone expected so much of her. Hardly anyone, except Francine, saw her for what she truly was underneath it all. A fourteen-year-old girl.

3

The next day at school was just as routine as the day before. Third period was Kelli's free period so she used the time to finish her calculus homework. When she was done with that, she put in a little work on her philosophy paper that was due on Friday. She put the final touches on the closing argument as the bell rang. She gathered her things and headed out of the classroom. She turned right after she crossed the threshold into the hallway but then paused for a moment, turned around and headed in the other direction. Today she would take a different route. Darius' locker was on this floor, and if she happened to run into him along the way, she could pretend it was a coincidence.

She moved through the crowded corridor quickly. Most of the other kids that attended school here were two to three years older than Kelli, so most of them were taller as well. When she first arrived at the school, she was slightly disoriented by the bigger kids and found herself getting bumped around as she navigated the hallways. Kelli didn't like that one bit. She learned quickly to be alert and nimble. Now, maneuvering through teenagers and crowded cliques had become a game she played. It was sort of like human dodge ball, but with the other students substituted for the ball. Kelli knew it was silly, but it helped her get to her classes more rapidly. It also helped in the event that she wanted to make a quick detour.

Kelli rounded the corner at the end of the hall and came face to face with Bling. She stopped and looked at him.

As usual, a pair of earbuds was inserted into his ears. He pulled them out and let them dangle around his neck as he stepped in front of Kelli. Hard and rhythmic Hip-Hop beats could be heard flowing from his miniature speakers. Kelli didn't hide the fact that she was annoyed.

"Hey, girl."

"What do you want, Bryan?"

"Bling," he corrected her.

"Whatever."

"I just wanted to tell you Mr. Huntley assigned me anotha' tutor for English," he explained.

"Oh," she responded, surprised. "Okay." She shrugged and began to walk off.

"Wait," he said and grabbed her arm. She turned to him and yanked her arm from his grasp. He handed her a piece of paper. There was a number scribbled on one side of it. "We live in the same neighborhood so I was wonderin' if you wanted to *kick it* sometime."

Kelli shoved the piece of paper back into his hand. "Why? You don't even know my name," she said scornfully. "You don't even know *your* name." She turned to walk away. He grabbed her arm again.

"Oh, so it's like *that*?" he asked, angered slightly. "What, you too smart for me?"

"Let go!" she yelled at him. She yanked her arm free again.

Bling took a step towards her. Just then, someone stepped between them. It was Darius. Darius was very handsome and very muscular. His skin was as smooth and dark as chocolate. His teeth were sparkling white. To Kelli, Darius was perfection personified.

"Is there a problem?" Darius asked Bling.

Bling wasn't fazed in the slightest. As intimidating as Darius might have appeared to others, Bling wasn't the type of kid who shied away from confrontation. After all, he had a reputation to uphold, even though he was trying to leave it behind. The thumping track that emanated from his earphones only served to fuel his attitude.

"I don't know," Bling answered and stepped within an inch of Darius' nose. "What do you think?"

Darius raised his voice. "I think the girl said to leave her alone."

"Funny," Bling said sarcastically, "I didn't hear that exactly. Maybe you should have your hearing checked."

Neither seemed likely to back down. Students began to congregate around them quickly. A female teacher, who was passing by, stepped through the small gathering and approached the two boys. She was approximately five feet tall, which was, at least, six inches shorter than either of them.

"Don't you both have somewhere you need to be?" she asked in a thick, Hispanic accent.

Both Bling and Darius looked at the teacher. Despite her small stature, her demeanor commanded respect and obedience. Darius stepped away first. "Yes, ma'am," he said.

"Go," she ordered. Darius turned and walked away. Kelli turned and followed him. Again, Bling stood there and watched Kelli walk away. The teacher stepped in front of Bling. "Go," she repeated.

Bling nodded. He did a one-eighty and sauntered away. The teacher looked around her. Several students were still standing there, transfixed. "Okay, clear the hallway!" she shouted. "There's nothing here to see."

Bling shook his head as he walked away. 'What was I thinkin'?' he thought to himself. 'This school crap. . . I tried. . . sorry, Mom. . . but I just can't do it.'

The students scurried away towards their classrooms. The teacher tugged on her blouse triumphantly and continued on her way up the hall.

ം⊷ക

Jaleesa maneuvered her small, red Toyota slowly through the traffic on Carpenter Avenue. Kelli sat in the passenger seat, recounting the event that brought Darius to her rescue.

"Then, out of nowhere, he was there," Kelli said proudly.

"Were they really going to fight?" Jaleesa asked.

"I don't know. It looked like it."

"I guess chivalry isn't dead," Jaleesa shot Kelli a look and laughed. "Look at you, got these brothas fightin' over you."

Kelli grinned from ear to ear.

Jaleesa's tone became more serious. "First of all, you need to stay away from Bryan Ling. That boy is always getting into trouble."

"He always finds me–"

"Second," Jaleesa raised her voice, interrupting Kelli, "Darius, as fine as he is, is too old for you."

Kelli rolled her eyes. "Yes, I know. I know."

"Not to mention I think he's messin' with Shanita Rogers," Jaleesa said off-handedly.

"Shanita Rogers?" Kelli asked with surprise. "She's ugly."

"She's easy," Jaleesa corrected her. "For guys, easy supersedes ugly. Don't forget it."

The light at the intersection changed to yellow. Jaleesa glanced in both directions quickly before pressing the accelerator. The car lunged forward and sailed into the crossroad. Without warning, a black SUV entered the intersection. Kelli saw the truck heading straight for them. Before she could call out Jaleesa's name, the SUV slammed into the driver's side of the Toyota, just behind the driver's door. The sound of metal colliding with metal echoed through the air. The Toyota was pushed out of the intersection into a parked car. The black SUV bounced off the end of the Toyota, careened off to the side of the road and skidded to a halt.

It took Kelli a few moments to come to her senses. The right side of her head was in pain and there was a ringing in her ear. She opened her eyes. She glanced to her right to realize that the Toyota was pressed against another vehicle. She looked to her left. Jaleesa was out cold. The driver's side air bag had deployed. Jaleesa's head rested against it. Kelli reached out and touched her.

"Jaleesa," she called to her. "Jaleesa. Wake up!" Nothing. No movement whatsoever.

Fear inundated her. It was only then that she realized that she, too, had sustained an injury. The warm blood from several lacerations on the right side of her head began to pour down her face. Kelli wiped at the blood. She looked at her hand and became terrified at the sight of it. She looked at Jaleesa again. Still, no movement.

Kelli looked out the rear window. She could see the black SUV resting motionless behind the Toyota. Kelli scanned the area. Oddly enough, there was no one around.

No one was there to play Good Samaritan and help her out of the mangled wreckage. The feeling of terror in her chest grew heavier. She burst into tears as a wave of hopelessness washed over her. Then, she looked around again. She noticed that the rear driver's side window had been shattered in the collision. She had a way out if she could manage to pull herself into the backseat and crawl through the window.

She unfastened her seatbelt. She lifted her right leg, then the left. Good. Both of her legs seemed to be working properly. She placed her right leg against the passenger side door and pushed herself towards the rear of the vehicle. Glass from the window was all over the seat. Kelli had to be extra careful not to injure herself further. She found leverage with her right leg and pushed once again, this time, harder. She landed in the backseat with a thud. Broken glass snapped and clattered under her weight. Kelli looked up. There were still several shards of glass hanging in the space where the window used to be. If she had any hopes of climbing through that window, she had to get rid of the glass. Kelli turned her body around so her feet faced the driver's side of the Toyota. She placed her feet against the remaining shards of glass and began to kick. Bit by bit, the glass fell from the frame. The space was cleared. Kelli reached up and pulled herself onto the door frame. A stray piece of protruding glass cut into the flesh of her left forearm. Kelli screamed in pain. The glass fell onto the seat. Kelli pulled herself through the frame of the car and fell towards the pavement outside. She howled in pain as her body came in rapid contact with the road. For a moment, she remained still. Then, something else caught her attention. 'What is that smell?' she thought to herself. She looked at the rear of the car. She noticed a waterfall of fluid leaking from some unknown compartment. Though she was, in fact, a genius, it wouldn't have taken one to figure out what it was. 'Gas!'

"Oh God!" she exclaimed. Without another thought, she pulled herself to her feet. She turned and saw an elderly man emerge from a corner bodega. "Call for help! Please," she yelled to him.

The elderly man waved to her, turned, and hobbled back into the store quickly.

Kelli turned her attention back to the Toyota. She moved to the driver's door. The window was partially shattered. From her point of view, she could see that Jaleesa's face was bleeding severely. Instinctively, Kelli grabbed the door handle and pulled. The door didn't budge. The metal frame was bent and contorted from the force of the collision. Kelli knew it would take more strength than she could muster to get that door opened. She looked towards the rear of the car again. The gasoline continued to gush out onto the pavement. She tried the door again. Nothing. She tried once more. Still, the door would not give. "Somebody, help me, please! Anybody."

Kelli peered through the broken driver's window. Jaleesa stirred slightly. Kelli called her name. "Jaleesa! Wake up! Jaleesa!" No response. Whatever level of consciousness Jaleesa had attained in that brief moment, it was gone. Kelli threw reason to the wind. She pulled on the door with all she had. It didn't budge. Still, she kept trying. Tears gushed from her eyes as she struggled relentlessly to jar the door free. She pulled again. A warm sensation began to coarse through her body. For a moment, she thought she would faint. She fought against the feeling.

She knew she couldn't lose consciousness as well. Not now. Not with Jaleesa's life at stake.

The warmth spread throughout her body. The pain in her head intensified. She wanted to give up, but she couldn't. She yanked at the door again. This time, it moved an inch. Encouraged, Kelli kept pulling. The temperature in her body spiked. The pain in her head began to throb. Her limbs grew strangely heavy and began to ache. Her entire body tightened as a wave of pain cascaded through her system. Kelli screamed at the top of her lungs. She felt the door give a little more. She continued to pull. The pain became excruciating. Her heart raced erratically. Kelli screamed again. She felt a cloak of blackness approaching. Though she tried to fight it, the throbbing increased. A sharp pain stabbed at the back of her eyes. Instantly, Kelli's world went black.

⊱⊰

The veil of darkness lifted. Kelli's eyes began to focus. She looked around. To her amazement, she was no longer standing next to the wrecked Toyota. Instead, she was standing approximately twenty-five feet away. She looked down at her arms. She was carrying Jaleesa. 'That's impossible,' she thought to herself. Jaleesa weighed well over one hundred pounds, Kelli was certain of it. 'How am I doing this?' Even more troubling was the fact that she didn't remember it happening. Kelli couldn't believe it, but somehow, during her blackout, she continued to function. She managed to open the car door, which, in itself, was literally incredible. Then she lifted a teenage girl, one who was bigger and heavier than she, out of a car and moved her to safety.

Kelli could hear the sirens approaching in the distance. She looked down at Jaleesa. Though Jaleesa's eyes were opened, Kelli could tell she was disoriented. Jaleesa looked up at Kelli. She smiled and whispered to Kelli softly, "Thank you." Then, as quickly as she had awakened, she fell unconscious once more.

Kelli stared at Jaleesa for a moment. 'She's still breathing,' she thought to herself. 'Good.' Kelli continued to stare at Jaleesa, but then, something strange caught her eye. Her arms. They looked different, both of them. No longer did they look like the sleek, feminine arms of a young girl. No. These arms were much more masculine, with bulging biceps and triceps.

Kelli looked at the SUV that had slammed into them. She was standing close enough to it to see her reflection in the driver's side window, but the reflection she saw was not what she expected. Instead of seeing herself as Kelli Freeman, a beautiful, young fourteen-year-old girl, she saw a tall, handsome, teenage boy. Kelli's jaw dropped. She had to be imagining it. She looked away quickly. She stared across the street at the road sign. "Carpenter Ave." Yes, she was seeing clearly. She turned and looked back at her reflection. Again, the face of a boy stared back at her, a boy that was holding the unconscious body of her friend, Jaleesa. Kelli couldn't believe her eyes. What's more, her eyes began to focus beyond her strange reflection and into the driver's seat of the SUV. The driver was still in the car. Not only was he still sitting there, but he was staring at Kelli in disbelief.

The sirens were within a block. The wailing sound burrowed into Kelli's skull, sending another wave of pain

through her head. Her stomach turned over and she began
to vomit. Her knees became weak, and her vision started
to become blurry. She felt as if she were going to faint
again. This time, there was no stopping it. Kelli fell to
the ground, dropping Jaleesa onto the pavement next to
her. As the darkness settled in, she saw the gleaming red
fire engine come into view. Kelli felt another sharp pain
zap her behind the eyes, and then. . . oblivion.

৯৯৯

Kelli woke with a start. Her breathing was heavy and
erratic. She tried to sit up but felt a pair of arms restraining
her. Suddenly, everything snapped into focus. She was in
the hospital, lying on a bed. The arms she felt holding her
down belonged to her mother.

"Calm down, Baby." Diane's voice was steady and reassuring. "You're all right."

Kelli stared at her mother. Behind her mother, Arthur
stepped into view. Kelli raised her arms and looked at
them. They looked normal again. Kelli tried to get up,
but her mother continued to hold her down. "Relax, Baby.
Don't try to get up. Everything's okay."

"Ma. Dad," Kelli looked at her parents nervously.
"Give me a mirror."

"What?" her mother questioned.

"Ma, please. I need a mirror."

Arthur surveyed the room quickly. "I don't see one."

"Baby, what's wrong?" her mother asked again.

"How do I look?" Kelli asked.

"Well," Diane began, "you have a bump and a few scratches on the right side of your face, and a deep gash on your left arm. Other than that, you look fine."

"But I'm me, right?"

"Well, yes," Diane answered her, confused.

A nurse stepped into view on the opposite side of the bed. She was a Caucasian woman with short, blonde hair. "She might be a little disoriented from the accident," the nurse explained. "It's very common with head injuries." The nurse leaned in closer to Kelli. "Do you know where you are, Sweetie?"

Kelli nodded. "I'm in the hospital."

"Can you tell me your name?"

"Kelli Coretta Freeman." She looked at her mother. "Where's Jaleesa?"

"Jaleesa is fine," the nurse answered. "A little banged up but. . . she's being admitted so we can keep an eye on her tonight."

"Can I see her?" Kelli asked.

"Dr. Moore should be in to see you shortly. He'll be able to answer all your questions. Okay, Sweetie?"

Kelli nodded. The nurse winked at her and exited the room. Kelli's breathing had returned to normal. She placed a hand on her head and rubbed the fresh bandage. Arthur poured some ice water into a white Styrofoam cup and handed it to Kelli. She put the cup to her mouth and didn't stop drinking until the cup was empty.

"How are you feeling?" her mother finally asked.

"Um," Kelli thought about it for a moment, "I feel okay. I'm just worried about Jaleesa."

"She's going to be fine," her mother assured her.

"Do you know what happened, Dad?" Since Arthur was NYPD, she knew he would have the official facts of the accident by now.

"Yeah. It turns out that the driver of the SUV was intoxicated. A full point over the legal limit."

"He came out of nowhere," Kelli explained. "Where is he now?"

"On his way to lockup," Arthur said proudly. "They carted him off as soon as the doctor released him. This guy was a piece of work. He was babbling the entire time."

Kelli's ears perked up. "What did he say?"

"Nothing really," Arthur said. He shot a quick look at Diane. Their eyes met. Arthur shrugged casually. "Just the normal, drunken chatter."

"He didn't say anything strange?"

Arthur's demeanor remained casual but his tone was much graver. "Strange like what?" Arthur sat on the end of the bed. Diane sat next to Kelli and squeezed her hand softly.

"I don't know," Kelli said. She wasn't sure if she should tell her parents what she saw. What if it was a hallucination that resulted from the bump on her head? What if she imagined the whole thing? "Strange like–out of the ordinary?"

Diane looked at Arthur. Again, he met her gaze. Kelli took notice.

This time when Kelli spoke, her voice was almost a whisper. "What did he say, Dad?"

"It's nonsense really," Arthur said dismissively. "But you're bound to hear about it. He claimed that he watched you–turn into a boy."

Kelli sat there, speechless. 'Oh, God! It was true. I didn't imagine it.' A million thoughts ran through her head, each of them colliding into one another, preventing any logical explanation. The only thing Kelli could muster was, "What? A boy? That's stupid."

Arthur chuckled lightly. "That's what he claims. He said you morphed into a boy, ripped the car door open and carried Jaleesa to safety."

"Yeah, right," Kelli said with sarcasm. "Like I can carry Jaleesa."

"Don't worry about it," her mother advised her. "It's so absurd; no one's going to believe him anyway."

Kelli didn't like the sound of that. "Who else has he told?"

"Everyone who would listen, I'm afraid," Arthur said, then he added, "Including the media."

"He told the news?" Kelli exclaimed. "Just great. Now it's going to be all over TV."

"Relax," her father said calmly. "As long as you know it's not true, you have nothing to worry about."

'Great,' Kelli thought to herself. 'Just great.'

శ్రీ

Washington, D.C.

A few hours passed. An elderly man in his mid-seventies strolled down a dark corridor. He wore a dark blue suit and a boring light blue tie. His wrinkled, worn face and his shallow, knowing eyes tell a story of long life with great victory, enormous sacrifice and tragic loss. His silver-gray hair was parted on one side, and he used a cane to mobilize himself. When he arrived at the third door on the left, the door was already ajar. Cautiously and quietly, he entered the room. He looked across the large desk that sat in the center of the room. There, in the dark, seated on the other side of the desk, was another man. This man had gray hair, as well. He was dressed in all black. Black suit, black shirt, black tie—everything. He was not a happy man.

The man in the blue suit crossed the room to the window. He didn't bother to sit. He knew he wouldn't be there long.

"Did you get a chance to see the news, Mr. Two?" the seated man asked.

"Yes," Two answered. "As a matter of fact, I did."

"What do we have so far?"

"A name. A fourteen-year-old girl." Two turned to him. "It's worth investigating."

"I agree," said a third voice from the doorway. The two men inside turned to see another man standing there. This man, who appeared slightly younger than the other two, sported a blue suit also. He stepped into the room. "Mr. One, Mr. Two. I'm rather surprised that we are convening on this matter. I thought this was taken care of."

One nodded in agreement. "As did we, Mr. Three. But here we are."

Three smirked. "Indeed. So, who do we have in the area?"

"Special Agent Towers of the FBI," One answered.

"Is he one of *us*?" Two asked.

One nodded. "He has been for quite some time now."

"Very well," Three said. "If this turns out to be true—"

"Then we'll make it untrue," Two assured him. "If this was to get out and the public believed it. . . "

"One thing at a time, gentlemen," One advised stoically. "Let's get our facts first. In the meantime, I'll contact Four. We may need to employ a specialist." One stood. "We'll meet again after the initial report."

The men nodded at each other. Two and Three exited the room and went their separate ways. One remained in the office.

He moved to the window and peered out over the city. The moon was full, and the sky was clear. From his vantage point, he could see more than half of D.C. One loved this city. He'd spent the greater part of his professional life working here, being an active and productive part of the system. Over the years, he had helped to ensure that the policies and standards that made the United States a thriving power were upheld, respected and, most importantly, protected. Not every man was willing to do whatever it took to protect a nation, regardless of the cost. Not every man could make the decisions that allowed the citizens of the United States to sleep peacefully in their beds at night. No. There were very few who would shoulder that burden willingly. There were very few like Mr. One.

4

West walked the corridor of Brooklyn Hospital. His partner, Agent Towers, was being released today. While waiting for medical help to arrive, Towers had lost a significant amount of blood from the two gunshot wounds inflicted by Keith Waters. The doctors felt it best to keep him under observation for at least a day before letting him go. West had called ahead and apologized to Towers for not visiting him during his short hospitalization. West spent the majority of the night and the next day at the Police Department. It took the NYPD some time to verify West's identity and, even then, he was asked to stay and fill in the blanks. West, proud of his solo capture, was more than happy to oblige the local law enforcement. After leaving, he checked into a Manhattan hotel and attempted to get some much needed rest. He was unsuccessful. The excitement of the previous day had West too riled up to sleep. It was only after a 'Will Smith' movie marathon on Showtime that he managed to doze off at four in the morning. Now, five and a half hours later, he was back in Brooklyn to retrieve his partner.

West entered Towers' room. Towers was already dressed. He was sitting in a wheelchair, talking on his cell phone. His left arm rested in an over-the-shoulder sling. The television in the room was on but the sound was muted.

"Yes, sir," Towers said into the phone. He glanced over at West. "He's here now."

West's curiosity was instantly piqued. Was Towers talking to Assistant Director Marsh, their boss? West had tried to get in contact with Marsh the night before. He had needed Marsh to verify his employment and assignment with the Bureau. He never reached Marsh. Instead, Assistant Director Ross called from the New York field office and gave the NYPD all the answers and verifications they needed. Ross congratulated West on a job well done. Perhaps Marsh was calling to do the same. But then, why wouldn't he have just called West himself?

"I understand, sir," Towers said. It sounded as if he was wrapping up his conversation. "Again, I'm sorry that I can't tend to this myself." A short pause. "I'll make sure he knows. Thank you, sir." Towers tapped a button on his cell phone and ended the call.

"Marsh?" West asked.

"Who else?" Towers lied.

"How are you feeling? You ready to get out of here?"

"I've been ready since I got here."

"Well, let's get you signed out," West said eagerly.

"I did it already," Towers responded quickly. "Donald, Listen. There's something that has come up and, because of my injuries, I can't tend to it."

West stepped closer. "What's up?"

"I don't know if you've been watching the local news, but there's a young girl that was involved in a car accident in the Bronx yesterday." Towers handed him a sheet of paper. There were several names and addresses written on it. "The Bureau has reason to believe that the girl may be in danger."

"Danger? From whom?" West asked.

"Possibly from the driver of the other car. His name set off a few alarms when they ran it through NCIC. All the names are there– his, the girl's, their addresses. . . " Towers adjusted his position in the wheelchair. "This guy needs to be interrogated. The girl needs to be checked on, as well."

West nodded. He was excited to get something else to work on so quickly. Maybe the news of Water's apprehension had garnered a little more trust in his abilities amongst the higher-ups. "Sounds easy enough."

Towers continued. "By now, there should be a fax for you at the nurse's station. Everything you need to know about the accident and this guy is there."

"Great," West said as he approached Towers. "Let's get you out of here and then I'll go check it out."

"Not necessary," Towers protested. "I can take care of myself. Go take care of this."

"Uh, okay. No problem."

"Listen," Towers began. "All the Bureau wants is information. Interrogate the guy, take his statement, check out the girl, then report back. Got it?"

West smiled confidently. "Got it." He turned and headed for the door.

Towers called to him. "West." West turned to him. "Good job handling Waters. I'm glad you're okay."

West's smile grew wider. "Thanks, partner." With that, West turned and disappeared into the hallway.

Towers allowed a small smile to grace his lips. West *did* do a good job. Towers liked having him as a partner. He was young, but he was a good agent. Towers knew, with more experience on the job, West had the potential to be a great agent. Taking Waters down was a big first step. Today could be a huge second.

Towers turned his attention to the TV. Local news anchor, Cloris Carver, was broadcasting a story that had the entire Tri-State area buzzing. Towers picked up the remote control and tapped the mute button. Carver's voice came blaring through the speakers.

". . . and even though Markham was charged with driving under the influence, he stands by his original statement. Markham claims vehemently, and I quote, *'She turned into a boy, right in front of me. I don't care how drunk I was. I know what I saw'*. End quote."

❧

The man known as Mr. One walked to the door of his D.C. office. He pushed it closed and secured the lock. He pulled a cell phone from his pocket and tapped in a series of numbers. He waited patiently as the phone rang. After the third ring, a line clicked open.

"I didn't expect to hear from you so quickly," the voice of Two said to him.

"Under normal circumstances, you wouldn't have."

"Oh?"

"I'll be brief," One stated. "It appears our operative in New York is currently incapacitated."

"Incapacitated? How?"

"The details aren't important," One assured him. "He sent his partner to gather preliminary information on the situation. His partner is not one of us. I suggest we send two of our own agents to take over the investigation."

"Agreed."

"I'll call you when I know more." With that, One disconnected the call.

∽∾

It was close to ten in the morning. Normally, Kelli would be in her free period at school. She'd be working on whatever homework assignment she decided not to do the night before, or reading a book while listening to her iPod. Not today. Today, her parents insisted she stay home. After the car accident yesterday, followed by Chad Markham's statement to the press, the phone had not stopped ringing. Although Kelli was a minor and her identity hadn't been publicly released, different news stations and newspaper reporters had been calling incessantly, trying to get a comment, any comment at all, from Kelli or her family. Sending Kelli to school today would have been like dropping a piece of meat into a den of hungry lions. They thought it wise to keep her home until they figured out the best way to handle the current situation. Diane called in to her job at the Middle School and took the day off. Arthur, on the other hand, decided he'd be more useful on the streets. As usual, he put on his uniform and went to work.

Kelli strolled into the kitchen. She found a note from her mother stating that she'd gone to Kelli's school to pick up any assignments that she was going to miss today. 'Principal Mom is on the job,' Kelli thought. Across the bottom of the note, Diane had written in large letters: DON'T GO OUTSIDE. DON'T ANSWER THE DOOR. 'No problem'.

Kelli picked up the phone and began to dial. Jaleesa was still at Our Lady of Mercy Medical Center. She wanted to make sure that Jaleesa was okay. Kelli saw her before she left the hospital last night, but Jaleesa was still only semi-conscious. She was hoping that she was more coherent today. Kelli prayed that Jaleesa wasn't going to tell the media what she saw in the brief instant that she opened her eyes. Maybe she didn't see anything. What if Jaleesa was so disoriented that she won't remember anything at all? Kelli could only wish. She was confused and, quite frankly, frightened. She didn't know what to make of any of this. And what about her parents? She allowed them to believe that the drunk driver was a rambling, deranged idiot. She's never lied to them before, not about anything as serious as this. And what if it happens again? What if she continues to change genders uncontrollably? What was she going to do? She sighed heavily. She wished that Francine was home from school. Francine would know what to say to her.

The phone clicked on the other end. A female voice confirmed that Kelli had reached the hospital. "Jaleesa Crosby's room, please. Room 310." The phone clicked and went silent. A few seconds passed before Jaleesa's voice came through loud and clear.

"I'm so glad you're okay," Kelli said. "How do you feel?"

"Like I got hit by a car," Jaleesa responded. "I've got a few broken ribs and a crazy case of whiplash. How about you?"

"I'm okay," Kelli confessed. "A little bump on the head and a scratch or two." Kelli paused. "You had me really scared. After the crash, you were just sitting there next to me, so still. . . I thought you were dead."

"I don't remember much of anything. One minute we're talking about Shanita Rogers, the next minute, nothing."

"So you don't remember how you got out of the car?" Kelli asked.

"My parents said you pulled me out."

"Me?"

"Yeah," Jaleesa said. "There were a couple of bystanders who saw us both lying outside of the car."

"Oh," Kelli said for lack of something more appropriate to say.

"Hey, girl," Jaleesa said sassily, "I was just about to thank you for saving my life. If you didn't do it, let me know so I can look for the real hero."

"What?" Kelli asked reflexively. Jaleesa's statement caught her off guard. "Oh, yeah. Of course it was me, girl. I was just a little dazed at the time. I don't really remember doing it."

"Whatever," Jaleesa said. "Thanks, Kell. I owe you one."

Kelli laughed. "Yeah, you do."

Jaleesa began to giggle. She winced in pain. "That hurt. Don't make me laugh."

Kelli felt a little more at ease. Jaleesa didn't seem to remember seeing her as a boy. Maybe she never would. Kelli wanted to mention the media coverage and the wild story surrounding the accident, but she decided against it. Jaleesa was going to hear about it eventually. When she did, Kelli was hoping that Jaleesa would think it was as ridiculous as it sounded. Then, the drunk driver's statement would be dismissed by the general public and she could get on with her life.

Kelli changed the subject. "When are you getting out?"

"Some time today," Jaleesa said. "My mother is on her way now."

"Good. Call me when you get home," Kelli said, and then added, "get some rest."

"I will," Jaleesa replied. "Thanks again. I really do owe you one."

"No problem." Kelli pressed a button and severed the phone connection. She went back into the TV room and sat in her father's big chair. As usual, the TV remote was within reach. Kelli picked it up and aimed it at the television. The screen flickered. The channel was set to one of the syndicated networks. An old rerun of 'ER' was playing. Kelli relaxed into the chair and made herself comfortable. It wasn't long before the drama of her life was replaced by the drama on the television. Before she knew it, she had fallen fast asleep.

Her slumber was uninterrupted. When she woke, she felt refreshed. A quick look at the clock revealed that she had been asleep for about an hour. 'I wonder if Ma is back yet'. Kelli stood. She stretched her tired body. Her bones made small cracking noises as her body was extended to its limit. Outside, she heard the familiar sound of her mother's car pull into the driveway. She crossed the TV room and headed for the kitchen. As she passed the mirror, she caught of a glimpse of her reflection. Kelli screamed in horror. It happened again. She had changed into a boy. Her initial reaction was to run, but she didn't. She couldn't. Kelli was transfixed by the image that stared back at her. She stared at her pajamas. On this body, they were exceptionally tight. She began unbuttoning her top. She wanted to see the body underneath. Then, she heard the key slide into the keyhole in the kitchen. Kelli's heart jumped. She was so distracted by her recent transformation that she had already forgotten her mother had arrived home.

The door opened. Kelli turned and headed for the stairs. She couldn't let her mother see her this way. Not now. Not yet. Kelli didn't know what she was going to do. Whatever it was, she had to figure it out. Fast.

࿊

"I'm Special Agent West. I'm with the FBI." West sat down at the small table in the center of the room. The room, like most interrogation rooms, was sparse and gray. Across from West sat Chad Markham.

Markham was a Caucasian male, thirty-six years old. According to his rap sheet, this wasn't the first time he'd been a guest of the New York Police Department. Markham had been convicted of armed robbery at the age of twenty-one. He served five years. Also, driving under the influence was a habit of Markham's. This time, there was a chance he was going to get more than a slap on the wrist for it. This time, Markham was going to do a little more jail time.

"FBI?" Markham asked, confused. "Where's my public defender?"

"He's outside," West answered, and then changed the subject. "What can you tell me about the accident the other day?"

"Are you for real?" Markham questioned. "Why does the FBI care?"

West paused for a moment. In truth, he didn't really know the nature of the Bureau's interest in Markham. He'd looked over the fax he received. He scanned the information three times. There was nothing in there that would indicate why a random, fourteen year old girl from the Bronx would be in any danger from the likes of Chad Markham. Except for the three times he'd been arrested for driving while intoxicated, Markham's record showed no known criminal activity since his release from prison ten years ago. Still, Markham had asked West a pointed question. West didn't want to let on that he was as much in the dark as the convicted drunkard that sat in front of him. "That's not your concern at the moment," West managed to say. "Just answer my questions and I'll be out of here."

Reluctantly, Markham nodded. "Apparently you don't watch the news?"

"I do," West countered. "And I'm aware of the public statement you made concerning the accident–"

"Then why are you here?" Markham interrupted. "My story isn't going to change. I saw what I saw."

"A girl who turned into a boy?"

"Look, Agent uh…"

"West."

"Agent West. I know how crazy it sounds," Markham confessed. "I know that, because I was loaded, people aren't putting too much stock in what I've said. But I'm telling you, I saw it."

West remained silent. Skepticism was written all over his face.

"You familiar with the Incredible Hulk, Agent West?"
Markham asked.

"I am."

"Well, let me tell you," Markham said as his tone became
more serious. He wiped a drop of saliva that had formed in
the corner of his mouth. "Slamming your car into another
vehicle while doing sixty is a pretty sobering experience.
I've gone through this song and dance before so I knew,
as soon as I heard the big crunch, I knew that this wasn't
going to end good for me. My air bag deployed–saved my
life–again! I knew I was a lucky bastard. I looked out my
window at the other car, and I'm prayin' that I didn't kill
anybody. I could just hear the charges in my head–vehicu-
lar manslaughter, reckless endangerment. . . hell, gettin' a
DUI would have been the least of my worries."

"So?" West asked, urging Markham to continue.

"So I sit there for a few minutes. I'm thinkin' to myself,
'You are so screwed this time'. Then, I see glass being
kicked out of the rear driver's side window. This young,
black girl pulls herself out of the car and falls to the ground.
Now, I'm thinkin' I'm really screwed. A white guy injures
a black girl in the Bronx. . . now there's a racial twist to it.
You followin' me, Agent West?"

West nodded. "Go on."

"The girl gets up and starts tuggin' at the driver's door.
The metal is bent, the door, as far as I can see, is jammed.
There was no way in hell this little girl was going to pull
open this door. No way. But she kept pullin'. Every time
she yanked at that door, it looked more and more like the
Hulk. She changed. She grew taller, sprouted muscles, and
she opened that door. She pulled her friend from the car
and. . . " Markham stopped.

"And what?"

"She just walked backwards away from their car," Markham said. "It looked like she was in a trance or something. Then, she turned and looked right at me. I'm tellin' you...there is no mistaking what I saw. She had become a he."

"What happened next?"

"She, or should I say, he collapsed right there in the street. Next time I looked in that direction, he was a girl again."

West was speechless. He wasn't sure if this guy was serious or if someone was playing a huge joke on him. There's no way Markham could have seen what he claims to have seen. West shook his head slightly. "That's quite a story."

Markham slapped the table. "And I'm sticking to it."

"Can anyone else corroborate your story?" West asked. Not because he expected an affirmative answer, but because it was standard protocol to ask the question.

Markham nodded. "As a matter of fact, there is."

"Really?" West asked, surprised.

"The girl that was rescued. When the girl, uh, boy, was carrying her, she woke up." Markham began to nod more rapidly. He smiled. "You want corroboration? Go talk to her."

ॐॐ

Kelli locked herself in the upstairs bathroom. She paced back and forth nervously. She stopped and looked in the mirror once more. Still a boy. 'Oh, God, this is really happening', she thought. Tears burst from her eyes as the terrifying reality set in. "How can this be happening?" she said aloud, only the voice that came out of her mouth wasn't familiar. This voice was deeper, more masculine.

There was a knock at the bathroom door. It was her mother. "Kelli?" Diane called out to her.

Kelli panicked. 'I can't answer her. She'll hear my voice.'

Another knock. "Kelli, baby, are you okay?"

Kelli sprang to the shower and turned it on. Maybe if her mother thought she was taking a shower, she would go away. No such luck.

Her mother knocked again. "Kelli, can you hear me?"

Kelli swallowed hard. With all that was going on, Diane had every right to be concerned about her. She knew she had to answer her. Maybe if she disguised her new male voice, perhaps she could convince her mother that everything was okay. Kelli wasn't sure if it would work, but she knew she had to risk it. She choked back the tears. When she spoke, she tried to make her voice as feminine as possible.

"I can hear you," she answered, keeping her response brief.

"Is everything okay in there?"

'Good grief, Ma,' she thought to herself, 'can't a girl take a shower?' Kelli cleared her throat and attempted the high voice again. "I'm okay, Ma."

"Okay," Diane replied. "Just checking."

Kelli waited a second. She heard her mother walk away from the bathroom door. Kelli released a long sigh of relief. For the moment, she would be left alone.

Kelli began to take long, even breaths. It was a calming technique she learned in her ju-jitsu class. She exaggerated the expansion of her diaphragm as she drew air in, then exhaled nice and slow. When she felt she was as calm as she was going to get, she opened her eyes and looked in the mirror. She noticed that she was at least an inch and half taller now. Her hair, while still long, looked somehow shorter as it hung from this new head and new face. Kelli leaned closer to the mirror. She saw a resemblance to her female self in the face of this boy. She opened her pajama shirt completely. She marveled at the strong, masculine chest that rested high where her breasts used to be. She analyzed her powerful-looking arms. She touched her right shoulder. It was round and strong. Her skin held the same beautiful brown tones as before, but in this body, the skin somehow seemed a little tighter, and a tad bit more firm.

Kelli's tears had stopped flowing. Her mood had transformed much like her body, from intense fear to growing curiosity. Kelli looked at her pajama bottoms. She bit her bottom lip. Though she had never seen a naked boy in person before, she was well aware of what to expect should she decide to explore further. Her nerves began to get the better of her. She breathed deeply to calm herself once again. Finally, she slid her thumbs underneath the elastic of her bottoms and, in one motion, pulled them down past her hips. The bottoms fell to the floor and Kelli stood there, naked. Strange. Kelli never imagined that the first penis she'd ever see would be her own. She touched it. It jerked up at her involuntarily in response. Kelli reached down to her ankles and pulled up her bottoms immediately. "Whoa!" she said as she looked around the bathroom. Even though she was alone, she felt embarrassed just the same.

She knew she had to do something. She didn't know how long it would be before she transformed back into her female self, but she knew she couldn't hide out in the bathroom all day, either. The shower trick was only going to work for so long. "Think, girl. Think."

Kelli turned to her reflection once again. "Maybe I can control it," she said softly to herself. "Maybe if I use the breathing technique. . . " Kelli placed her hands on either side of the sink. She concentrated on the rate of her breathing and focused her thoughts on her appearance, her female appearance. She stared at herself in the mirror, visualizing her former self. She slowed her breathing even more. She blocked out every stray thought that passed through her mind and focused on the task at hand. At first, she felt nothing. She saw no change. Then, she felt it. A warm surge of energy began to sweep over her body. It was similar to the sensation she felt right after the car accident. Kelli struggled to maintain her focus. She concentrated on the image in her mind. Her skin began to tingle. Slowly, the transformation began to take place. The masculine facial features began to soften, her height began to diminish, and her breasts began to take shape once again. Unfortunately, her metamorphosis did not come without a measure of discomfort. Her muscles ached and her head throbbed. The warm sensation was almost overwhelming and she began to perspire. Kelli was uncertain if she'd remain conscious. She steadied her breathing and continued to fight to maintain control regardless of the pain. Within seconds, Kelli was back to her normal self. All traces of her male alter-ego were gone. The discomfort subsided as quickly as it had begun. The perspiration ceased. Kelli gathered the shirt to her pajamas and put it on. She stepped to the shower and turned it off. She turned to the mirror once again. She wanted to make sure that she was still 'Kelli' before she opened the door and ventured out into the house.

Kelli still did not know what to make of what was happening to her. Throughout all of her academic studies, she had never come across anything as bizarre as this. Kelli felt that she should tell her parents, but she was afraid. It's not that she thought they would reject her. It was nothing like that. She was afraid that her parents would be at a total loss in helping her. 'I mean, let's face it,' she thought to herself. 'How many parents deal with this every day?' She did not know. But maybe, just maybe, she knew how to find out.

∂∞∂

"I'm sorry," Jaleesa said. "What did you say your name was again?"

West smiled at Jaleesa. "Special Agent West. I'm with the FBI. I just have a few questions," West said as he turned to Jaleesa's mother who had just arrived at the hospital to take her home. "It will only take a few minutes."

Jaleesa's mother, Elnora Crosby, was a stern looking African-American woman. She was the kind of woman who always had a hand on her hip, and her attitude at the ready. "What's this about?"

"I'm doing some follow up on the car accident that your daughter was involved in, ma'am," West explained.

"She told the police every thing that happened," Elnora interjected.

"I'm sure she did," West said politely, "but I wanted to make sure we didn't miss anything."

Elnora looked at Jaleesa. Jaleesa shrugged. "Okay."

West smiled warmly. "Thank you. I've read the report that recounts the accident, but I wanted to ask what you remember."

"Nothing. Kelli and I were talking about school, the next thing I know I'm waking up in an ambulance."

"And you don't remember anything that happened in between?" West questioned.

"Does this have anything to do with the drunk guy who hit my daughter?" Elnora asked.

Jaleesa smiled. Her mother had just filled her in about the story that was circulating through the media. Jaleesa thought it was pretty far-fetched.

"I'm just trying to get a clear picture of the events," West said in an attempt to dodge the question. He turned back to Jaleesa. "What about when you were being pulled from the wreckage? Did you recall seeing anything?"

Jaleesa opened her mouth to respond. Suddenly, an image of a young, handsome boy appeared in her head. He was carrying her. Jaleesa remembered feeling very safe in his arms, as if she trusted him even though he was a stranger. She recalled looking up at him. Their eyes met. Then, nothing.

Jaleesa snapped back to the present. She thought about the ridiculous story that her mother had relayed to her. "This man claimed that Kelli turned into a boy. There are some crazy-ass people in the world," Elnora had said. Jaleesa dismissed it as nonsense when she first heard it, but now she didn't know what to think. This was an FBI agent sitting in front of her, for God's sake. 'What the hell was going on?' Jaleesa wondered. She wasn't sure, but there was one thing she did know. Kelli was her friend. Jaleesa didn't want to do anything that would cause her any trouble. Jaleesa shook her head. "No. Like I said, I don't remember anything."

West nodded his head. Although he smiled warmly at Jaleesa, for some reason he couldn't explain, he didn't believe her. Maybe it was the way she answered the question. He could see her wheels turning right before she responded. It was almost as if she wanted to say one thing, but decided on another. Still, except for his gut feeling, West had no other reason not to believe the young girl. After all, the story Markham told was outrageous. Nevertheless, call it instinct, West was not convinced.

"Thank you for your time," West said politely. His work here was done. He excused himself and exited the room.

Elnora looked at Jaleesa and shook her head. "White people," she said, chuckling.

అ~ఆ

West drove his government-issued sedan strategically through the Bronx traffic. With his 'hands-free' device inserted firmly in his ear, West pressed a number on his cell phone and the speed dial function did the rest. A moment later, Towers was on the line. West updated him on his progress.

"Good work, Donald," Towers said. "You can come in now."

"Come in? Why?" West asked, confused. "I haven't questioned the girl yet."

"It's okay," Towers assured him. "The Bureau decided that this isn't worthy of our concern."

"Did Marsh say why?"

"No. Just that we were to fall back and leave it alone."

West wasn't ready to let it go. "But what about Markham? I thought there was concern about the girl's safety."

"Apparently that's a moot point, Donald. Markham was just released."

"What?" West exclaimed. "This guy needs to be taken off the street. He's going to kill somebody."

"It's not our concern anymore," Towers repeated sternly. "We've been ordered to forget it. I'll see you back at the hotel."

West sighed heavily. He didn't understand what had just happened, and he didn't like it one bit. Unfortunately, orders were orders. "Fine. See you soon." West disconnected the call. He shook his head in disbelief. He slowed the car and took the next right turn. He was taken off the case so there was nothing left to do but return to the hotel and leave it alone.

∽⬧

"An FBI agent? No way!" Kelli exclaimed. Kelli rolled onto her bed as she talked on the phone to Jaleesa. Jaleesa had made it home safely. Kelli was the first person she called. "What did he say?"

"He was asking me what I remembered," Jaleesa replied.

"Oh," Kelli said. Her heart jumped into her throat. "What did you say?"

"I didn't tell him anything."

Kelli relaxed. "Oh, good. I mean, what's there to tell?"

"Exactly," Jaleesa said. There was a short pause. Then, Jaleesa spoke. "You know, Kelli. I know that I'm a little older than you, but I want you to know that I've always thought you were special."

Kelli giggled. "You don't have to do this, Jaleesa. You've already thanked me for saving your life."

"I know," Jaleesa said. "I just want you to know. . . if you ever want to talk, your secrets are safe with me."

Kelli remained silent. 'Jaleesa knew,' she thought. 'What should I do? Do I tell her the truth?' There was a part of Kelli that wanted to ask those questions, but there was another part that was afraid to reveal her startling new development. The silence extended beyond the realm of comfort. Kelli had to say something. "I know. Thank you."

"No problem, girl," Jaleesa said lightly. "Listen, my mom is all over me to get some rest so I've gotta go."

"Okay."

"You going back to school tomorrow?" Jaleesa asked.

"Yeah. I'd be happy to grab your homework for you," Kelli offered.

"That would be great. Thanks, girl."

"No problem," Kelli said. "Hey. I'm glad you're okay."

"Thanks to you. Talk to you tomorrow." Jaleesa blew her a kiss through the phone and ended the call.

Kelli rolled over onto her back. She lay there, staring blankly at the ceiling. The last few days had been unbelievable. First, Darius had come to her rescue at school. He walked her to her next class and promised to come to her track meet on Saturday. That put her on cloud nine. Then, she was involved in a car accident on the way home. She could have been killed. Still, that event paled in comparison to what happened to her next. Her mind was flooded with questions, but there was one that stood out amongst the rest. 'How is this possible?'

After 'escaping' the bathroom earlier, Kelli went to the computer and surfed the internet. She searched for anything that would explain what was happening, some clue as to why and how. More importantly, Kelli looked for any evidence that would indicate if this had happened before. She found nothing.

There was a knock at the door. Kelli sat up. Her parents had been checking in on her quite frequently. Her father had come up to her room three times since he arrived home from work. Truthfully, Kelli didn't want to be bothered right now. All she wanted was to be left alone so she could figure out what she was going to do. Her feelings changed as soon as the door opened and Francine entered the room.

Kelli jumped off the bed and ran to her friend. She hugged her tightly. "I'm so glad to see you," Kelli said happily.

"Are you okay?" Francine asked. She looked at the small bandages on Kelli's forehead and forearm.

Kelli closed her bedroom door and locked it. She wanted to tell her parents what was going on, but she didn't know how. She had wanted to tell Jaleesa, but the words just wouldn't come out. But Francine was a different story. She could tell Francine anything.

Kelli grabbed her by the hand and pulled her to the center of the room. "I'm fine. Well, no, I'm not."

Francine looked confused and concerned at the same time.

"I've got something to tell you," Kelli said. "You've got to promise that you won't say anything. Promise me."

"Always," Francine said, excitedly.

Kelli took both of her hands. She began to speak but she couldn't find the words.

"Kell, what's up?"

Kelli took a deep breath. "I can turn into a boy."

Francine's expression remained blank. "What?"

"I know it sounds crazy, but it's true," Kelli said.

Francine stood there quietly. Then, she laughed. "You had me goin' there for a minute."

"Francy, listen to me," Kelli insisted. "It's true. It's happened twice already."

"You can turn into a boy?"

"Yes," Kelli replied. "Keep your voice down."

Francine was not convinced. Kelli knew it.

"Okay. Fine," Kelli said, resigned. "I'll show you."

"Show me what?" Francine asked skeptically.

"Promise me you won't freak out."

"I promise," Francine laughed. "What?"

Kelli shook her head. She couldn't believe she was going to do this. She took a step back, steadied her breathing, and focused.

The warm sensation began to spread throughout her body. The perspiration followed. The throbbing pain in her head followed that, but, to Kelli's surprise, it wasn't as painful this time.

Kelli felt her body changing. As it did, Kelli watched Francine. At first, Francine just stood there. As the seconds passed and the transformation began, Francine's mouth dropped. She backed up slowly until she pressed against the bedroom door. Her eyes grew wider and her mouth became dry. Where Kelli stood only a moment ago, now stood a boy.

Francine didn't speak. Instead, she turned around, unlocked the bedroom door, opened it, and ran.

❧

Something didn't sit right with West. Though he couldn't put his finger on it, he felt that something was wrong. He sat in his Manhattan hotel room and reviewed the facts available to him. Over and over he tried to make some sense of it. First, the Bureau sent him to question Markham because of his past criminal history. Markham told him an outlandish story but showed no indication of being a danger to Kelli Freeman except when he's drunk and behind the wheel. Then there was the girl in the hospital, Jaleesa Crosby. Though she failed to corroborate Markham's story, West could tell she was keeping something from him. Lastly, while on his way to question Kelli Freeman herself, he was pulled from the case and told that Markham was back on the street. There's no way, given Markham's record, that he should have been released. It just didn't make sense.

West tried to relax. He and Towers were scheduled for a flight back to D.C. in three hours. West wanted to let this 'thing' go, but he couldn't. Before he knew it, he was putting on his jacket and heading for the door. He grabbed the few belongings he had with him and stepped into the hallway. He checked his watch. 'If I hurry,' he thought, 'maybe I can still catch the flight.' He laughed to himself. 'In New York traffic? Yeah, right.' Still, West had made up his mind. Sixty seconds later, West exited the hotel.

5

Kelli headed for Francine's house. After Francine bolted out of her bedroom, Kelli morphed back into a female and ran out after her. By the time she made it outside, Francine was nowhere in sight.

Kelli crossed to the next block and made a beeline to where Francine lived. Francine's sister, Zenaida, said that Francine had gone out and had not yet come back. Kelli didn't know what to do. She had scared her best friend, and now she couldn't find her. Kelli had no choice but to continue to search for her. Kelli felt pretty safe in her neighborhood during the day, but it wasn't the type of area she wanted to be out in at night. It would only be another thirty minutes or so before the streetlights would come on. Kelli had to find Francine, and she had to do it fast.

Kelli continued up the block. There was a bodega on the northeast corner. She and Francine went there quite often to buy candy for themselves or pick up whatever little things their parents may need. Maybe Francine was there. If not, maybe someone had seen her in the area. No such luck. The clerk hadn't seen her. In fact, the clerk claimed that no one, save Kelli, had been in the store in the last ten minutes. Kelli was at a loss. She turned left out of the store and headed for the park.

Kelli sprinted to the park in no time flat. Despite everything that had happened to her in the last two days, physically, she felt great. She made it to the park without breaking a sweat. Her track coach would've been proud.

The sun had set. Kelli crossed onto the big field. She could see park benches and picnic tables set up in the distance. Francine was sitting there. Kelli increased her pace. Francine was off in another world and didn't see Kelli approaching. It wasn't until Kelli was twenty yards away that Francine looked up in her direction. Francine stood. She began shaking her head and backing away quickly. Kelli accelerated. Before Francine could get up any speed, Kelli was on her. She grabbed Francine's arm and stopped her best friend in her tracks.

"Francine, wait!" Kelli pleaded.

"No. Get away from me," she yelled. "I can't believe you."

"I'm sorry, Francy. I didn't mean to scare you."

Francine turned and looked at Kelli. "Scare me? Are you kidding?" Francine stepped closer to Kelli. "Do I look scared?"

"Then what is your problem?" Kelli asked desperately.

"You don't know?" Francine countered. "All these years we've been friends and you don't know? All those sleepovers where we would change clothes together–"

"What?" Kelli tried to interject.

"All the times we took showers at school, this whole time, you're really a boy? You were my best friend. I trusted you with everything."

"Francine, please," she begged her. "You still can."

"How can I? No wonder you haven't gotten your period yet. You're a boy."

Kelli froze. With all the different possibilities she'd entertained concerning her transformations, she never once stopped to consider that this one problem could be connected to the other. Kelli took a step back. Her mind began to race.

Francine looked at Kelli. Even though she was angry with her, she knew Kelli well enough to know when something wasn't right.

"Aye, Dios. Kelli," she stepped closer. "You aren't lying, are you?"

"No," Kelli screamed. She began to cry. "You have to believe me. This just happened for the first time yesterday, right after the accident." The tears began to rush from her eyes faster and harder. "I was trying to save Jaleesa. The next thing I knew, I had changed." Kelli's legs became weak suddenly, and she dropped to her knees.

Francine didn't know what to say. She knelt beside her weeping friend and put her hands on her shoulders. "Kelli. . . I. . . what are you going to do? Did you tell your parents?"

Kelli choked back her tears. "You're the only person I've told. I thought if anybody would understand. . . "

Francine took Kelli's face in her hands. "Oh, Kelli. I–"

"Well, what have we here?" an unfamiliar male voice said.

Kelli and Francine looked up. There were two teenage boys standing there. They were adorned in black and red, the local gang colors. Smash was African-American, and the other, Toro, was Hispanic.

The African-American boy stepped forward. "It looks like we have a couple of damsels in distress."

Toro laughed, "They're *honeys*, too, Dawg."

"Leave us alone," Francine ordered.

"You on our territory, Chica," Toro responded. "You want to go home? You gotta pay the fare."

"For real," the other boy chimed in.

Kelli wiped her tears. She stood and faced them. "Just let us go. We don't want any trouble." Kelli grabbed Francine's hand and proceeded to push by the boys. Smash grabbed Kelli by the throat and pulled her to him.

"You must not have been listening, little girl," he sneered lasciviously. "We said you have to pay." His grip on Kelli's neck began to tighten.

"Let her go," Francine demanded.

"Shut up." Toro turned around. Another teenage boy wearing similar colors approached them. "Look what we found," Toro called out to him.

The third boy stepped into the light. Kelli recognized him. It was Bling. Bling looked at Kelli. His gaze shifted to his fellow gang member. "Let 'em go."

"What?" Smash questioned. "Forget that. These cuties got it comin' tonight."

Bling stepped closer. "I said let 'em go, Smash. Don't make me say it again."

Smash looked at Bling. There was a confused look on his face. "Last time I checked, you wasn't runnin' things."

"I don't care," Bling responded. He gestured to Kelli. "I know her. Leave her alone. Her friend, too."

Smash stared at Bling. He relinquished his hold on Kelli. She fell to the ground. She coughed uncontrollably as air escaped from her lungs. Francine knelt to comfort her.

Smash stepped closer to Bling. Their faces were merely inches apart. "It looks like you owe me, Bling." Toro stepped behind Bling. Bling could feel the hot breath on his neck.

"I guess I do," Bling responded.

Smash gestured to Toro. He kicked the dirt, sending a stream of sand at Kelli and Francine. "See ya around," he said.

Smash looked back at Bling again. "All of you." Without another word, Smash walked away with Toro in tow.

Francine helped Kelli to her feet. Bling stood there silently, watching them.

"Are you okay?" Francine asked Kelli.

"Yeah. I'm fine," Kelli answered. She turned and faced Bling. "Thank you."

Bling shrugged. "You shouldn't be over here."

"It's a free country," Francine snapped at him.

"Who told you that?" Bling snapped back. He shook his head in disgust at Francine. He turned his attention back to Kelli. "Let me walk you home."

"No, thanks," Kelli declined. "We'll be okay."

"You think those two niggas are the only clowns in the streets tonight?"

Both of the girls remained silent. They needed his help but neither one wanted to admit it. Luckily, they didn't have to.

"Come on," Bling said. "I'll walk you back."

Reluctantly, the girls followed Bling as he escorted them from the park. The girls chatted loudly amongst themselves. Bling spewed lyrical Hip-Hop vernacular under his breath. They crossed several blocks, maneuvering south then north through the vast neighborhood. Finally, they arrived at the intersection between Kelli and Francine's block. Kelli turned to Bling first.

"I think we can handle it from here," Kelli said.

"You sure you're all right?" he asked her. Kelli looked closely at Bling. For a brief moment, she thought she saw something in his eyes that was never mentioned in regard to his well-known reputation. Compassion. Then, as quickly as it appeared, it was gone.

"Yeah," Kelli nodded. "We're fine."

"All right," Bling said. "You really ought to be careful about walking the str. . . ," Bling's words trailed off. Something off to his right had caught his attention.

Kelli and Francine looked in the direction in which Bling was staring. Two Caucasian men, both dressed in dark suits, were approaching from across the street.

"Do you know them?" Francine asked.

"No," Kelli and Bling answered in unison.

"Miss Freeman," one of them called out. "I'm Special Agent Gillis. This is Special Agent Finch. We need you to come with us."

Kelli took a small step back. "Excuse me?"

"Your father, Officer Freeman, sent us to find you," Agent Finch explained. "There's been an accident."

"What kind of accident?" she asked.

"We'd prefer not to discuss it here," Gillis said abruptly. He stepped closer. An old scar could be seen across his left eyebrow.

Kelli tapped the small, thin bulge that rested beneath the denim shorts she was wearing. Her cell phone was there. Whenever her father needed her, he always reached her via her cell phone. It was the main reason Kelli's parents bought her a cellular phone in the first place. Kelli knew something wasn't right.

"Well, I just live up the street," she said. "I'll go home now."

"I'm sorry, "Agent Gillis said as he closed in on her. "We really need you to come with us."

"Wait a second," Bling said as he stepped in front of Gillis. "How about some I.D.?"

Gillis and Finch exchanged a look. Bling, no stranger to acts of violence, read their silent communication loud and clear. He looked back at Kelli. "Run!"

Gillis swung his right fist into the air. He caught Bling squarely on his jaw. The teen fell to the ground. Kelli and Francine turned tail and sprinted in terror in the opposite direction. Finch gave chase. Gillis followed.

Francine began to fall behind Kelli. Kelli grabbed her arm and pulled her along. As fast as Kelli was, it wasn't fast enough. Perhaps she could've outrun them if she were alone. But the fact of the matter was, Francine was slowing her down. Kelli looked over her shoulder. Finch was on top of them. He reached out and shoved Francine. The young Latina lost her footing and toppled over onto the sidewalk.

"Francine!" Kelli screamed. Without thinking, she stopped in her tracks. She turned to her fallen friend. Finch seized Kelli with both hands. A dark-colored car pulled up behind Kelli. It stopped suddenly. The door opened, and Special Agent West stepped out of the car. His weapon was drawn.

"Federal Agent!" West yelled. "Release her!"

Finch stepped to his right as Gillis approached from his rear. Finch's body, along with the struggling teen in his grasp, shielded Gillis' hands from West's view.

"Step away from the girl!" West shouted. Finch stepped aside. Gillis, with his gun leveled at West, fired off a shot.

West took cover behind his car door as the passenger side window shattered. Glass poured onto his shoulder and onto the ground beside him. West peered around the side of the door. He aimed his weapon at Gillis and returned fire.

Gillis dove to his right. West's focus shifted to Finch. Finch had retrieved his weapon and was attempting to draw a bead on West. West pointed his gun at Finch and fired two shots. The first shot sailed effortlessly through the center of Finch's trachea. Blood exploded from his throat. The second shot landed two inches below the first, embedding itself into Finch's Kevlar vest.

Kelli and Francine screamed in terror. Kelli turned and was instantly immobilized by the sight of the dead body in front of her. West moved his weapon in Gillis' direction. Gillis was already scrambling to take cover behind a tree. West fired two shots at Gillis. Both missed Gillis' head by a narrow margin as he dove behind the tree for cover. West turned to the girls. "Kelli! Run!"

Kelli pulled Francine to her feet. They took off running in the direction from whence they came. West jumped behind the wheel of his car. He pressed the accelerator. The government-issued sedan lurched forward and trailed behind the two terrified, young teens.

They reached the top of the block as Bling pulled himself to his feet. Kelli and Francine ran towards him, screaming. Bling's attention moved to the car that closed in behind the girls. Bling reached into his side pocket. Out of nowhere, he produced a .45 caliber handgun. West slammed on his brakes. The girls froze, terrified. West emerged from his car with his weapon drawn.

"Drop the weapon!" West ordered him.

Bling stood there motionless. He leveled his gun at West. Sweat began to bead down his forehead. During his association with the local gangs, Bling ran with the likes of thugs, bullies and hoodlums. Many times he had wondered what it would be like to pull the trigger and take someone's life. Recently, Bling had decided to try and turn his life around. He knew that a life on the streets would land him in prison or in the morgue. Still, while it seemed that the straight and narrow path of school was not for him, the care-free street life seemed a perfect fit. "This is what I'm cut out to do," he had told himself. Now, with a gun in his hand, and another being pointed at him, it seemed that the moment to reconsider may have come a second too late.

"Son," West yelled. "Drop your weapon."

Kelli turned and looked at Agent West. She didn't know who he was, but she did know that he had just saved her life. Kelli couldn't explain why, but she felt she could trust him. She turned back to Bling. "Bryan!" She called to him. "Put down the gun."

Bling looked at Kelli briefly, then back at West. His finger twitched slightly as it rested upon the trigger. His nerves got the better of him and his hand began to shake.

"I'm counting to three," West warned. "One."

"Bryan!" Kelli shouted. Francine began to cry harder. "Two."

"Bryan," Kelli pleaded. "Put it down."

"Three."

"Bling!" Kelli screamed. "Drop the gun!"

Bling's focus shifted to Kelli. He looked into her eyes. She held his gaze. Without a word, Bling opened his hand and let the gun fall to the ground. Kelli released a sigh of relief. Francine threw her arms around Kelli and continued to cry. Bling slumped to his knees. West circled the car and approached Bling. He kept his weapon steadied on Bling the whole time.

"Get on the ground," West shouted at Bling.

"No. Wait," Kelli said. "He's with us."

"Who is this guy?" West asked her. He turned to Kelli. His gaze drifted past her and focused on Gillis as he appeared out of the darkness behind her. Gillis' shoe scraped the pavement. Francine turned and saw him.

Instinctively, she pushed Kelli away from her. "Kelli!'

Gillis fired a shot. The bullet struck Francine in the chest and lifted her off her feet. Kelli turned as Francine's body sailed backwards through the air. Time itself seemed to slow down as Kelli watched her best friend plummet to the concrete sidewalk in a heap of torn flesh and spraying blood.

"No!" Kelli screamed.

West fired a shot into Gillis' chest. Gillis stumbled back and fell onto the sidewalk, dropping his weapon. Kelli ran to Francine's side. She knelt beside her friend. Blood poured from the corner of her mouth as she struggled to breathe. Her lips quivered. Her eyes were open. Kelli picked up her head.

"Francine?" she cried.

Francine gasped for air.

West approached Gillis slowly. He kept his gun in front of him as he reached Gillis' still form. Suddenly, Gillis' foot shot out. He struck West in his Achilles tendon, and West toppled to the ground.

Gillis rolled onto his stomach. He saw that West did not drop his weapon. He scrambled to his knees and dove on top of West. There on the ground, the two men struggled for control of West's gun.

Francine struggled to speak to Kelli through a flood of tears and blood. "Kelli. I'm sorry. . . I. . . didn't mean to. . . fr. . . freak. . . out. . . on. . . you. . . I–"

Kelli's tears streamed onto Francine's face. "It's okay, Francy. Don't talk. Everything's gonna be okay."

Gillis grabbed hold of West's wrist. He slammed the wrist into the pavement forcefully, trying to cause West to relinquish his hold on his firearm. No good. West held on. Gillis slammed his wrist into the pavement again. The weapon discharged a round into the rear tire of West's car. The car slumped to the side as the tire went flat.

Gillis raised his right hand into the air and slammed his fist into West's jaw. The hold on his gun loosened. Gillis hit him again. West's head reeled back from the blow and slapped against the sidewalk. West, dazed and disoriented, released the gun. Gillis lunged for the weapon. He picked it up, turned and pointed it at West. A gunshot rang through the air, then another. West looked up as Gillis fell to the ground in front of him. West peered past Kelli and Francine. Bling rested on his knees with a smoking .45 in his hand.

West jumped to his feet. He retrieved Gillis' weapon, then picked up his own. He ran to Francine's side and kneeled next to Kelli. West stared into Francine's eyes. He watched as the light dimmed, and then, finally, flickered away.

Kelli screamed at the top of her lungs. As she did, her body tingled and she transformed into her male form. Her voice dropped an octave as she continued to howl with every bit of strength she had. Then, her lungs ran out of air. Her voice cracked and her body relaxed. Instantly, she reverted back to her female form. West stared at Kelli in disbelief. Bling's mouth hung open in amazement. Kelli, seemingly unaware of her brief, moonlight transformation, continued to shed tears over Francine's lifeless young body.

West was the first to move. He touched her shoulder. "Kelli, we have to go."

Kelli ignored him. Instead, she chanted Francine's name softly over and over again through her tears. "Francy. Francy. . . Francy. . . "

West looked at Bling. Bling looked back in return. "What do we do?" Bling asked.

"We can't stay here," West said. "The guy you just shot is wearing a vest. I don't think he's dead."

"Well, go and kill him, man!" Bling screamed emphatically.

West stood up. "I've got a better idea." He walked back over to Gillis. He pulled a pair of handcuffs from the back of his belt. It only took a moment before Gillis was laying there with his hands cuffed behind his back.

Sirens could be heard in the distance. Apparently, the multiple gunshots were heard and NYPD had been notified.

West began rifling through Gillis' pockets. 'There has to be some I.D.', he thought. He found nothing. No wallet, no passport. Nothing to confirm this man's identity.

"He said his name was Special Agent Gillis," Bling said. West turned to him but said nothing. "What's going on, man?" Bling asked. "Who are you?"

Just then, a man in plain clothing came bounding up the block. He had a gun in hand. He pointed it at West. "Hands in the air," he screamed at West.

"I'm a Federal Agent." West explained, raising his hands. Like before, he knew the procedure.

"Keep your hands in the air."

Kelli looked up at the man. It was Arthur. "Daddy?"

"Kelli, Baby. Are you okay?" Arthur stepped closer. He saw that Kelli was covered in blood. He looked at Francine. He didn't have to ask.

The sirens drew closer. Within minutes, the entire area was filled with squad cars and ambulances. Lights flashed and bystanders gathered. New York's Finest cordoned off the entire block. They had the situation under control as the initial questioning commenced. It wasn't long before Francine's parents were notified and brought to the scene. That's when the hard questions began. Who? What? Where? When? Why? How? No one had the answers. But Special Agent West knew one thing for certain. There was more to this case than met the eye. He didn't have all the pieces to the puzzle or know how they would fit, but he did know that Kelli Freeman was at the center of it all.

6

The top brass of the NYPD were not happy to find out that the FBI was seizing control of the 'Bronx shootout' investigation. Once Special Agent West's identity was confirmed, again, it was only a matter of time before his mere involvement gave the case federal jurisdiction. Once that was established, all of the participants in the shooting were separated. Then, the interrogations began.

Towers entered Interrogation Room A. West had been in there all morning answering questions put to him by the FBI interrogator as best he could. West was being reprimanded for disobeying the order to leave the Markham incident alone. West, in his defense, admitted that he wasn't sorry he did. "I saved lives tonight," West had said. He only wished he could have saved young Francine Rodriguez.

"How are you feeling?" Towers said as he hobbled in with the help of a cane. He carried West's belongings: a jacket, his service weapon, and his identification. The NYPD had confiscated them from West when they brought him in the night before. Towers handed them to his partner.

"I'm good," answered West. "Should you be back on your feet already? Where's your wheelchair?"

"Screw the chair. What were you thinking, Donald?"

"What are you talking about?"

"I'm talking about this case, or whatever it is now." Towers pulled out a chair and sat. "You were told to let it go."

"Look, Jimmy. I've already been through this with New York's Assistant Director Ross." West pounded the table with his fist. "I felt that something wasn't right with this case, and I was right."

Towers shook his head and exhaled heavily. "If you had just left it alone–"

"Well, I didn't," West declared defiantly. "And it's a good thing. Those guys, Jimmy, they were not FBI or CIA–"

"How do you know that?" Towers interrupted.

"Because we don't operate the way they did, that's how." West pulled up a chair and set it close to Towers. He sat down and lowered his voice. "Those guys came to execute that girl."

"The Rodriguez girl?"

"No. Kelli Freeman. She was targeted. And those men had no identification or anything on them," West said. "When I asked A.D. Ross about it, he said that information was on a right-to-know, need-to-know basis."

"It was out of our hands, Donald," Towers said. "You should have followed orders."

"Orders? If I had, three kids would be dead instead of one," West said through gritted teeth. "No, Jimmy. This isn't right–" West stopped to gather his thoughts. His eyes shifted in Towers' direction. "Jimmy. What's going on? Are you *in* on this?"

"There's nothing to be *in* on," Towers swore adamantly. "Just because we're federal agents doesn't mean we're privy to everything that goes on."

"We're talking about a bunch of kids," West yelled. He stood and began to pace the room. "They were after her, Jimmy. I know it."

"Okay," Towers said finally. "Let's assume you're right. Two people are dead, and some unknown entity is trying to kill Kelli Freeman. Why?"

West stopped pacing. He shook his head slightly.

Towers, being a fifteen year veteran of the Bureau, picked up on West's apprehension. "West, what is it? I'm your partner. If we're going to help this girl, you need to tell me what you know."

West considered Towers' words. Towers had been his mentor in the Bureau for the three years since he was put on assignment. West admired Towers and his dedication to his job. He knew that if anyone could help him, it was Towers.

West turned back to Towers. He sat in the chair next to him. He took a breath. "Okay. But I need you to hear me out."

"You have my word, Partner."

West shook his head. His tone was gravely serious. "You aren't going to believe what I saw last night."

ৡৎগ্ৰ

Diane Freeman sat in a small, enclosed room. Her arms were wrapped tightly around Kelli who still wept over the loss of her best friend.

The door opened. Arthur, on duty and in uniform, stepped into the room. Kelli looked up and breathed a sigh of relief.

"You okay, Baby?" he asked.

"Yes," she nodded. "I thought it was one of the FBI guys coming to ask me more questions."

"They're not done yet?" Diane asked.

"For now," Arthur answered. He crossed the room and took Kelli's hand in his. "They've got their hands full with the Rodriguezes."

"I can't imagine what they must be going through," Diane said sadly. "What have you heard?" she asked her husband.

"Not much," he admitted. "The FBI isn't exactly forthcoming with their information, but from what I've gathered, the main focus is on Francine's death."

"I can't believe she's gone," Kelli said. Her voice cracked as a flood of tears began to stream down her face.

Arthur gripped her hand tighter. "Don't worry. We're going to get to the bottom of this, with or without the FBI. I promise."

Kelli continued to cry. Her sobs increased in intensity with each passing second. Her mother squeezed her tighter in an effort to console her eldest daughter. It didn't help. Kelli wasn't only crying over the loss of her best friend. Kelli had another reason. A reason she could keep to herself no longer. "It's my fault," she blurted out between sobs.

"Oh, Baby," Diane said as she rubbed Kelli's back, "it's not your fault."

"It is," Kelli insisted.

"You couldn't have known this was going to happen," her father pointed out.

"No," Kelli managed to say. "If I hadn't freaked her out, she wouldn't have run– and then I chased her. . . "

"What do you mean 'freaked her out'?" Arthur asked sincerely.

"I should have told you," Kelli said. "I should have admitted it when it happened, but I thought you would freak out like Francine did."

Diane took Kelli's face in her hands. "Should have told us what? Kelli, what are you talking about?"

Kelli tried to wipe her tears but they fell from her eyes faster than she could sweep them away. "It's true. It's all true."

"What's true, Baby?" Diane asked.

"What the man said . . . the drunk driver . . . it's true. . . I showed Francine and she ran out . . . if I hadn't shown her, she would've stayed in my room."

Arthur's eyes shifted to Diane. Her eyes were already burning in his direction. A silent communication passed between them. Finally, Arthur spoke again.

"Kelli. Kelli." He repeated her name several times in an attempt to get her attention. "Kelli, whatever it is, we're your parents. You can tell us anything. You know that. You know that, right?"

Despite what she was feeling, Kelli nodded.

"So tell us now," Arthur said quietly.

"The driver who hit us," Kelli began, "he was telling the truth. I don't know how it happened, I don't even remember it, but . . . I did it . . . I turned into a boy. And I can do it at will."

෨෯

The hallways in the police station were narrow. Towers maneuvered carefully towards the rear exit. As he passed a door on his right, it opened. Arthur stepped out of the room and closed it immediately. Arthur turned and bumped into Towers.

"Excuse me," Arthur said apologetically.

"No harm done," Towers responded.

Arthur, not hindered by a walking cane, moved down the hallway quickly. He reached the rear exit and stepped outside. He took a sharp right turn and headed to the side of the building. As he walked, he pulled out a cell phone.

Towers reached the exit one minute later. He stepped into the April breeze and turned left. Despite his cane in one hand, he managed to extract a cell phone from his pocket with the other. Within seconds, he was standing on the opposite side of the building from Arthur Freeman.

ॐ◈

The phone rang in Towers' ear. He looked around cautiously. 'For God's sake, pick up,' he thought to himself. His silent plea was answered instantly.

"It's Towers."

"I told you that *I'd* contact *you*," One scolded him.

"It couldn't be helped."

"Did you get the sample?"

"Yes. However, the situation–"

"The situation has become messy," One said. "Messy attracts attention."

"I know," Towers replied nervously. "But we have confirmation."

A slight pause. "Do we?"

"Yes. West saw it with his own eyes."

"That's good, but, unfortunate for Agent West."

Towers' lowered his head in anger. He had not wanted it to come to this. He choked back his emotions and replied with a simple, "I know."

"Good," One replied. "Here's what I want you to do."

৵৽

Arthur paced anxiously as the phone rang. He had just placed a phone call he'd hoped he would never have to make. He considered hanging up. Too late. The phone clicked and the line sprang open.

"Hello," Arthur said nervously.

"Yes," a male voice said in return.

"It's Arthur Freeman."

"I was wondering when you were going to call," the voice said.

"I didn't want to, but—"

"It was a wise choice."

"Then you already know?"

"Yes," the voice answered flatly. "Don't worry. I've already got someone in place to take care of it."

"You *do* know what you're doing, right?"

"I do," the voice answered confidently. "Now, listen carefully. Here's what I want you to do."

৵৽

West splashed cool water from the restroom sink onto his face. He'd been awake most of the night and still had to get up early to meet with Assistant Director Ross from the New York City field office. In the last three days, West had killed two men. The first, a serial killer named Keith

Waters. It was a fitting end to a long and horrendous investigation. When all was said and done, West felt justice was served. The second was a mysterious John Doe with clandestine connections to the government. West kept bouncing the facts around in his head. 'The teenage boy that was found with Kelli Freeman, Bling was his name . . . he recalled that our John Doe was identified as Special Agent Finch. When I asked A.D. Ross about it, he blew me off. And this other guy, Special Agent Gillis . . . he took three slugs in his vest . . . when I inquired about him, I was told it was being taken care of.' West grimaced at the thought. 'Swept under the rug is more like it.'

Towers entered the restroom. He made a beeline for West. West saw him in the mirror and turned to face him. Towers had a pair of car keys in his hand. He extended them to West.

"What's this?" West asked.

"There's a car out back. We need to move the Freeman girl and the Ling kid to the federal building in Manhattan."

"Why?"

"They're not safe here," Towers responded. "Take these and go. And keep it quiet."

West grabbed the keys. He placed a hand on Towers' shoulder. "Thank you."

Towers replied with a simple nod. West exited the restroom and disappeared into the hallway. Towers stood there in silence. "I'm sorry," he said softly. He turned and looked at his reflection in the mirror. He stared at himself for a brief moment. Then, he turned away. Towers needed only an instant to recollect his composure. "It's for the greater good," he told himself. That always made him feel better. Then, he straightened his tie, hobbled to the door, and exited.

•••

Diane Freeman charged through the rear exit of the police station. She looked right, then left. She saw no one. She turned and ran quickly up the hallway. Ahead, she saw Arthur approaching her.

"Arthur," she called out to him.

"Diane?" Arthur could tell something was not right. Diane was shaking. "What's wrong?"

Diane ran into Arthur's arms. She began to rant hysterically. "I went to the bathroom. I was only gone for five minutes."

"Diane, slow down. What's going on?" Arthur looked up the hall towards the interrogation room where Kelli was being questioned. "Where's Kelli?"

Diane stepped back. "That's what I'm trying to tell you. She's not in there anymore. I asked everyone but no one has seen her."

Arthur grabbed Diane by the arms and shook her lightly. Her eyes, swollen and full of tears, focused on Arthur. He moved his face closer to hers. "What do you mean no one has seen her?"

"She's gone, Arthur. Kelli's gone."

7

The entire police station had been searched. It was soon discovered that Kelli wasn't the only person unaccounted for. Agent West could not be found, nor could the teenage boy, Bryan Ling.

Assistant Director Ross made a few phone calls and emerged from the police captain's office with an explanation. "For the safety of all concerned, we have placed Special Agent West, Kelli Freeman, and Bryan Ling into protective custody."

Diane Freeman listened to the announcement from the corner of the crowded room. Arthur entered and crossed the distance to where she was standing. They embraced. She buried her face in his shoulder and continued to cry. Arthur led her out of the room and proceeded to take her outside to get some fresh air. Once there, Diane looked up at her husband.

"Do you think they bought it?" she asked, wiping her tears.

"It looks like it. We were pretty convincing," Arthur said.

"Thank the Lord! Did we do the right thing?"

Arthur managed a small smile. "I hope so. She wasn't safe here."

"How did you get the FBI guy in on it?" Diane asked.

"What do you mean? Which FBI guy?"

Diane gestured towards the glass door. Assistant Director Ross was walking through the lobby. "Him. Just before you came in, he made a statement saying they were in protective custody."

Arthur's eyes widened. "Something's wrong. I didn't get him in on it. Except for you and Kelli, I told no one else."

"Call Kelli on her cell phone," Diane said urgently. "Call her now."

⊱⊰

West drove the black sedan towards the Cross Bronx Expressway. Kelli and Bling sat in the back seat quietly. Finally, Kelli broke the silence that hovered in the car since they left the police station.

"Where are we going?" She asked West.

"To the New York field office in Manhattan," he answered. "We think you'll be safer there."

"Yeah, right," Bling said sarcastically.

"Is my dad going to meet us there?" Kelli asked.

West looked in his rear-view mirror at Kelli. He wasn't certain how to answer that question without alarming the young girl. After all, in the last few days, she'd had more hardship than any teenage girl should have to bear. How could he tell her she had been taken from the police station without her father's knowledge? "Uh, yeah," West lied. "I'm sure, once he's informed of the situation, he'll be right down."

A confused look crossed Kelli's face. "What do you mean? My father is the one who told me to come to the rear of the station. He said someone he trusted was going to take me to safety."

"I've never even met your father," West blurted out. His mind began to race as he pondered yet another piece of information that didn't add up correctly. According to Towers, no one was privy to this recent turn of events.

Kelli became more confused. She turned to Bling. "Didn't my father escort you outside?"

"No," Bling answered, shaking his head negatively. "It was some guy with a cane."

The black sedan approached an intersection. At the stop sign, West brought the car to a halt. Kelli's cell phone began to ring. She reached into her pocket and retrieved it. The screen read: DAD. West, again, glanced into his rear-view mirror. As he did, he saw a grey sedan closing rapidly. The approaching vehicle accelerated.

"What the–?" West exclaimed.

The grey sedan slammed into the rear of the car that West, Kelli, and Bling occupied. In the front seat, West's air bag deployed. Kelli and Bling were jerked forward violently by the collision. Kelli dropped her cell phone on the floor. It continued to ring.

West's neck ached. He was injured. He turned and looked out the rear window. As he did, the door to the grey sedan opened. A man stepped out of the car and into view. It was Gillis. Kelli turned and screamed as Gillis pointed his gun at the car.

"Get down! Now!" West yelled.

Everyone in the car ducked behind their seats. Gillis unleashed a barrage of bullets at the black sedan. The rear window exploded into a sea of shattered glass. Gillis walked towards the car, continuing to fire one shot after another at the car. The driver-side window broke apart, followed by the driver's rear window. The rear-view mirror above

West's head took a bullet. The front windshield cracked as three bullets impacted the surface. Gillis stepped next to the rear driver's side window. He raised his weapon and released the empty clip. Almost simultaneously, he shoved a loaded clip in its place. Gillis peered in at Kelli. He leveled his weapon at her head. Three gunshots rang through the air. Kelli could see Gillis stumbling forward as something impacted him from behind. Kelli's heart jumped. It was her father. She knew it. He had realized something was wrong and came after her. But then, if that was her father, why was her phone still ringing?

West opened his door. He hopped out of the sedan with his weapon drawn. He grunted as a sharp pain stabbed at his neck. He was certain he had whiplash, but now wasn't the time to worry about it.

Kelli turned and looked to the rear of the car. Standing with a gun pointed at West, was a man she'd never seen before.

"Drop that weapon," West ordered.

"In case you hadn't noticed," the man said calmly, "I just saved your life."

"Put your weapon down," West ordered again, then added, "I *will* shoot you."

"What about him?" The stranger gestured to Gillis who was rolling around on the ground in agony. West saw no blood so he assumed Gillis was still wearing a bullet-proof vest.

Bling exited the car from the passenger side. He pointed at Gillis. "Damn! Why doesn't somebody just shoot that guy in the head?"

"Officer," the stranger said to West, "or Special Agent-whoever-you-are. I am not here to harm you. Believe me or shoot me but we must come to a quick resolution."

"Shoot him," Bling advised.

"Shut up," West ordered.

"Fine," the stranger said.   He relaxed his grip and released his gun. It fell and landed at his feet. He, then, gestured towards Gillis once again.

West turned to Gillis. He gripped his gun by the barrel and struck Gillis in the back of the head with the butt of the weapon. Gillis fell unconscious.

Bling breathed a heavy sigh of disgust.   "What the hell? Kill his ass, yo!"

"Bryan, shut up!" West yelled at him. He turned his attention back to the stranger. "Who are you?" he asked.

"My name is Nicholas Connelly. I'm a friend."

Kelli shifted her gaze to West. She shook her head.

"Kelli," the stranger called out to her.

She looked back at him with surprise. 'Who is he and how does know my name?'

The man said calmly, "Answer your phone."

Kelli looked at West. West, once again, had his weapon trained on their unknown savior. He nodded to her. Kelli turned and retrieved her phone from the floor.

"Hello," she said anxiously.

"Oh, thank God you're all right," her father's voice said to her. "Where are you?"

"Not too far from the police station," she answered.

"Who's with you?" Arthur asked.

"Agent West and Bryan–"

"Bling," Bling corrected her.

"And some other man named Nicholas Connelly."

At the mention of his name, Nicholas and West exchanged a look. Nicholas could tell that, with all West had just been through; all he needed was a good reason to pull the trigger.

"Daddy," Kelli continued, "do you know him?"

"He's the one I told you about," Arthur said. "He promised he was going to take you somewhere safe."

"Can I trust him?" Kelli asked.

"Yes, Baby," Arthur answered. "You can."

"We're wasting time," Nicholas said aloud.

"Daddy—"

"Baby, go with him. You'll be safe. I'll be in touch." Arthur paused. "We love you."

"I love you, too." Kelli said. She closed her phone. She nodded at West. "He's telling the truth."

West looked at Nicholas with caution. Nicholas raised an eyebrow. "Can I put my hands down now?"

Reluctantly, West nodded. He kept his gun aimed at Nicholas as the man bent over and retrieved his gun. Nicholas slid the weapon into a small holster on his belt. He turned to West. "We should probably take my car. Yours might draw too much attention. And remove the batteries from your cell phones. They can be used to track you."

West gestured to Kelli and Bling. Kelli exited the car. They followed Nicholas to a silver SUV which was parked a few yards away. The car was still running. Nicholas slid into the driver's seat. Kelli and Bling took the rear seats. West, after handcuffing Gillis to the stop sign, rode shotgun. Nicholas put the car in gear and sped away from the scene.

"You really should have killed him," Bling said to West. West turned to Bling. There was a look of contempt on his face. Bling shook his head in disbelief. "Whatever, man. If that dude shows up again and kills you . . . well, you know."

Kelli leaned forward and spoke to Nicholas. "So, you know my father?"

"No. But your father is an old *acquaintance* of my father," Nicholas said.

Kelli nodded. She wasn't exactly sure she liked the sound of that. "Oh. Where are we going?"

Nicholas took a sharp right and headed for the Van Wyck. "The airport."

"What's at the airport?" Kelli asked.

Nicholas smiled. "My private jet. As a matter of fact . . . " Nicholas grabbed an earpiece and shoved it in his ear. He pulled a cellular phone out from under his seat and pressed a number. He remained silent while the phone connected and began ringing. Then, he spoke. "It's me. We're en route. Is everything ready for departure?"

"Fueled and ready, sir. We're just waiting for your arrival," the response came.

"Excellent. We'll be there shortly." Nicholas ended his call. He turned to his passengers. "Fasten your seat belts. It's the law." He smiled smugly.

Kelli and Bling exchanged a disconcerted look. West sat quietly in the passenger seat. His mind reviewed the most recent events. One question kept coming to his mind. 'How did Gillis know where to find us?' West had a few theories, but only one of them made sense. And Special Agent West didn't like it one bit.

৵৹৻

Gillis sat at the intersection. He was still handcuffed to the stop sign. Sirens in the distance were getting closer. Gillis pulled a cell phone from his pocket and speed-dialed a number. He wasn't looking forward to making this report.

"Tell me you have good news," the voice of Two said.

"I lost them again," Gillis said.

"Is there a reason why you can't seem to finish this assignment?"

Gillis took a breath. He didn't want to answer that question the *wrong way*. "I'll get it done. I need a replacement for Finch."

"Consider it done. Meet them at the usual rendezvous."

"About that," Gillis said as he tugged at his handcuffs. "I'm going to need another extraction." Gillis knew that his recent predicament was not going to be received well. He knew, also, that if he didn't produce results, and quickly, he would find that his services were no longer required. Gillis had been with the Agency for quite some time, and he wasn't too fond of their severance policy.

࿎

Nicholas led Kelli, West, and Bling to a private runway that sat off in the distance at John F. Kennedy Airport. Nicholas' jet was a Gulfstream IV model. It could hold up to fifteen passengers and had a cruising speed of up to 527 miles per hour. He used it primarily for business trips but wasn't above using it for any necessary personal or private endeavors that came along. Nicholas grinned from ear to ear at the sight of it. It was a beautiful and impressive machine. Nicholas loved it.

As they approached the aircraft, they were met by a pilot wearing a white polo shirt and a pair of jeans. He had a headset wrapped around his neck and a lollipop hanging from his mouth. Nicholas' greeting to him was all business.

"What's the word from the tower?" Nicholas asked.

"We're all clear for take-off," the pilot answered. "Just give the word."

"Consider it given," Nicholas said. He gestured for Kelli and the others to follow him as he climbed the stairs of the jet rapidly. Moments later, everyone was on board.

Kelli pulled Bling to one side and spoke quietly. "Have you contacted your parents during all of this?"

Bling stepped away from her. "What? *Now* you're all concerned about my personal life?"

"Well, we've been through a lot together lately," Kelli answered. "I mean, you saved my life, more than once."

"Yeah," Bling scoffed, "and look how long it took you to ask about mine." Bling walked past Kelli and plopped himself down into the first seat to which he came.

West leaned closer to Kelli as he walked by. "Is he okay?"

Kelli shrugged. "I barely know him." She turned and walked towards the narrow aisle in search of a seat.

"Really?" West said, puzzled.

A slender, young woman in her late twenties exited the cockpit and hurried over to Nicholas. Her blonde hair was tied back in a bun and she wore a casual-looking, blue skirt with a white blouse. "Everyone should strap in for take-off, sir," she said.

"Thank you, Courtney," Nicholas replied. He turned and walked into the passenger area. "Time to buckle up," he said to his guests.

"Let me guess," Bling said. "It's the law."

Nicholas smiled. "No, but it's recommended."

"May I ask where we're going?" Kelli spoke up.

"Forgive me, Miss Freeman," Nicholas said. "We're going to Los Angeles."

"California?" Kelli asked, surprised.

"Is there another?" Nicholas responded sardonically.

"Wait," West interjected. "What's in California?"

Nicholas looked at Kelli. "The answers." Nicholas took a seat at the front of the cabin. He strapped himself in and tapped a button at the base of his seat. The seat swiveled until Nicholas was facing his three anxious passengers. He took notice of the fact that West was suddenly preoccupied.

"Penny for your thoughts, Agent West," Nicholas said to him.

West wasn't exactly certain that he wanted to share his suspicions. Sharing them would mean he was considering the unthinkable. "Just have some things on my mind."

"I imagine you would," Nicholas said. "You almost died today."

West nodded. 'I almost died yesterday, too,' he thought to himself.

Bling leaned forward in his chair. "Speakin' of which, Agent West. This guy, Gillis—how did that dude find us so fast? I mean, we had just left the police station."

"Yeah," Kelli said angrily. "He killed my best friend. Why isn't he locked up somewhere?"

"I don't know," West answered.

"Oh, come on now, Agent West," Nicholas said, "you can't be that naïve."

"It doesn't make sense," West said. He shook his head, trying to organize his thoughts before articulating them. Nicholas saved him the trouble.

"Surely you know that there are forces in our government that operate outside the law," he said to West.

"What are you talking about?"

Nicholas chuckled. "You really *are* naïve. Are you so brainwashed into being a good agent that you can't see the writing on the wall? Or is it that you're just blinded by your love for this country?"

West grew angry. "Don't make fun of me," he snapped. "You don't know anything about me."

"I know that you were set up," Nicholas said flatly.

"By who?" West asked furiously. "The FBI? No way!"

"No, not the Bureau itself," Nicholas retorted.

"Then what are you saying?" West yelled.

"I'm not sure you want to know," Nicholas countered.

West began to answer but stopped himself. He was fully aware of what Nicholas was implying. The problem rested in the fact that West wasn't certain if he was ready to believe it. Unfortunately, West was no dummy. He knew from the beginning that something wasn't right with this case. His being a witness to one of Kelli's transformations only served to confirm it. And then there's Gillis. Kelli was right. There's no way in the world that man would be walking around as a *free* man after murdering a teenage girl in cold blood. Even the Bureau couldn't pull strings like that. No, Gillis' release was orchestrated by someone far more powerful than the FBI. It was time West found out who.

West held Nicholas' gaze. "I want to know," he said sternly.

"We all do," Kelli said. Her eyes shifted to Bling. He nodded in agreement.

"Very well," Nicholas said calmly. "There is a group of men in this country, whose identities are known only to one another . . . these men . . . these twelve men—four heads, each with two subordinates . . . handle things."

"What types of things?" West asked.

"Things those other agencies like the FBI or the CIA won't touch. This *Agency* – they do the *real* dirty work. The kind of work no one ever wants to hear about. There are no heroes on the news, there are no twenty-one gun salutes for their operatives, and there's no glory. And usually, no evidence."

"And the United States government sanctions this?" West asked skeptically.

"Most people in our government are ignorant of their existence. Those that are not get to turn a blind eye," Nicholas said. "Don't hold the government at fault, Agent West. If they were to acknowledge the acts of this Agency, they would have to admit that everything upon which our country was built is a lie."

Kelli shook her head in astonishment. All of her life, she was raised to believe that law enforcement officers were trustworthy and honorable; her own father was an example. She found it difficult to believe that any part of the government would allow such a betrayal.

"So operatives like Gillis get to run around murdering people, unchecked and unpunished?" West asked.

Nicholas shrugged. "It's a small price to pay for the peace of mind of three hundred seven million people . . . *their* mentality, not mine."

"Twelve men? That's a lot of power for twelve men," Bling said.

"Too much," West added.

"Yes, it is," Nicholas agreed. "The country's very own secret, little jury."

"That's disgusting," West sneered.

"How do you know so much about them?" Kelli asked.

Nicholas stifled a frown. He had wondered when one of them would get around to asking that question. He wasn't proud of the answer. "My father used to work for them."

Each of Nicholas' passengers stared at him blankly. Nicholas understood. It wasn't easy for someone to hear the information that Nicholas had revealed and then process it easily. Nicholas wasn't surprised that each of them was at a loss for words. In fact, he expected it.

"This Agency you spoke of," West began, "if it's so secret, how does one become one of their operatives?"

"Their operatives are usually ex-military—most of whom are thought to be dead. But, at times, they groom their prospects while they're employed with the more well-known agencies."

"Like the FBI?" West asked.

Nicholas nodded. "The CIA, DEA, NSA…pick an acronym." Nicholas waited while West digested that last tidbit of information. Then, he spoke again. "You asked me earlier if I knew who set you up."

West turned to Nicholas. "Do you?"

"Not directly," Nicholas answered honestly. "Do *you*?"

West didn't respond.

Nicholas let his eyes wander to Kelli, and then to Bling. "Make yourselves comfortable," he advised them. "It's going be to a while."

Kelli sat back in her chair. Due to the events of the morning, she found it difficult to find any comfort at all. Bling reclined in his chair, popped his earphones into his ears and lost himself in the music.

West looked aimlessly out of the small cabin window. The jet was taxiing down the runway. West had been so enthralled in the conversation that he hadn't noticed when the aircraft began moving. West swallowed hard. He was beginning to wonder what else in his life had gone unnoticed.

$\sim\!\!\sim$

It was almost five o'clock in the evening. Gillis stood in front of the Hudson Hotel on 58th Street in Manhattan. He scrutinized each car as it moved past him, waiting for the right one to pull up. He rested against the wall next to one of the potted pines that lined the front of the building. Gillis was exhausted. Today had been a long, unproductive day. After being detained by the NYPD for as many times in two days, Gillis waited for his release into the custody of the federal authorities. Once transported to the FBI's New York field office, it was only a short time before the man known to Gillis as Mr. One orchestrated his extraction once again. After a lengthy walk to 58th Street, Gillis was ready to call it a day. Unfortunately for Gillis, there would be no rest until his assignment was completed successfully. Gillis was eager to get back on the hunt.

A black, late model Crown Victoria slowed in front of the hotel. The rear windows rolled down, then, just as quickly, rolled up again. Gillis recognized the signal.

He approached the car, opened the door, and slid into the passenger seat. He turned to the man sitting behind the wheel. Like Gillis, the man was a Caucasian male. His haircut smacked of military and his suit was pristine and pressed. He nodded as Gillis closed the door. The man pressed the accelerator and the car cruised forward.

Without looking at Gillis, the man spoke. "Gillis?"

"Yes."

"I'm Valverdi."

Gillis almost smiled. He thought Valverdi was an interesting choice for a name. He was well aware that Valverdi wasn't the man's real name. After all, the name Gillis was just a pseudonym that was given to him when he was drafted by the Agency.

"I've been briefed," Valverdi continued to say, "and I've been assigned as your partner for the remainder of this assignment. All of the standard items are in the manila envelope under your front seat."

Gillis said nothing. Instead, he reached under the passenger seat and pulled out the manila envelope. He opened one end of the paper sack and poured the contents onto his lap. There he found a .40 caliber Glock, a passport, an airline boarding pass, and a sizeable amount of cash divided into four stacks of one hundred dollar bills.

"All here," Gillis confirmed. He flipped over the boarding pass and looked at the destination: Los Angeles.

"Good," Valverdi responded. "I've been instructed to bring you up to speed on our situation. As you can see, we're being sent to Los Angeles. Our employer believes that is where our target is headed. When we arrive, we are to check in with Designate Four, at which time we will receive further instructions. Any questions?"

"No," Gillis responded.

"Excellent," Valverdi said, and then added, "don't screw this up. Good operatives are hard to come by."

Gillis managed a small grin. He knew that that was a warning from One. This was Gillis' last chance. If he didn't put the target down, he knew he was going to take her place.

ॐ

Los Angeles, California

The cross-country flight was long and grueling. Though Kelli was completely drained, she couldn't get herself to fall asleep on the jet. Every time she closed her eyes, visions of Francine being struck by Gillis' bullet flashed in her mind. Kelli wasn't the only one who had trouble getting rest. West was bothered by Nicholas' revelation about the secret agency that plays God with the lives of United States citizens. Bling was preoccupied as well. To Kelli, the only person on the flight who seemed at ease, besides the two pilots and the flight attendant, was Nicholas. Kelli wondered how often he did this sort of thing. She wondered if this was something to which one could grow accustomed. A life of intrigue and danger seemed romantic on television, but in real life, it was downright scary.

The jet touched down at a small airport in Van Nuys, just north of Los Angeles. Then, a private town car transported Nicholas and his three companions to the beautiful, cultural town of Pasadena. Kelli was in awe of how different the landscape of California was from that of New

York. It was surreal for her to look up and not see the towering, concrete and steel monstrosities with which she had grown familiar. The pedestrians of New York City seemed to step to an unheard beat, a rhythm that dictated the hustle and bustle that was their lifestyle. Here, as Kelli observed the people walking down Colorado Boulevard in Old Town Pasadena, she sensed a carefree attitude, a laid-back existence that seemed to lack urgency, or drive. Kelli glanced over at Bling. The look on his face seemed to convey the very thoughts she was thinking. He looked at her. He grimaced, gestured to the pedestrians, and then shook his head disapprovingly. In spite of herself, Kelli allowed a small grin to grace her lips. She was still troubled slightly by her verbal exchange with Bling as they boarded the jet back in New York. Maybe she had judged Bling too hastily when he'd asked for her help at school. Kelli wasn't certain. Bling did have a reputation for being a bad seed that ran with the wrong crowd. Perhaps Kelli shouldn't have assumed his reputation was completely accurate. Perhaps, as Bling had suggested, she should have asked.

The town car turned off the main boulevard. It headed into a more secluded-looking neighborhood with tall trees, green grass and metal gates. The car made a few more turns before pulling up to large gate in front of a massive estate. Kelli peered through the forward window and tried unsuccessfully to take in the entire house with one glance.

"Why didn't you just park your jet in the backyard?" Bling joked.

"I'd have to move the amusement park first," Nicholas said with a smile. West and Kelli looked at Bling. Bling smiled with a nod.

The large metal gate parted. The town car crossed the threshold and rolled onto the expansive property within. The long driveway was aligned with small trees and budding flowers on either side and was reminiscent of a narrow, country road in a small, southern town. Kelli looked ahead as the large mansion grew even larger by the second. The 24,000 square foot estate sat upon ten acres of green grass, broad fields and hidden trails. As they approached the house, three young children, two girls and a boy, were playing in the yard. The oldest child, a girl, turned and waved to Nicholas. He smiled and maneuvered the car to a halt in front of the grand steps.

Bling, being completely out of his element, began to feel uncomfortable. "I think I'm underdressed," he joked again.

"Yeah," West said in agreement, "Me, too."

Nicholas opened the door and exited the car. The three passengers followed suit and fell in behind Nicholas as he headed for the heavy-looking front door. The door opened and everyone entered the house. Kelli spied a golden plaque on the right side of the door frame that read: THE WOODS. She turned and looked back at the children. The oldest girl stared back at her. Her blonde hair strayed in the warm breeze and blew across her face. The girl didn't seem to notice. Kelli turned away and continued into the house. The door closed behind her with a soft hush.

Nicholas led them in to a large foyer. There was an oak, spiral staircase to the right, and a spacious library that opened off to the left. A man in a wheelchair rolled towards the unsuspecting trio. West saw him first. He resisted the urge to reach for his weapon. Bling saw the man next. Bling looked at the man and then followed the man's gaze to Kelli. Kelli froze in her tracks as the man glided to her feet and stopped before her. The man in the wheelchair, Dr. James Connelly, beamed with glee.

"Welcome, all of you," James said. He extended a hand to Kelli. "Kelli Freeman, I presume. It's such an honor to finally meet you. I'm James Connelly."

Kelli looked at Nicholas. Nicholas said to her, "My father."

Kelli turned back to James nervously. She accepted his hand and shook it gently. "Nice to meet you," she responded politely.

"I'm sure you have a multitude of questions," James said as he turned and acknowledged West and Bling, "all of you. After you've had a chance to settle in, I'll do what I can to fill in the blanks."

"With all due respect, sir," West spoke up. "Two attempts have been made on our lives in the last two days. We've travelled a long way to get these 'so-called' answers, and I think we've waited long enough."

James began to respond. Just then, the front door opened and the three children from the front yard hurried in. The oldest girl moved to James' side and hugged him. "How was your nap, Daddy?" she asked.

"Just fine, my dear," James answered. He gestured to the three newcomers. "Calliope, I'd like to introduce you to Special Agent West, Bryan Ling and—"

"I know who this is," she interrupted. The two other children gathered timidly behind Calliope as she stepped closer to Kelli and extended her hand in greeting. "I'm Calliope Woods. I can't believe that you're actually here."

Kelli looked around Calliope and focused on James. James giggled, "I promise I will explain everything. Please, settle in first. Relax. There is much to tell."

West looked at Kelli. She glanced at him and nodded.

Nicholas gestured towards the staircase. "You'll find your rooms up these stairs, and down the first hallway to the left. Feel free to freshen up. There is a change of clothing for each of you."

"Blanca is preparing a late lunch for us," James explained. "It should be ready in about an hour."

Calliope touched Kelli's arm. "I can show you to your room if you'd like."

Kelli smiled. "Sure. Okay."

Calliope led the group up the spiral case and directed each of them to their respective rooms. The last room on the left was Kelli's. As they reached the door, Kelli turned to Calliope. "Thank you. I was wondering . . ."

"Yes?" Calliope responded eagerly.

"You said your name was Calliope Woods, but Nicholas and your father–"

"Woods is the name I was born with," she explained. "My father legally changed his name from Connelly to Woods a few years before I came along."

"Oh," Kelli said, still confused.

"I'll let you get settled," Calliope said before excusing herself. She skipped down the hallway and disappeared down the stairs.

Kelli entered the room. It was a spacious room with a high ceiling. The lavender walls were decorated with wrought-iron butterfly sconces with multi-colored stained glass wings. The valences that hung over the large windows were white lace embroidered with a rich lavender and green trim. A large, king-sized bed sat against the far left wall. The right wall extended beyond the back wall into an opened-air bathroom that smelled of fresh lilacs. The carpet was plush and as white as a fresh field of snow. Kelli closed the door. A large, 12th century mural of Galen and Hippocrates had been replicated on the far wall. Kelli recognized this work from her accelerated studies curriculum. A large mirror sat above a long dresser that stood opposite the bed along the right wall. The furnishings in the room were immaculate.

Kelli sat at the foot of the bed and took in her surroundings. The house, the room, everything was beautiful. It was like a dream. Her mind drifted to Francine once more. She wished Francine was there to see this house. What she wouldn't give to have her best friend again. And what about Jaleesa? She hadn't even had time to think about Jaleesa since Francine was killed before her eyes. Kelli wanted to call her, but she couldn't. Nicholas had advised all of them to turn off their cell phones to prevent their signals from being traced. Kelli hated this. She had been separated from her family, her friends and her life. Why was this happening to her? How could her life go from normal one day then completely out of control the next? Kelli hoped that James Connelly had more than just the answers. She hoped he had a solution.

8

Despite her nerves, Kelli managed to enjoy the late lunch that Blanca, the live-in nanny and housekeeper, had prepared for them. After taking a long, hot shower, Kelli felt refreshed and revived. In the large walk-in closet, she found a casual, white, form- fitting shirt. Though smooth, the texture of the fabric felt unusual to her, almost elastic. A pair of blue sweatpants made from the same material adorned her lower body. She tied her long, straight tresses into a bun and slipped into a comfortable pair of sandals. She was the last to arrive at the lunch table. Bling, now dressed in a white polo shirt and a pair of jeans, sat next to West. The Special Agent was wearing a blue polo of the same design, but instead had donned a comfortable pair of khakis. As usual, his gun was holstered to his side.

After lunch, the group, including Calliope, adjourned to the grand study towards the back of the house. There, James Connelly wheeled his chair into the center of the room. Everyone sat in the chairs and on the sofa around him in order to have a front row seat. Finally, James turned to Kelli. "So," he began, "it's time you learned the truth. Ask me anything and everything."

"I don't know where to start," she said honestly. "So much has happened to me in the last few days, I . . . " she inhaled deeply. As she exhaled, her eyes met James'. "Can you explain the transformations?"

James' expression softened. He nodded slowly. When he spoke, he chose his words very carefully. "I did that to you."

"What do you mean? When?"

James chuckled. "Twenty years before you were born."

"I don't understand," Kelli said.

"It's been almost thirty-five years since I first met one of the most brilliant minds I have ever encountered," James smiled as a memory filled his mind. "I remember it clearly. I was working as a geneticist, employed by the government. Given my prior accomplishments in the field, I was selected to complete unfinished work on a military intelligence project." He leaned towards Kelli. "Are you familiar with eugenics?"

Kelli nodded. "Human manipulation of the gene pool."

"Very good," James praised her. "But then I expected nothing less from one whose intellect I suspect is becoming increasingly immeasurable. Yes?"

Kelli smiled modestly. "Since I was nine years old."

"Really?" West asked, surprised. "You're a certified genius?"

Kelli nodded. "Please, Doctor. Continue."

James cleared his throat. "Well, the practice of eugenics was supposedly abandoned after the horrific events that took place in Nazi Germany. Hitler's racial hygiene program might have been abolished, but the theory was still an intriguing one."

"Wasn't the Nazi program derived from the forced sterilizations that were initiated by the United States?" Kelli asked.

"You've done your homework," James said. "Only years later, the United States felt that the world's technological advances could ultimately evolve the eugenics programs of the past. This is why I was brought into their employ. I, too, believed that this medical breakthrough could be achieved. I was partnered with one of the few men whose intelligence surpassed even my own . . . Dr. Marcus June."

"Never heard of him," West said.

"Neither have I," Kelli admitted.

"That's not surprising," James said. "His very existence was wiped out by the very Agency that is now pursuing Miss Freeman here. Needless to say, before his tragic death, Dr. June and I succeeded. We created a stable, viable genome for a super soldier."

"Super soldier?" Bling questioned.

"Indeed. Superior in every way, mentally and physically...enhanced intellect, eidetic memory, enhanced strength, heightened resistance to disease and sickness . . . genetically engineered humans that were bred with all the desirable traits without any of the undesirable ones . . . science working in perfect accord with nature. We called it the Harmony Project. It was quite remarkable."

"What happened next?" West asked.

"We manipulated all the traits we could, but Dr. June knew that the experiment had a better chance of succeeding if the fertilization and incubation processes were as natural as possible."

"Meaning?" West asked.

"We inseminated an actual woman with the enhanced genetic material," James said. "The woman had been injured in a fall and was brain-dead. What did we have to lose?"

"And it worked?" Kelli asked.

"Like a charm," James said proudly. "However, because we used an actual female as opposed to a laboratory incubator, the X chromosome found a way to dominate. Our super soldier was born female." James laughed. "Marcus was a descendant of civil rights activists. He was very adamant about producing an African-American soldier. I didn't care one way or the other. Imagine Marcus' pride when the child was born black *and* female."

"What happened to her?"

"We named her Harmony in honor of the project's name. We gave her Marcus' surname because someone had to raise her and educate her outside of the lab. It just so happened that Marcus' wife, Serena, was unable to have children. It seemed like a win-win situation."

"Until?" West knew the downside of the story was soon to come.

James remained silent for a moment. Not all of the memories that were flooding his brain were pleasant. "Until we realized that we had done our jobs too well."

"Explain," Kelli said.

"We had designed Harmony to be resistant to disease and illness. Every strain of the flu we threw at her, Harmony's immunity attacked and destroyed it. What we didn't realize was this: by manipulating the genes that enhanced her immune response, we, inadvertently, activated a dormant immunity gene that was somehow linked to hormonal balances that, ultimately, regulates the sex of an unborn fetus. This gene, later named the June Gene, allowed Harmony to shift from one gender to the other."

Kelli gasped heavily. All eyes in the room landed on her. Her cheeks became warm as she closed her eyes in embarrassment.

After a moment, James continued. "Each time Harmony shifted genders, certain immunity based cell groups would identify and eradicate any foreign bodies that were present during the regeneration process."

"Whoa," said West. "You lost me."

Kelli spoke up. "When the body shifts genders, certain body parts are regenerated or diminished, depending on which sex is prevalent." She looked at James.

"You're on the right track. Go on," James urged her.

"If the body is switching from male to female, the uterus and female reproductive organs have to be regenerated. When this happens, the immune response goes into overdrive to keep the body from harm. If there are any bacteria or viruses present during this time, they are identified as foreign and destroyed."

James smiled proudly. "That's it exactly."

"I don't get it," said Bling, scratching his head.

"It means that Harmony's body eradicated any and all diseases every time she shifted genders," Kelli explained.

"We injected her with several known diseases, a variety of strains, exposed her to cancer-inducing levels of radiation," James said. "Every time she shifted, the diseased cells were destroyed."

"That's, uh . . . cool," Bling said for lack of a better adjective.

"It's more than cool," James said. "Dr. June and I had stumbled upon the cure for all known diseases. It was the most amazing breakthrough in medical history. When our employers found out what we had done, we were ordered to scrap the project and terminate Harmony."

"Kill the girl?" West asked. "That's barbaric!"

"Barbaric is an understatement," James said to him. "Harmony was a ten-year-old girl at the time."

"I don't understand," Kelli said. "Why? I thought that finding a cure for diseases was a good thing."

James turned and faced her. "Let me ask you all a question. What do you think would happen to this country's economy if all diseases were suddenly cured? What? If all the pharmaceutical companies were no longer needed, what do you think would happen to this country?" West, Bling, and Kelli stared at him blankly. "I'll tell you. The government would go broke. Our government profits from the country's illnesses. When they realized that we had developed a cure for *everything*, they shut us down."

"That's why they're after me," Kelli surmised.

"But wait," West interjected. "Harmony was killed. Right?"

"Yes," James answered, "but we had extracted stem cells from Harmony shortly after she was born."

"You cloned her," West said.

"Yes. We had to," admitted James. "We were doctors. We had found a way to cure humanity of every ailment—cancer, AIDS, the common cold— and they wanted us to destroy it all and walk away. We couldn't do it. So, in secret, we used Harmony's stem cells and cloned her, but this time, we did something different. This time, we found a way to incorporate some of Dr. June's DNA. Previously, during the initial Harmony experiment, we found that our genetically enhanced fetus had healed some of the scar tissue that we'd found in the uterine walls of our brain-dead host. We theorized that if we engineered the cloned embryos to repair damaged reproductive tissue, we could inseminate a woman who couldn't otherwise carry children."

"So you implanted it into Dr. June's wife," Kelli deduced.

"Precisely," James said. "And this time, the clone was born male. The Junes named him Christopher. He was a handsome young lad, so full of energy. It was our expectation that his ability to shift would manifest itself during his early pre-pubescent stage."

"You said, earlier, that Dr. June was dead," West said. "His family, too?"

"I'm afraid so," said James solemnly. "Christopher had just celebrated his first birthday. We don't know how they found out about him, but they did. They came after Marcus and his family. They were killed right in front of me. All three of them. It was the saddest day of my life. Dr. June was a good man who only wanted to serve humanity with his extraordinary gifts. He was a wonderful friend. He didn't deserve that fate. None of them deserved it. The Agency destroyed our lab. They killed our assistant, Dr. Simons, as well."

"How did you survive?" asked West.

"I have leverage," James revealed. "I made detailed copies of all our research, along with DNA samples, and I stored them in a safe deposit box. I gave the key to someone I could trust. In the event of my untimely death, the evidence was to be leaked to the press and the authorities."

"I thought these people were untouchable," West countered. "Surely you had more than that."

James ran his fingers through his graying brown hair. "I did have one more thing. These twelve men I mentioned, they all have numeric designations that they use in the presence of one another. It's a precautionary tactic in the unlikely event that their conversations are recorded."

"They don't trust each other?" Kelli asked.

"They trust each other as much as they have to," James answered. "But it's in the Agency's best interest to protect each other. At any rate, there is one designate in particular, Mr. One—I know who he is."

"What!?" West exclaimed. "Why haven't you gone public with that information? We can stop these guys."

"No, we can't. Not like that," James told him. "If I expose him publicly, the Agency will just replace him with someone else. This is a hand I can play only once, Agent West. I must pick that particular battle very carefully."

Kelli was becoming more and more anxious. Though she was waiting for the part of the story that pertained to her, she already suspected what James was going to say. "Okay, Mr. Connelly," Kelli spoke loudly, "so you managed to stay alive. What happened next?"

"I couldn't continue working for them," he explained. "It was too dangerous. So I disappeared. Nicholas was seven years old at the time, and I had to think of his safety. I changed our names and I moved to the Midwest for a while. I found a job teaching at a small university and I stayed off the Agency's radar."

"But you continued to work on the Harmony Project, didn't you?" Kelli asked pointedly.

James' eyes dropped to his lap. He nodded, slightly ashamed. He could sense Kelli's growing frustration. "Yes, I did. I know that I should have abandoned the research, but I couldn't. Dr. June's sacrifice had been too great and I couldn't sit idle and allow his legacy to die." James looked up at Kelli. Her eyes were locked onto his. James continued his tale. "It took me almost five years to find a couple with the right profile: young, African-American, with difficulties conceiving children. I'd almost given up, and then one day, I came across the Freemans—"

"You must be mistaken," Kelli interrupted him. "I have an older brother. My mother was able to have children."

"Yes, she was," James said, "but there were complications with her first pregnancy that prevented her from being able to conceive again. Your parents wanted desperately to have more children. I approached them and proposed a solution. I was very candid about all that had transpired with the Harmony Project. Your parents were still willing to proceed. I did not ask for money. I was a millionaire several times over so I didn't need it. All I asked was that, if ever your family was in danger because of our arrangement, they send you back to me."

Kelli became outwardly incensed. "My parents would never have agreed to that."

"But they did," James insisted. "They wanted to have more children. Remember, the cloned embryo from Harmony repaired reproductive tissue. I did not give them promise for having just one more child, I gave them hope to have as many as they wished. Do you have younger siblings?"

Kelli tried to smother her rage. "A brother and a sister."

West stood and began to walk the perimeter of their little circle. Finally, the pieces began to fall into place. "Kelli's involvement in the car accident exposed her ability to shift genders. The Agency gets wind of it and they send someone to investigate, but . . ." West grew hot under the collar as realization began to set in, "but the person they called was incapacitated, so . . . my partner sent *me*."

"Your partner?" Bling questioned aloud.

West accepted the only truth that made sense. "Yeah, my partner. If he hadn't been injured the day before, he would have investigated this himself. That's why he tried to pull me back. He knew the Agency had decided to target Kelli, but I wouldn't listen."

"It's a good thing you didn't," Nicholas stated.

Kelli sat there and listened, fuming silently.

"That's why they are so adamant to catch her," James said. "Imagine what would happen if the citizens of this country found out the government had found a cure for all known diseases, but kept it from them. Think about how many people have lost their loved ones—fathers, mothers, children—you name it. Now imagine how angry those people would be if they discovered that none of their loved ones had to die."

"An entire country pissed off at the government," West surmised aloud, "would mean the beginning of the end of life in the U.S. as we know it."

"And Kelli is the key," James said.

Kelli could contain her fury no longer. She rose from her chair and took a step towards James. "You did this, all of this! I've been feeling guilty over Francine's death, but you . . . playing God with other people's lives," she began to cry incessantly. "You killed Francine! You've put us all in danger. This is your fault!" She stepped closer and pointed a finger at James. "I hate you!" she yelled. "Do you hear me? I hate you!"

Kelli turned and stormed out of the study. All eyes stared as she disappeared around the corner. Silence fell over the gathering. One by one, each of them turned and rested their gaze on James Connelly. James' eyes were lowered towards his lap once again. He had wanted Kelli to understand. Unfortunately, she understood all too well. James didn't blame her for hating him. After all, Kelli was right.

Finally, Bling rose from his chair. Quietly, and without uttering a sound, he left the room in search of Kelli. The silence still hung uncomfortably in the air. Calliope moved to her father's side and wrapped her arms around him. James felt the dampness from her tears as they rolled onto his face. He closed his eyes and wished that he could make all of this go away. However, James knew that wishing wasn't going to be enough.

"So what do we do now?" West asked James.

James didn't open his eyes. He put his arms around his young daughter and hugged her tight.

"James?"

"I don't know," James said finally. He opened his eyes and looked up at the young FBI Agent. "I really don't know."

൧൦ഄ൦

Kelli sat under one of the large trees that lined the driveway. Her mind raced as tears poured from her eyes uncontrollably. She sobbed so hard that she found it difficult to catch her breath. She had come across the country to find out the truth, only to learn that truth is wrapped around a big lie. She pounded her bare fist against the rough bark of the tree. She did it again, and again. Each time, she cried harder and harder. A noise behind Kelli made her jump in fear. She turned. There stood Bling.

He placed a hand on her shoulder. Kelli shrugged it off forcefully.

"Go away, Bryan! Just leave me alone!"

"You sure?" he asked.

"Am I sure?" she repeated his question through an increasing barrage of tears.

"Yeah. Sometimes when I'm upset, I say I want to be left alone, but I don't . . . I know how it feels."

Kelli whipped around and faced Bling. "Do you know how it feels to learn that you're a third generation clone of a freaking science experiment?"

"Well, no, but—so what?"

"So what?" she yelled back at him. "My life is a lie, Bryan. I wasn't conceived out of love, I was engineered in a Petri dish. I'm not Kelli Freeman, I'm not Harmony June . . . and the whole super soldier thing, that's a laugh! I'm four-teen. I've always been told that I was gifted because of my aptitude for learning; it turns out that that's a lie, too. It's not a gift if that's what I was genetically predisposed to be."

Bling didn't know what to say to console her. It wasn't as if her argument wasn't valid.

"And then there's my parents," Kelli said with dis-dain. "They've known my entire life that this was going to happen to me. They've been lying to me the whole time. When I didn't have my period, my mother knew why."

"Whoa," said Bryan as he threw up a hand in uncom-fortable protest.

Kelli ignored him and continued her rant. "And do you think she said anything?"

"What was she supposed to say?"

"Something . . . anything!" Kelli yelled. "Instead, she pretended she had no idea what was happening."

"Maybe she didn't," Bling said in Diane's defense. "Your mother ain't a scientist."

"No, she isn't," Kelli agreed. "She's a mother. That's what I needed."

Bling moved closer to Kelli. "I know what it's like to feel betrayed by a parent. My dad took off when I was little and never came back. Even though my mom tried to hold it down, I–"

"Don't try and compare our lives, Bryan," Kelli screamed. "And don't try to console me, okay? We're not friends. Three days ago you tried to give me your number so we could *kick it*, as if it was my friendship you were interested in. Then, this morning, you bit my head off when I tried to show a little concern, so don't pretend that we're friends. You're just a guy who was in the wrong place at the wrong time. So, just . . . go away, all right?" With that, Kelli turned her back to him.

Bling stepped back. Though he didn't want to admit it, his feelings were hurt. He stared at Kelli's back for an instant before turning and heading back to the house. As he turned, he resisted the urge to call her a bitch. Bling knew that she was hurting. In truth, he couldn't imagine having to deal with such an enormous problem. Her very existence represented a medical miracle that could change the world. Consequently, someone was trying to rob her of that existence. Bling sighed heavily as he approached the house. He pulled open the door; he turned and looked back at Kelli. He shook his head in sadness. She was right about what she said earlier. He was simply a guy in the wrong place at the wrong time. His involvement in this matter was insignificant. He was collateral damage, expendable, unimportant. 'Yeah', Bling thought to himself, 'the story of my life.'

❧❧

Arlington, Virginia

Special Agent Towers occupied the passenger seat of the grey sedan that was cruising north on the George Washington Parkway. Assistant Director Marsh from the D.C. field office was behind the wheel. Towers had much on his mind. He had betrayed his partner, Special Agent West, and allowed him to walk into an ambush. By a strange turn of events, West survived and then vanished from the radar. His cell phone was turned off so Towers had no way to reach him or track him. Towers' conscience wouldn't let him relax. His betrayal of West bothered him. If only he could contact him, maybe then he could try to get West to come in. Maybe he could save West's life before the Agency caught up with him.

At the moment, however, West was the least of Towers' worries. When A.D. Marsh picked him up from Reagan National Airport, Towers could tell it was going to be a long ride back to the office. Marsh had received the same report that was now circulating through the Bureau. Marsh was livid. Not only was he upset that West had gone unaccounted for, but it was suspected that West was with the two minors who were eyewitnesses to the murder of Francine Rodriguez. The FBI was catching major heat on this one, and no one knew where to point the finger.

"When was the last time you spoke to Agent West?" Marsh asked.

"Shortly after the Rodriguez girl was killed. We were at the police station in the Bronx," Towers answered.

"What did he say?" Marsh probed. "Did he give you any idea that he was going to bolt with those kids?"

"No," Towers barely had enough time to say.

"And how did he manage to sneak two teenagers out of a police station undetected, anyway?" Marsh questioned.

Towers shrugged. "I have no idea, sir." Of one thing Towers was certain, Marsh had no connection or knowledge of the Agency. 'Then again,' Towers reconsidered suddenly, 'What if Marsh knows what's really going on, but he doesn't think I do? That's the problem with this type of covert activity. You never know who you can trust.' Towers decided to do a little probing of his own. Perhaps if he asked the right questions, he could siphon information out of Marsh.

"Who relayed the report about West, sir?" Towers asked.

"Baldwin told me," Marsh answered unsuspectingly.

"Well, he's the director," Towers stated. "Who did he get the info from? Ross, maybe?"

"He didn't say," Marsh answered with a distinct air of irritation. "In fact, he made a point of saying that he couldn't say. Makes me think it came from the Pentagon."

"The Pentagon?" Towers' feigned ignorance. He was pleased that Marsh seemed genuinely unaware of the Agency's existence. The only thing he had to do was play along. "Why would the Pentagon be involved in a murder in the Bronx?"

Marsh looked at Towers. The look on his face was intensely grave. His wheels were turning as if he knew something but was reluctant to enlighten Towers. Then, finally, he spoke. "What I'm about to tell you doesn't leave this car," Marsh said.

"Of course," Towers agreed immediately.

"I'm telling you this only because we've known each other for so long," Marsh added.

"You can trust me, sir," Towers lied.

Marsh nodded. "You know the corpse that West handed us? Finch. He's a ghost."

"What?" Towers exclaimed, simulating surprise.

"No hits on his prints. No hits on his DNA, dental records, or body markings—nothing. It's like he never existed."

Towers let his jaw drop slightly. He expected this. He knew how the Agency operated. "What do you think it means?"

"It means there's a player in the game that we're not aware of," Marsh responded. "Which subsequently means West is either involved, or in danger."

Towers didn't comment. He couldn't. This situation had grown out of control. Towers' knew that, wherever West was, he was in way over his head.

❦

Los Angeles International Airport

Gillis and Valverdi disembarked from the plane and moved down the long ramp to the gate inside the airport. They maneuvered inconspicuously through the moving crowd of weary travelers, oblivious to the normal hustle and bustle of the airport. As they passed through the security gate, Valverdi tapped Gillis and gestured to his left. A man in a dark suit approached them.

"Agent Valverdi, Agent Gillis," The man said. "I'm Agent Lind. Designate Four sent me to bring you in and debrief you."

"Excellent," Valverdi responded robotically.

"I trust your flight was a comfortable one," Lind said pleasantly. "Los Angeles is beautiful this time of year."

"Believe it or not," Gillis said, "I've never been." A lie.

"Oh," Lind said gleefully. "Hopefully we'll wrap up our business quickly, and you'll have some time to relax."

"Yeah," Gillis replied. "That would be nice." Gillis' concern wasn't on rest and relaxation. He wanted to find the girl, finish the job, and make it through this situation alive. It wasn't customary for Agency operatives to ask why a given person becomes a target. It is understood that the less one knows, the better. But this time, Gillis' curiosity was getting the better of him. He had never known there to be three active agents working the same assignment. Too many agents presented the possibility of too many loose ends. For some reason, this assignment seemed to be the exception. Or was it just that the Agency was unsure of Gillis' ability to complete the mission? Gillis pushed that thought out of his head. 'No room for paranoia,' he told himself. 'Just finish the job, and everything will be fine.' Now, if he could just get himself to believe it.

છે

Kelli had wandered the grounds for a while and then managed to make it back to the front porch. She followed the porch as it extended around the side of the house.

There, she found a comfortable-looking swing. She sat in the chair and pushed against the floor of the porch lightly. The gentle swaying soothed her and calmed her enough to the point where she was beginning to think from a place of logic, not emotion. She thought of her parents and the decisions they made, both past and present. She was still angry with them, but Kelli's maturity allowed her to, at least, try to see it from their point of view. It wasn't easy.

Kelli heard the front door open. A second later, she heard it close followed by light footsteps that travelled in her direction. Kelli suspected it was Bling coming back outside to give her a piece of his mind. She didn't care. She was ready for him. But Kelli was wrong. Instead, Calliope rounded the corner. She smiled sweetly at Kelli and approached her slowly.

"May I join you?" Calliope asked in a sweet tone.

Kelli gestured to the open space next to her. Calliope's smile widened and she plopped down in the seat without making a sound.

"Are you okay?" Calliope asked.

"I don't know," Kelli answered honestly. "I'm not sure what I'm feeling."

"I understand why you're mad at my father," the young girl said, "but he really does have your best interest at heart."

Kelli turned to her. "How old are you?"

Calliope grinned bashfully. "I'm twelve and a half."

"Where's your mother?"

"Gone," Calliope said. "She moved back to England about two years ago. She and my father were not getting along."

"Oh. I'm sorry to hear that," Kelli said. "Didn't you want to go live with her?"

"We couldn't," Calliope answered sadly. "It was part of the agreement."

"What agreement?" Kelli asked. She knew she was prying.

"It's complicated," the girl responded.

Kelli touched the girl's arm. "I understand," she said, then added, "you're pretty mature for your age."

"My father says it comes with the territory."

Kelli smiled, but then, Calliope's words sunk in and took on another meaning. "Calliope, what's your I.Q.?"

"170 and climbing," she said proudly. Then, she looked directly into Kelli's eyes. "I really do understand what you're going through, or, at least, I will very soon."

"When you reach puberty," Kelli surmised.

Calliope nodded.

"And your sister and brother?"

Again, Calliope nodded.

Kelli couldn't believe it. Dr. Connelly didn't stop after he engineered her. He continued and went on to genetically enhance his very own children as well.

"We were born the same way," Calliope said. "Our mother carried us just like your mother carried you."

"Are you . . . clones?"

"No," Calliope answered. "My father extracted eggs from my mother's ovaries and then re-inserted them." Calliope moved closer to Kelli. "Don't you understand? That's why it is so great to have you here. Me and my brother and sister, we exist the way we are because of the Harmony Project. For years now, our father has been telling us about Harmony June and what an amazing girl she

was. He spoke of her with such pride and adoration...
and sorrow. I used to dream about meeting her, getting to
know her...thanking her."

"Thanking her? For what?"

"I love my life," the young girl answered. "You may see
my father as a monster, but he's the best father a girl could
ask for. I'm grateful to be alive, and I'm happy to be who and
what I am. I owe much of that to him, but I owe a great deal
of it to her–Harmony June. My little sister, Clara, and my
baby brother, Joseph–we're all just products of the Harmony
Project, but you–you're more than just a product of it, you're
more than just a clone, you're the embodiment of this wonderful girl. When I look at you, I see Harmony June."

Kelli was at a loss for words. She was amazed at Calliope's
intellectual capacity. Though Kelli was older than she,
Calliope seemed far more advanced than Kelli remembered
being at that age. Perhaps it was because Calliope grew up
knowing who she was, and having a father who was a scientific genius in his own right was surely a benefit. A mere
moment ago, when Calliope confessed to her that she, too,
was genetically enhanced, Kelli felt pity for her because she
was an innocent victim of Dr. Connelly's obsession. But
now, after hearing Calliope speak so fondly of her life, Kelli
was overwhelmed with envy. Calliope was certain of her
identity. Kelli, for the first time in her life, was not.

A single tear welled up in Kelli's right eye and rolled
down her cheek. She lowered her head. "I appreciate what
you're trying to do. I wish I knew what to feel about myself
right now."

Calliope sat next to Kelli in silence. They rocked in
the swing holding each other's hand. After some time had
passed, Calliope tilted her head to one side. "Does it hurt?"

Kelli turned to her. "What?"

"When you become a boy."

Kelli could tell that Calliope was anxious about the experience. She knew that, one day, Calliope would be going through it as well. "A little," she told her honestly. "But it gets easier every time, or, at least, when I'm a little excited."

"My father would say that's due to a rush of adrenaline." Calliope's eyes widened. "Can you show me?"

Kelli stopped breathing. The image of Francine's reaction in the bedroom came rushing back to her in full force. It took a few seconds for her to take a deep breath and relax. She liked Calliope. It was nice to have someone close to her own age with whom she could talk. That's how it was with Francine. But this girl wasn't Francine. Francine was gone and she was never coming back.

Kelli managed a small smile. "Maybe some other time."

Calliope was content with that. She beamed at Kelli. "Cool." An excited look crossed Calliope's face. "Do you want some dessert? Blanca makes the best cheesecake."

Kelli relaxed a little more. "Sure. I'd love some."

∂∞⌐

James and Nicholas were in the den. The large plasma screen television was tuned to a local news station. West entered. His eyes were drawn immediately to his own image being displayed on the screen. The FBI had released an official statement announcing the disappearance of Special Agent West and two minor children involved in the

Bronx shooting the night before. A telephone number was superimposed under West's picture. Anyone who had seen or had any knowledge of West's whereabouts was being instructed to call that number. West was not happy.

"What the hell is the Bureau doing?" West asked angrily.

"Covering their asses," Nicholas responded.

West's eyes shifted from the screen to James. James nodded in concurrence.

"There is a dead girl in the Bronx and two eyewitnesses have miraculously gone missing. They needed to put someone's face to it."

"So they picked mine?" West asked, growing more furious by the second.

"They can't blame it on this Gillis character you mentioned, now can they?" James spun his wheelchair around to face West. "He's surely not in their custody anymore, and the FBI isn't going to lay claim to him. Your face is the only one available."

West knew he was right. West imagined that, no matter how powerful the Agency really was, the shooting death of Francine Rodriguez received too much coverage to be swept under the rug. When crimes such as this occur, the public needs a scapegoat, someone to vilify. Tonight, it was West.

≈∽✑

Kelli and Calliope ate cheesecake in the dining room. Clara, the second eldest child, and Joseph, the youngest, bounded into the room cheerfully. Clara sat next to Calliope while

Joseph positioned himself in the chair directly opposite Kelli.

"Hello, there," Kelli greeted them politely. "You must be Clara and Joseph."

Clara nodded happily. Joseph extended his arm towards Kelli. Gripped between his fingers was a photograph. "I found this."

"You can't find something that wasn't lost, Joseph," Clara corrected him.

"What's this?" Kelli asked as she took the photo from the young boy. She flipped the photo around and stared at the image. The expression on her face went blank. Kelli stared at photo of a young, black girl that looked exactly like her. Kelli turned the photo over and looked at the inscription on the back. It read: Harmony, nine years old. Standing next to Harmony was a handsome black man wearing a long, white lab coat. Kelli surmised that it was Dr. Marcus June. She searched his face for any resemblances that she might have to him, any similarities in the smile, or the shape of the eyes. Kelli didn't have to look too deeply. She saw it all.

Kelli placed the photograph on the table. Calliope peered at the old photo and then shot a nasty glare at Joseph. "Why did you do that, Joseph?"

"Do what?" he asked innocently.

"It's all right," Kelli assured her. "It's just weird seeing my face. . .*our* face."

"Father has one of baby Christopher, too," Joseph said proudly. "Want to see it?"

"Joseph Colin Woods!" Calliope snapped at him.

"Yes," Kelli said abruptly. "I'd like to see it, and any other pictures you might have." Kelli wasn't certain if she was ready to see old pictures of her predecessors, but she knew running from the truth wasn't going to make it go away. She learned that from her father, Arthur Freeman.

Joseph leapt from his chair and dashed out of the room. Kelli glanced at little Clara. Her eyes watched Kelli intensely. "You have pretty hair," Clara said. Kelli smiled at her meekly. "Are you going to stay here?" Clara asked.

Kelli shook her head. "I don't know. For a little while." Kelli's gaze dropped to the photo that sat in front of her. A chill shot up her spine. As she looked at the man who gave her life, literally, her thoughts traveled back to the man and family with whom her life made sense. More than anything, Kelli wanted to go back home. But she couldn't. Doing so would bring certain danger to her family. It terrified her to think that she may never see them again.

꙳

FBI Field Office,
Washington, D.C.

Towers limped slowly through the corridors. He didn't like using the cane. It felt clumsy and it made him feel like an invalid. He didn't want to admit that, for now, he needed it. The cane was the only way he could get around.

Towers entered the central hub of activity in the office. He looked around the room. His attention zeroed in on a young, attractive brunette by the name of Monica Davies. Davies had been with the Bureau almost five years. Towers had partnered up with her once or twice on assignments before West came aboard and became his permanent sidekick.

Right now, Davies was working on the communications end of this investigation. Towers made a beeline for her desk.

"Hey, Monica. How's it goin'?" he asked politely as he neared her.

Davies looked up from her computer console. "Jimmy, ouch," she said as she spied the sling on his arm. "You just got shot three days ago, what are you doing here?"

"You know I can't just sit around," he responded.

"Then go home and lie around," she joked.

"Soon enough," he said dismissively. "Hey, any hits on West's cell?"

Davies gestured to her computer. "No activity on his cell, no signal at all. Wherever he is, his cell is off."

"How about the two missing kids? We know the Freeman girl has a cell phone, but what about the other one?"

Davies tapped a few strokes on the keypad. "No signal on the Freeman girl's cell, and, yes, the Ling kid has a cell but there's no activity showing there, either."

"Damn," Towers cursed.

"Any idea what's going on?"

"Uh, no. I'm just worried about Donald," Towers said. "He's a good guy."

"He is," Davies agreed. "If anything comes up I'll let you know."

"I appreciate it," Towers said. With that, Towers hobbled across the room and found a desk behind which to relax. His shoulder and thigh ached with every step. Davies was right. He should be at home relaxing. But right now, he wanted to find West. Towers wanted to save him if he could. More importantly, he wanted to do what he had to do to help clear up this mess before evidence of his own involvement came back to haunt him.

৵ঙ

Bling sat on the floor at the foot of the bed. The bedroom that was assigned to him, like every other room in the house, was enormous. Despite the handsome oak furniture, the beautiful paintings on the walls, and the large personal bathroom, Bling was most impressed by the floor-to-ceiling closet that lined the left wall. He could only imagine owning enough clothing to fill that closet. Running the streets of New York and committing petty crimes would never afford him the life about which he fantasized. Only a true master of gangster life could ever hope to attain a fraction of the wealth Bling was witnessing here. He was smart enough to know that his present course in life was a destination to nowhere.

Luckily, Bling had another plan. Like many young street thugs, he had often dreamed of becoming a famous Hip-Hop artist and making it big in music, raking in the money, and then living the life of luxury. Until now, he never really had a clear picture of what that luxury looked like. Now, Bling wondered if he really had what it took to master the street game and live a thug life that was worthy of Hip-Hop rhymes and commercial success.

In the past two days, Bling had been shot at more than once. The experience brought his mortality into very clear perspective. Still, the events of the last forty-eight hours were over-shadowed by something else that was far more important to Bling. Through it all, one thought kept creeping into his mind. 'I'm never gonna see my *moms* again.' Bling was worried about her. The sad part was, his mother probably had no idea that he was missing. How

could she? Her chemotherapy made her extremely sick.
On the day that he was supposed to meet Kelli for their
first tutoring session, his mother collapsed in their kitchen.
Bling hotwired the car and drove her to the hospital himself. His mother had been in the hospital getting pumped
full of morphine ever since. He felt horrible that he wasn't
there for her. In a way, he hoped that she was still unconscious. That way, she wouldn't know that he wasn't by her
side. She wouldn't know that her son was wrapped up in
the murder of a neighborhood girl and was now missing.
With his connection to the local gang, he knew that his
mother would only think the worst. Bling didn't want to
lose his mother, and despite his rough, gang attitude and
exterior, he loved her more than anything in the world.

Bling reached into his pocket and pulled out his cell
phone. Nicholas had told them to keep their cell phones
turned off. The danger of being tracked was too great. Still,
Bling wanted to call the hospital and check on his mother.
'It will only take a minute. They can't trace a call that fast,
can they?' Bling decided that knowing about his mother's
condition was worth the risk. He pressed the power button.
The backlight illuminated the numbers and the small screen
lit up. Bling waited as the phone rebooted and searched
for service. He watched as the bars appeared on the phone,
indicating the signal strength. Bling dialed his mother's
room directly. Two rings later, the phone was answered.

"Hello," he said eagerly. "Is this Michelle Ling's room?
Room 514?"

"Yes," a female voice responded.

"This is her son, Bling, uh, Bryan. Who's this?"

"I'm Ms. Ling's nurse," the voice said.

"How is she? How's my moms?"

"I'm sorry, but Ms. Ling's condition hasn't changed. She's been in and out of consciousness for the last few days."

"Has she–you know . . . asked for me?"

"Yes, she has," the nurse responded. "You really ought to come and see her."

Bling became choked up. He cleared his throat in an effort to sound unaffected. "Uh, I will. When she wakes up again, tell her I'll be there as soon as I can."

"I sure will."

Bling started to lose it. He uttered a quick, "Thank you. Goodbye." He pressed the 'end' button and disconnected the call. He buried his head in his hands and did something that he hadn't done in a long time. He cried.

❧

Gillis groaned as he took a seat at the table. His body was sore from all the bullets that had slammed into his vest over the last few days. He swallowed hard and tried to ignore the pain. Valverdi pulled up a chair and sat next to him. The small apartment was sparsely decorated and it was evident that no one had taken up residence here in quite some time. This was a briefing station for the Agency. It was a small, insignificant rest stop along the way where operatives could receive and relay sensitive information to the Designate who oversaw that respective region. The southwestern region fell under the 'care' of Designate Four.

In the center of the table rested a speaker phone. Lind entered the room and stood by the table. A second later, the phone rang. Lind pressed the button and spoke aloud. "We're here."

"How's the weather?" the voice said.

"Highs in the mid 80's with a low of 76 today," Lind responded.

There was a brief silence as the coded response was verified. Then, the voice came back. "Confirmed. This is Mr. Four. Listen carefully. Your mission objective has been altered. Special Agent West and the girl are to be captured and brought in alive. Everyone else is expendable."

"Understood," Lind responded. "Do we have a location?"

"Yes. Wait until midnight, go to rendezvous point thirteen and pick up the Specialist. You will receive the location at that time."

Lind paused. He wanted to ask a question, but then thought better of it. "Understood."

"Good luck, gentlemen." The phone clicked and the call ended.

Gillis was confused. This method of operation was far from standard. Gillis could not contain his curiosity. "The Specialist? Since when do we have four agents on one case?"

Valverdi rotated his head slowly and glared at Gillis. "Since when do we ask?"

"The Specialist is not an operative like us," Lind offered. "They don't usually accompany us."

"Why now? Why is this girl so special?" Gillis knew he was crossing a line.

"You know that I'm not privy to that information," Lind responded stoically. "I suggest you stifle your penchant for asking questions that will get you killed, Agent Gillis. You know the rules."

Gillis did know the rules. He knew that four operatives on one case was a clear violation of every rule he was

trained to follow. Still, Gillis bit his tongue. He nodded and remained silent. Gillis didn't like this situation.
There were too many variables, and he knew that something other than the mission was at hand. Suddenly, Gillis
knew what he had to do. 'After we get the girl, I'm going
to kill Valverdi and Lind. If I don't, I'm sure they're going
to kill me.' Paranoia or not, Gillis wasn't going to take any
chances.

∾∽

Towers slumped over onto his desk. The events of the day
had taken their toll. He was tired. He had tried to fight the
fatigue but he couldn't hang on. 'Maybe it's the vicodin,'
he wondered to himself as he slipped into slumber. A sharp
knock at the door snapped him back into coherency. He
jumped. Davies chuckled as she leaned in through the
doorway.

"We got a hit," she announced. "Bryan Ling's cell
phone placed a call about an hour ago. His cell signal was
transmitted by a cell tower in Pasadena."

"California? Does Marsh know?"

"Yep," Davies answered. "He's already contacted the
L.A. field office."

Towers pulled himself to his feet. He grabbed his cane
and limped out of his office. He needed to talk to Marsh.
Only Marsh could give him what he needed now. Two minutes later, he was in front of Marsh, posing his question.

"Are you out of your mind, Towers?" Marsh asked.
"There's no way I'm sending you to Los Angeles. Even if
you weren't injured, the answer would still be 'no'."

"Please, sir," Towers begged. "West is my partner. If there's any way I can convince him to come in . . ."

Marsh didn't budge. "What part of 'hell no' did you not understand? Besides, you're supposed to be on medical leave."

"Sir, I can do this," Towers protested.

"No you can't," Marsh retorted. "You're on medical leave as of three days ago. I don't want you anywhere near this, you hear me? Go on, get out of here. Now!"

Towers wanted to push a little more but he knew his efforts would be futile. Marsh had made his decision and that was that. Towers went back to his office and gathered whatever personal items he would need while on medical leave. He knew Marsh would flip if he saw him in there again before he was cleared to return to duty.

Davies entered the office and slapped an envelope on his desk.

"What's this?" he asked.

"The exact location of the cell tower in Pasadena," she said.

Towers looked at her, surprised. Davies laughed.

"Come on, Jimmy," she said. "I know you well enough to know that you're not going to go home and do nothing."

Towers leaned closer to her. "If Marsh finds out—"

"He won't," Davies said confidently. "Just watch your butt and bring West back in one piece. I don't care what the news is saying, West is one of the good guys."

Towers smiled. "Thanks, Monica. I'll keep you posted." Towers hurried out of the office and then out of the building. He caught a cab out on 4th Street and ordered the driver, "Reagan National Airport."

"No problem," the cabbie said, starting the meter.

Towers leaned back in the seat. He checked his watch. It was time to change his bandages. 'I'll do it in the bath-room on the plane,' he decided. The only objective on Towers' mind was to get to California. He hoped he could get to West before it was too late. Towers knew he had to play his cards right. He knew how the Agency operated. One false move, and he'd wind up dead alongside Special Agent West.

9

Midnight arrived. Despite any jet lag she may have been experiencing, Kelli could not get herself to fall asleep. She tossed and turned for what seemed like hours before surrendering the fight for rest and getting out of bed. Back home in the Bronx, it was three in the morning. Normally, Kelli would be out cold, dreaming of Darius and the date they never had. She wondered what Darius was doing right now. 'Sleeping, of course,' she told herself. 'I'm the only idiot who's awake at this hour'. Kelli stared out of her large window. The moon was full in the night sky. She attempted to count what flickers of stars she could see in hopes that it would fatigue her. She quit after forty-two. Finally, she slipped on a pair of shoes that James had left for her, and stepped into the hallway.

Small lights aligned the baseboards along the corridor, illuminating the way to the stairwell. Kelli descended quickly and as quietly as she could. She hit the last step and headed for the kitchen. Surely, in a house this size, there must be something in the fridge worthy of a midnight snack. As Kelli neared the kitchen, she heard voices. She rounded the corner. West, standing by the sink, turned and looked at her. Kelli noticed that West, even this late at night, still kept his gun holstered to his body. Bling, who sat at the table, glanced in her direction. Franco, a male member of James' house staff was in the kitchen as well. He sat next to Bling while drinking a cup of hot tea. When he saw Kelli, he stood.

"Can I make you something to eat, my dear? Or perhaps something to drink," he asked.

"Uh, no, thanks," Kelli said. "Just point me to the peanut butter, I guess."

Franco crossed the kitchen and opened the pantry door. He stepped inside and reemerged as quickly as he had entered. He held a jar of peanut butter in his hand.

"Any bananas?" Kelli asked.

Franco gestured to a series of multileveled baskets that hung from the ceiling next to the refrigerator. The second level held apples, oranges and bananas. Kelli retrieved a banana. Franco handed her a butter knife, and Kelli sat at the table opposite Bling. Reluctantly, she looked up at him. Bling avoided eye contact. Kelli exhaled lightly and began peeling back the banana skin.

West stepped to her side and placed a hand on her shoulder. "How are you holding up?"

Kelli shrugged. She didn't have a definitive answer to that question. Instead, she posed one of her own. "What are we supposed to do now? Hide out here forever?"

West sat next to her. He held a glass of ice water. "No. But we need a way to resolve this issue without any more bloodshed."

"I'm all for that idea," Kelli said. She opened the jar of peanut butter and stuck the butter knife deep inside. She scooped up a heaping glob of the brown substance and smeared it carefully on the tip of her banana. She took a bite.

"Can't you just call someone from the FBI?" Bling suggested.

"I don't know who to trust," West admitted.

"Come on, man. You can't be the only honest agent in the world," Bling said to him.

"I'm the only one I know right now," West responded. He took a sip of his water. He eyed Kelli's peanut butter covered banana. "I used to love to eat that when I was a kid."

"Grab a banana, help your self," she offered. "In fact," she said as she pushed the jar towards West, "take it. This isn't what I was craving after all." Kelli stood. "I'm going back to bed. I'll see you all in the morning."

"Good night," West said to her. Bling remained silent. Kelli turned away without looking in Bling's direction. She exited the kitchen and made her way back to the stairs.

She climbed them slowly. As she reached the top, she yawned. 'Good,' she thought. 'Maybe I'll get some sleep, now.'

Kelli crept silently down the hallway. She pushed her door open and crossed the threshold. Her attention was drawn instantly to the man in the dark suit standing in the center of her room. He was holding a gun that was pointed directly at her.

Kelli gasped and darted out of the room. Valverdi pulled the trigger. Kelli yelped as a dart flew from the gun and embedded itself in her left shoulder as she turned the corner.

Kelli raced down the hallway. Her vision began to blur. Each step she took seemed harder and harder to take. She stumbled slightly. She could see the top of the stairs coming into view off to the right, but she wasn't sure if she was going to make it. The man had shot her with some type of drug, she was certain of it. She tried to scream, but it was becoming increasingly difficult to breathe. Kelli thought of her ju-jitsu training and how useless it seemed at this moment. She fell just a few feet short of the stairway. Her breathing had grown heavy and her vision became fuzzier. Still, her sense of hearing was working just fine. Kelli heard the man approaching her from behind. In a second, he would be on her, and there was nothing she could do about it.

Valverdi reached Kelli as she flipped around on the floor, struggling to remain conscious. He grabbed her forcefully by the neck and turned her over. He looked into her eyes. They were glassy and unfocused. 'The tranquilizer is working just fine,' he thought. He pulled her face closer to his. "Don't fight it," he whispered to her.

Kelli began to lose consciousness. Her mind raced with images of the past two days. Voices rang in her head as she fought to stay in control. Her arms and legs began to lose strength and go limp. As Kelli's vision faded to black, she remembered hearing James' voice saying, ". . . certain immunity-based cell groups would identify and eradicate any foreign bodies. . . " Kelli tried to focus on the words. Again, she remembered James' voice. "Every time she shifted, the diseased cells were destroyed." Kelli knew she was losing this battle. In an instant, she knew what she had to do. 'Would it work?' She didn't know. But it was worth a try. The veil of black began to consume her. Kelli focused in the darkness. She could feel her body being hoisted up onto the man's shoulder. She concentrated even harder. The familiar warmth moved throughout her body. She felt her physiology morph from female to male. Kelli guessed that her male form weighed considerably more than her female one. The voice of her captor confirmed it.

"What the hell?" Valverdi said. The sudden increase in weight surprised him. With one motion, he repositioned the body on his shoulder and continued back down the hall from whence he came.

Kelli's vision began to clear. Her breathing returned to normal. She wiggled her fingers frantically. It worked. Somehow, her gender shift neutralized whatever it was her captor shot into her. Kelli was amazed, but she knew everyone in the house was in danger. She had to do something.

Kelli lifted her legs suddenly. Her weight shifted behind Valverdi and he lost grip of her. Kelli fell to the floor face first. She extended her hands and fell into a forward roll as her gymnastics training came into play. She continued her roll until she was facing forward. She pushed herself to her feet and turned. Valverdi, though confused, had already turned around to confront her. When he saw a male standing in front of him, he couldn't hide his surprise.

Kelli launched a right hook that caught Valverdi on his left temple. Valverdi stumbled to his right. Kelli followed him and hit him again. Valverdi fell unconscious.

തംൽ

West walked towards the kitchen entrance. "Did you hear something?" he asked as he stepped into the small passage that connected the kitchen to the dining area.

"No," Bling said.

West stood in the darkness. His eyes darted from one direction to the next. He saw nothing out of the ordinary. He shrugged and stepped back into the kitchen. When he turned, he saw a man standing outside on the porch. It was Gillis.

"Get down!" West yelled. He lunged in Franco's direction. Gillis fired several rounds through the window. Franco's chest exploded as the bullets penetrated his back and exited the front of his body.

Gillis continued to fire into the kitchen. Bling took cover under the table. Wood splintered next to Bling's head as bullets were forcefully imbedded into the tabletop.

West stood to his feet. With his weapon leveled, he unloaded several rounds at Gillis. Gillis dove onto the porch for cover. Glass shattered over Gillis' head as West kept the lead flying.

"Bling! Move!" West ordered. Bling jumped to his feet and raced for the kitchen exit. West fell into step behind him, all the while keeping his gun aimed at the shattered windows overlooking the porch area.

In the small hallway, West raced in front of Bling. He had to get upstairs. They had come for Kelli. For all West knew, they had her already.

"Where are you going?" Bling asked him nervously.

"I've got to find Kelli," he said as he reached the stairs. "Stay close." West bounded up the stairs with Bling closely in tow.

❧

Kelli had raced by the stairwell and continued towards the hallway to the right. As she moved into the hall, she heard gunshots coming from downstairs. Kelli froze. 'West is down there. Bling . . . ' Kelli stood there, transfixed by fear. Then, more gunshots followed by sounds of glass breaking. Kelli turned and continued down the corridor.

As she reached the first door, it opened. Nicholas emerged with a .38 in his grip. He swung the large gun in Kelli's direction. She threw up her hands immediately.

"It's me. Kelli," she said, though the voice that came out was deeper and masculine. "They're in the house."

Nicholas lowered his weapon. "We have to get the kids to the panic room," he said to her. He stepped into the hall and moved away from the stairwell. "Follow me."

చ∙ఈ

Valverdi rubbed his face. He couldn't remember the last time he'd been hit that hard. 'Where did that guy come from?' he wondered. Valverdi noticed his weapon laying a few feet from his head. 'Whoever he was, he wasn't smart enough to take my gun. Sucker.' Valverdi grabbed his gun. A noise from the stairwell grabbed his attention. West and Bling rounded the corner. Valverdi raised his weapon. West had already drawn a bead on him. West squeezed his trigger and sent a single bullet into Valverdi's forehead. The gunshot echoed throughout the house.

చ∙ఈ

James pushed his wheelchair through his upstairs office. The gunshots woke him out of a sound sleep. They had found them. After twenty years of evading the Agency, all of a sudden, they were here. Something wasn't adding up correctly. James pushed that thought out of his mind. His only concern now was finding his children and getting them to safety. He thought of Kelli. He prayed that she was okay. James exited the office and headed for the east corridor. His arms, having pushed the wheels on his wheelchair for the last eighteen months, had grown considerably stronger. Still, he cursed his chronically arthritic knees for giving out on him. James rounded the corner to the hall. There, a man in a dark suit waited for him. James gasped. The man raised his weapon and pointed it at James. James, preparing for the inevitable, closed his eyes.

"Wait," a female voice said from within the darkness.

James opened his eyes. The man was still standing there with his gun ready to unload. Then, James saw another figure approaching him. Though it was dark, he could tell that the figure was that of a female. As the mysterious female moved closer, the lights from the baseboard illuminated the corridor enough for James to discern the distinct features of her face. His jaw dropped. A look of shock crossed his face and a hurricane of anger welled up inside of him.

"Amanda?" he said. He saw her standing there, but he didn't want to believe it.

"Hello, James," she said sweetly.

"Amanda, no. You're dead."

Amanda Simons pulled out a small handgun. "I think you have me confused with someone else," she responded smugly. Amanda gestured to the man behind her. Lind stepped into the dim light. "Get the son and the children."

Lind nodded and moved into the darkness towards the children's bedrooms.

"Amanda. I don't understand. How are you alive? Why—"

"I know you have a million questions for me, James. I wish I had time to answer all of them."

A single gunshot sounded from somewhere in the house. The acoustics of the structure carried the sound clearly throughout the empty hallways.

"It was you all those years ago. You informed the Agency about our research."

Amanda smiled. "It only took you twenty years to figure that out. I'm impressed."

"But why?" James asked earnestly. "You were our assistant."

"Your assistant," Amanda scoffed at him. "I was planted by the Agency to keep tabs on your work."

"I don't believe you," James snapped.

"Believe it," she said. "At first, I admit that I had my doubts. I didn't really believe that you and Marcus could pull it off. . . advanced eugenics, the super soldier program. It sounded like a science fiction movie. But you did it. I was genuinely impressed. And when we discovered what we had really created–the gender shifting, the cure for infirmities–I considered keeping silent and not reporting our findings to the Agency. I had found new hope and I loved the work we were doing."

"Then why did you betray us?"

"Because once you and Marcus found your boon, your prized creation, nothing else mattered. You let all other research fall to the wayside, your concerns were for Harmony and nothing else."

"You mean no one else, don't you?" James sneered at her. He rolled his wheelchair closer. "You felt neglected, pushed aside."

"Not to mention receiving minimal to no credit for my contributions to the success of the Harmony Project."

"You betrayed us because you didn't receive accolades? How petty."

"Maybe so," she said angrily. "But after Harmony, you and Marcus shut me out. Christopher was almost a year old before I discovered what he truly was. And to think, I actually felt bad when Harmony died."

"When she was murdered," James corrected her. "It may have been ruled an accidental overdose, but Harmony was much too intelligent to have ingested those narcotics on her own."

"It doesn't matter anymore, James. When I found out that Christopher was Harmony's clone, I decided to stick to my original assignment."

"Marcus and his family were slaughtered," James yelled.

"And I'm here to finish the job," Amanda screamed in return. "I wish I could say I'm sorry." With that, Amanda squeezed the trigger. A bullet perforated James' chest. His eyes opened wide as the pain and reality set in. Blood began to leak out of his wound slowly and soak into his night shirt.

Amanda didn't wait to watch him die. She turned around and walked back into the shadows of the corridor.

James sat in his chair. Alone and dying.

৵৽৽৵

West and Bling searched Kelli's room. They checked under the bed, in the closet and in the bathroom in the event that she was hiding. Nothing. She was nowhere to be found.

West feared the worst. He had already survived another confrontation with Gillis, and he just killed another man in the hallway. There was no way to tell how many operatives were in the house.

West moved towards the door. A single gunshot reverberated through the house. This shot sounded different to West. It sounded more like a firecracker, as if it was fired from a lower caliber weapon. He paused at the door and peered into the hallway.

"How'd they find us?" Bling whispered behind him nervously.

"Doesn't matter at the moment," West answered. "We need to find Kelli."

West stepped into the doorway, glanced in both directions quickly, and then lunged into the corridor. He pressed his back close to the wall as he moved back up the hallway. Bling stayed close behind him. They came to the top of the stairs. Bling glanced back at the dead agent lying close by. He spied the agent's gun still clutched in his hand. Bling sprinted to the agent and wrenched the gun from his grasp.

"What are you doing? Put that down!" West ordered him.

"Fuck you," Bling snapped in return. "People are shootin' at me, man. I'm shootin' back."

West didn't argue with him. Frankly, there was no point. Usually, West would have back up for situations like this. Towers and ten other agents in tactical gear would be on scene and ready to go into battle. But this wasn't a usual situation. Tonight, West had no one save Bling. If West was unsure about anything else, he was, at least, confident that Bling was on his side.

West nodded. "Stay low. Stay alert. Let's go."

❧❦

Nicholas raced down the back stairwell that descended just
north of the kitchen. Kelli, still in her male form, dogged
his heels. Calliope held his hand. Blanca, the housekeeper,
held the hands of Clara and Joseph. All three of the children
were crying. Nicholas stepped off the bottom stair. He
threw up a cautionary hand while he surveyed the area.
He saw nothing. He signaled the group to proceed. They
crossed under the stairs and headed for the small passageway
that led to the study. As Nicholas stepped into the narrow
passage, he came face to face with Lind.

Nicholas lunged at Lind, colliding with his body and
pushing him backwards into the passage. Each man held
the wrist of the other, while trying to wrestle away the other's weapon.

The children screamed in terror. Blanca tried to shield
the younger children's eyes from the gruesome battle that
ensued in front of them.

Calliope screamed, "Nicholas!"

Kelli pushed Blanca forward. "Get them to the panic
room. Go!"

The two men thrashed about in the narrow passageway.
First, they slammed into one wall, then the other. Lind's
weapon released a round. Everyone screamed. Blanca
hoisted Joseph into her arms. She tugged at Clara and ran
by the struggling men as they fell to the opposite side of
the narrow space.

Blanca entered a room down the hall. Kelli ran and
launched herself into the air at Lind. She was astonished
at how much stronger she felt in this male body. In truth,

the feeling was quite intoxicating. It almost made her feel invincible.

Kelli's dense male form fell onto Lind and Nicholas, knocking both men to the floor. Kelli struck Lind with a flurry of fists. Nicholas rolled to his knees and secured Lind's wrist. As Kelli continued to pummel Lind, Nicholas attempted to pry Lind's gun from his hand. Lind held on tight.

Nicholas turned and picked his gun from the floor, aimed it at Lind's hand and fired a round into his wrist. Lind howled in pain. The gun sprang from his hand.

Kelli pounded Lind once more. Lind succumbed to the pain of the bullet wound in his wrist and Kelli's repeated battering against his face, and plummeted into unconsciousness.

Footsteps approached from the rear. Nicholas swung his gun in the air and pointed it at the entrance to the passage. West and Bling froze in their tracks. "Don't shoot!" West yelled. "It's us."

West approached Kelli. He was slightly disconcerted by her male appearance but was happy to see her nonetheless.

Bling, covering West's back, pointed his weapon towards the back stairs. Without warning, he began squeezing off shots into the darkness. "That's right," he screamed. "I see you. Come and get it." Gillis, who had attempted to sneak up on them, dove for cover through the double doors that led to the kitchen.

West turned to Nicholas. "We've got to move. Where's your father?"

Nicholas' face turned to dread. "I don't know. You didn't see him?"

West shook his head.

"We need to get to the panic room," Kelli insisted urgently.

Bling let off a few more shots. "I can't hold him off forever," he shouted.

"This way," Nicholas said. He sprang to his feet and headed for the safe room.

West grabbed Lind by his feet. "Kelli, help me!" he ordered.

"What are you doing?" she asked.

"We need some answers." West explained. Without hesitation, Kelli grabbed Lind's other foot. They dragged him down the hall and into the room on the left. A trail of Lind's blood was left in his body's wake. Bling backed down the passage behind them. He kept an eye on the opening to the passage. He was prepared to shoot Gillis or anyone else who dared to follow them.

Bling rounded the corner and entered the large study. Nicholas crossed the room to a large, plush recliner. He knelt before it and reached his arm under the front of the chair. He appeared to be feeling for something. Suddenly, he jumped to his feet and pushed the chair. The large chair fell onto its back to reveal a trap door with a descending flight of stairs. The bottom of the chair was suspended to thick springs and several locking mechanisms.

"Everybody in," Nicholas ordered.

West kept his gun trained on the door as, one by one, the group lowered themselves into the trap door and descended down the stairs. West pushed the unconscious Lind into the open space. Soon, only West and Nicholas remained.

"Nicholas. Go!" West commanded.

"I can't. I have to find my father."

West grimaced. He knew that allowing Nicholas to search for his father would be a death sentence for the young Connelly. In good conscience, he couldn't let him go. "We may not be able to help him," West said.

Nicholas thought for a moment. Then, he turned and descended down the stairs. West followed quickly. As West descended the stairs, Nicholas yelled back to him, "Hit the red button." West complied. The springs activated and the chair was pulled back into place and the locks engaged. With the trap door closed, West descended safely to the bottom of the stairs.

West followed Nicholas down a short, dimly lit hallway. A quick right turn later and West found himself in a room with no visible exit. He looked around the room. Everyone was accounted for. Everyone except James Connelly.

A small light fixture on the wall had been pulled out of its socket. Blanca was tapping numbers into a keypad in the space that was occupied by the fixture. A door, one that was not visible a second ago, popped open in the wall. Nicholas moved to the door and pulled. West could tell the door was extremely heavy. He moved to Nicholas' side and helped him. As soon as the door was ajar, each person ran in. Soon, the heavy door was closed behind them.

The panic room measured approximately one thousand square feet. The front of the room was lined from floor to ceiling with several flat screen televisions. Each monitor was receiving a closed-circuit feed from cameras throughout the house. There was a control station positioned in front of the screens. Nicholas moved to the station and began tapping buttons.

There were several comfortable futon chairs lining the walls. Off to the far right was a refrigerator which sat next to a walk-in pantry. On the opposite side of the room was a restroom.

The children sat in the chairs. Their faces were covered with tears. Kelli sat with them. Blanca held young Joseph in her arms. Bling kept a gun trained on the unconscious Agent Lind. West moved to Nicholas' side.

"There!" Nicholas pointed at the monitor. "He's in the East Hallway." The screen displayed an image of James. He sat in his wheelchair motionless. Nicholas manipulated a lever on the console and zoomed in on his father. He slapped another button and the night-vision popped on. "He's bleeding. Those bastards shot him and left him for dead."

All eyes landed on the monitor. Everyone witnessed the brutality of the Agency as James Connelly sat alone in the dimly lit corridor.

"I've got to go get him," Nicholas said.

"Wait a second," West said, and pointed at another screen.

"No, I have to g—" Nicholas' gaze followed West's finger to a screen in the middle of the wall. This screen displayed an image of Gillis and a woman. They were outside of the house, walking along the side yard. Gillis was holding a large container, emptying a liquid along the perimeter of the house. "Oh my God," Nicholas uttered.

"They're going to set the house on fire," West said.

"They can't. We've got their boy," Bling reasoned, gesturing to Lind.

"They don't care about him," West said. He turned to Nicholas. "Tell me there's another way out of here."

"It wouldn't be much of a safe room if there was," Nicholas responded.

"We're going to be trapped," Blanca cried.

"What do we do?" Kelli asked aloud, her voice still deep and masculine.

"You're the genius," Bling reminded her.

"I'm only fourteen," she snapped at him.

"Still," Bling snapped back. "And can you please turn back into a girl? You're freakin' me out over here."

Kelli stood. As a female, Kelli was an inch or so shorter than Bling. As a male, she was taller by half an inch. She took a step towards him. "Deal with it," she said.

West spied a number of walkie-talkies that were charging on the console. He grabbed one and twisted the small knob on top. The small red light flickered to life. He looked back at the monitors. "These cameras cover the whole estate?"

"Inside and out," Nicholas answered.

"From the looks of things, there are only two of them out there. Once the house starts to burn, they'll have to keep their distance. When they do, we can make a run for it. We'll have to split up. That'll make them split up and work for their targets. If we stay together they can pick us off more easily."

"But what about Daddy?" cried Calliope.

Nicholas eyed West. "Someone has to go get him," Nicholas said. "If there's even a chance that he's alive—"

"Fine," West agreed reluctantly. "You go for your father. Kelli and Blanca will take the children and make a run for it out back."

Nicholas pointed at one of the monitors. "See this paved walkway that leads to the lower yard in the back?" He moved his finger to an adjacent monitor. "Follow it to the car garage over here."

"I'll go out through the side and draw their fire," West said. He turned to Bling. "I'm counting on you to watch their backs."

Kelli moved closer to the large screens. "They must have already poured the gas in the house," she observed. "They're lighting it on fire."

All eyes focused on the monitor displaying Gillis and the woman. Gillis held a burning Zippo lighter in his hand. He stepped back and tossed the lighter onto the accelerant. Instantly, a fire blazed five feet in the air. The flames traveled around the house and into the front and back doors as it fed upon the fuel source that was poured out along the property grounds.

"We've only got a few minutes," West said. "We have to time it right. Once we're out, we can use the walkies to find each other."

"What about our friend here?" Bling said referring to Lind. There was a small pool of blood that had collected under his wounded limb.

"It's time we woke him up," West answered.

"Gladly," Bling said as he turned and kicked Lind in the stomach as hard as he could. "Wake up!"

Lind lurched and howled in pain on the floor. He cradled his injured wrist immediately. He looked up, only to be staring down the barrel of Bling's gun.

"We need some answers," West said to him.

"Too bad," Lind said through gritted teeth.

Bling pushed the barrel of the gun against Lind's forehead. "You might want to rethink that."

"Go screw yourself, kid," Lind sneered, and then grimaced in pain. "I have no answers for you."

"Where are the Designates?" West asked. "How many are here in California?"

"Don't you get it, Agent West?" Lind spat. "Even if I knew that, and I don't, I'd be committing suicide by telling you."

"Hell, let's just kill him then," Bling suggested. Carelessly, he turned his attention to West. Lind slapped the gun away from his forehead with his left hand and grabbed hold of Bling's wrist in one motion. He used Bling's weight as leverage as his right foot shot up and caught Bling squarely between the legs. Bling squealed and dropped to his knees. Lind stripped the gun from his hand. By the time West reacted and began reaching for his own weapon, Ling had the gun pointed at Bling's head.

"Don't try it," Lind warned West. "You may be fast enough to reach your holster, but not before I blow this kid's brains out." Everyone moved away in fear and gathered behind West.

"What are you going to do now?" West asked.

Lind surveyed everyone in the room. He saw that Nicholas was armed as well. Even if he shot Bling, Lind knew he wasn't fast enough on the draw to take out West and Nicholas before one of them dropped him where he stood. No. Lind had another idea. With his good hand, he yanked Bling to his feet and positioned himself behind the young teenager.

"I'm going to walk out of here," Lind said, "and I'm taking the kid as insurance."

"Don't let him do it," Bling said, trying to be brave.

"He can't stop me," Lind said confidently. "And he knows it."

Lind was right. West knew that if he tried anything, Bling was dead. West's wheels began to turn.

"If you're going, you better hurry," West said. He pointed a thumb at the displays to his rear. "Your friends have set the house on fire. It's only going to be a few minutes before we're all trapped."

"That was the plan, after you were all dead, of course." Lind took a step back. "Let's go, Aladdin," he said to Bling.

"Take me!" West said. "He's just a boy. Take me instead."

Lind thought for a moment. The orders were to bring West and the girl back alive and kill the rest. He decided to settle for bringing West back alive. "No problem," Lind said. His eyes scanned the others. "Where's the girl?"

Kelli's heart jumped. Lind was talking about her. Up until this point, she hadn't realized that the operatives were unaware of what she could do. Lind didn't recognize her in her male form. He didn't realize that she was the target.

"I don't know," West lied.

"Your friends got her," Kelli blurted. "The other guy dragged her off."

Lind glanced at the monitors. The house was beginning to burn quite nicely. He could see Gillis and the Specialist moving away. 'They must have put her in the truck already. Good. All I have to do is deliver Agent West.'

"Okay," Lind said. "Let's make this switch nice and easy. First, drop the hardware."

West reached for his gun slowly. Lind watched him carefully. He pressed the weapon firmly against the back of Bling's head.

"No tricks," Lind advised. "I have no qualms about killing some kid."

West nodded. "Understood." West gripped the butt of his gun. He pulled it slowly out of the holster. He dangled it at arms length and then, as Lind instructed, dropped it on the floor.

"Now, you," Lind said to Nicholas. The younger Connelly complied and repeated the steps taken by Agent West. With both guns on the floor, Lind relaxed slightly.

West watched as Lind wiped a flood of sweat from his forehead. West had not yet begun to feel the heat from the burning house, so he surmised that Lind's perspiration was related to his wound and the amount of blood he had lost. When the time was right, maybe he could use that to his advantage.

"Okay, Agent West," Lind said triumphantly. "Time to switch. Hands on your head, both of you. Move!"

Bling stepped forward. West moved across the room to take his place as Lind's hostage. As West and Bling crossed each other's path, West whispered, "Take care of them."

"Kill the noise!" Lind ordered. A moment later, West was standing with his back to Lind. "If any of you poke your head out of this room, West is a dead man. Hear me?"

Everyone nodded.

"Good." Lind tapped West in the back of his head with the barrel of the gun. "Let's go, Hotshot!"

Lind backed up across the room. West remained in front of him. "Open the door," West said to Nicholas.

Nicholas tapped a button on the console. Across the room, the edge to the heavy door popped out of the wall. Lind placed his back against the door and pushed with everything he had. Once the door was opened, Lind turned his focus to Nicholas.

"I owe you one," Lind said. He took aim at Nicholas' left leg and squeezed the trigger. The discharge caused everyone to flinch. The children screamed. Blood shot out of the back of Nicholas's thigh as he crumbled to the floor in pain. West bit his lip in anger. Lind moved into the hallway. West followed compliantly.

The children continued to cry. Calliope ran to Nicholas' side. He moaned in pain. Blanca did her best to comfort the kids but nothing seemed to help. Bling eyed the multiple monitors. The blaze had spread across much of the lower level of the mansion. If they waited much longer, they would have no means of escape.

Kelli watched the screen that monitored the study. She saw the large chair spring onto its back and reveal the trap door. She watched as Lind climbed out. Lind kept the gun trained on West as the young FBI agent followed. Tears gushed from Kelli's eyes. She feared she would never see Agent West alive again.

Bling tapped Kelli's shoulder to snap her out of her trance. "We gotta go," he said to her. "It's now or never. If they make it outside before we get on the move, that guy is going to tell the others that we're in here. Once that happens—"

"They'll never let us out alive," Kelli finished his sentence. She wiped tears from her masculine face. "Let's go."

Nicholas rolled around on the floor. Blood poured out onto the hardwood under him. "Dad . . . we can't leave him."

"We have to," Bling said. "Kelli, help him up."

Kelli grabbed Nicholas by his shoulder. With one pull, she yanked Nicholas to his feet. He leaned against her for support. Bling held West's discarded firearm. He tucked

Nicholas' weapon in his sweatpants. Quickly, they moved
out of the panic room and through the dimly lit hallway.
Bling scaled the stairs first. Once in the study, he kept
his eyes peeled as the group emerged in rapid succession.
A heavy layer of smoke already covered the ceiling. The
temperature had risen remarkably and the sound of wood
burning could be heard coming from all directions.

"What's the quickest way to the backyard?" Bling
asked.

Nicholas struggled to answer him through his agony.
"Through the side door in the kitchen."

Bling cursed silently. The side door in the kitchen was
where Gillis launched his assault on him, West and Franco.
Bling didn't want to revisit that gruesome scene, but he
knew that time was of the essence.

The group dashed into the hallway. The walls on
either side were on fire. The thick, white smoke hung in
the corridor like an unwelcomed apparition that threatened to envelope them as they passed. Bling kept his gun
out in front of him, ready to shoot anyone with whom he
was unfamiliar. Nicholas thrashed in pain as they maneuvered through the long hallways. He was slowing Kelli
down.

Bling imagined that West and his captor had made it
outside by now. It was only a matter of time before their
only escape route would be cut off. He picked up the pace.
Blanca, carrying Joseph in one arm, pulled little Clara
behind her with the other.

They burst into the kitchen. Everything was aflame
from the floor to the ceiling. The sight of Franco's bloodied
body made Blanca scream in horror. She froze at the sight
of him. Kelli pushed into her from behind.

"Keep moving," she yelled with strong, masculine tones.

Blanca trudged forward. They pushed through the side door that opened onto the side porch. The open air filled their lungs. Kelli stepped to Bling's side.

"Get them to the garage," she said. "I'll be there in a second."

"Where the hell are you going?" Bling asked.

Kelli handed Nicholas off to him. "I'm going to find James."

"What?" Bling exclaimed. "You crazy, man—uh, girl? He's dead."

"I don't know that for sure," she said as she pushed Bling away. "Go. Get to the garage. If I'm not there in two minutes—"

"Two minutes? Nobody moves that fast," Bling yelled.

"I do," Kelli said confidently. "Go!" With that, Kelli turned and bounded up the rear stairwell. Bling turned and pulled Nicholas along. Nicholas hopped on his good leg. Blood continued to soak his pants as they moved through the backyard towards the large garage in the distance. Bling shook his head as he thought about Kelli. 'What is she thinkin'?' he wondered. The familiar feeling of uselessness began knocking at his chest. He was unable to protect his mother from cancer, and now, he was unable to protect Kelli. 'I should have gone with her.' He cursed under his breath. He and Kelli have never gotten along, not even back at school. Nevertheless, a lot had happened to them in the last few days. If something bad were to happen to her now, Bling knew he would never forgive himself.

10

West moved through the burning hallway. He coughed as smoke choked at his lungs and the heat from the flames licked at his sweating flesh. Lind followed close behind West, his gun trained at the back of West's head.

They passed the front staircase. The burning spiral structure resembled the phoenix rising from the ashes, leaving flames in its wake as it ascended towards the heavens. Unfortunately, there was nothing heavenly about this situation. This house was going up in flames and fast. Whoever didn't make it out was a goner.

West stopped short of the front door. Though it was slightly ajar, the door was engulfed in flames. West turned and looked at Lind. Lind did not look good. His skin was pale and his eyes appeared glassy. West considered making a move, but Lind still held the gun rather steady. West reconsidered.

"What are you waiting for?" Lind asked.

"It's on fire," West said.

Lind lifted the gun and leveled it between West's eyes. "Get burned or get dead."

West didn't like either choice but he decided to go with the former. He stepped close to the door. He raised his right leg and kicked at the door. The heavy door swung open. The top of the door frame succumbed to the flames and crashed to the floor. West didn't bother to look behind. He proceeded through the flaming doorway and emerged onto the burning front porch. The flames danced at his feet, forcing him to run into the yard. Lind stuck close.

West moved to a safe distance. He scanned the front yard quickly. There was no sign of Gillis or the mystery woman. West turned to face Lind. Lind staggered slightly. West seized the moment.

He backhanded Lind with a closed fist. Lind's head snapped back. West charged Lind and tackled him to the ground. Lind did not relinquish his weapon. He swung the weapon in West's direction. West caught his arm. There, they struggled for control of the weapon. Lind squeezed the trigger. Then again, and again. The shots echoed into the night air. West's ears rang. Finally, West shifted his weight. He lifted his body into the air just high enough to bring his knee forward. His knee landed hard onto Lind's wrist, sending more pain through an already excruciating wound. Lind screamed in agony. His resistance dropped. West pummeled his face with several blows from his fists. Again, Lind slipped into unconsciousness. West grabbed Lind's weapon. He stood and pointed it at the uncon-scious man's head. Then, he heard a sound. Someone was approaching him from behind. West swung the weapon in the air. He turned around in time to get a glimpse of Gillis. Gillis raised the butt of his weapon and struck West in the back of head. West tumbled unconsciously into the grass.

Kelli struggled to catch her breath as she rounded the corner to the east corridor. The heat and smoke stung her eyes, causing them to water. Flames from the first floor had crawled up the walls and begun their assault on the upper level. Kelli knew she was running out of time.

She reached the center of the corridor. There was no sign of James. Kelli saw a pool of blood in the middle of the hallway. Thin trails of blood travelled along the floor away from where Kelli stood. Some of James' blood must have gotten on the wheels of his chair. Kelli darted off in the direction in which the trail led. She tried to remain low to avoid the bulk of the rising smoke. It didn't matter. The entire corridor was blanketed and it was becoming increasingly difficult to see and breathe.

Kelli followed the trail around the corner to the right. After about forty feet, the trail turned left. Kelli squinted. This hallway was already aflame. The smoke was thicker and the heat was more intense. Kelli continued down the corridor. The darkness was now replaced by intense, brilliant flames. The wheelchair came into view. There, slumped backwards in the chair, was James. Before him, at the end of the hallway, was an elevator.

Kelli circled around and crouched in front of the wheelchair. James' face was covered with sweat. The front of his shirt was soaked in blood. She almost vomited at the sight of the bullet wound in his chest. She wanted to run, but she had come this far. She needed to know if she had arrived too late.

She placed a hand on either side of his face. She shook him lightly. "James!" she called to him. "James. Oh, please be alive. James!"

James' eyes opened. He looked at Kelli. Though he had never seen Kelli in her male form, he smiled. "Christopher," he said softly.

Kelli breathed a sigh of relief. "James," Kelli said. "It's me. Kelli."

James nodded. Kelli could tell that even that small movement caused him pain. "I know," he managed. "The last time I saw that face was twenty years ago. He . . . he was . . . the cutest little boy."

Kelli had seen pictures of young Christopher earlier in the day when young Joseph brought them to her attention. She had seen the resemblance to her male alter-ego almost immediately. Still, it was strange to be referred to by that name, especially by a man who'd actually known him.

Kelli chased those stray thoughts out of her head. The house was coming down around them and she had to get James and get out. "Hold on, James. I'm going to get you out of here."

"No," James protested.

Kelli ignored him. She squeezed an arm behind James' back and placed the other under his knees. She pulled him close and stood to her feet. In that moment, déjà vu set in as the image of Jaleesa being carried away from the wreckage in the Bronx flashed through her mind. Before the events of that day, Kelli had never rescued anyone from anything in her short life. Now, in a matter of three days, she'd done it twice. For reasons Kelli couldn't explain, it felt right, almost innate.

Kelli focused once again. She considered the elevator but decided against it. Perhaps James was trying to reach it because he had no other choice. He was in a wheelchair, and the elevator may have been his only means of getting to the lower levels. Fortunately, Kelli had no such restriction. She turned and bolted up the hallway towards the rear stairwell. She prayed that her escape route had not been cut off.

❧⬥

Gillis opened the back door to the large SUV. He tossed West's unconscious frame into the open space. Amanda Simons sat in the front passenger seat. She turned to Gillis. "What's the hold up?" she asked, checking her watch.

"This is one of our targets," Gillis answered. "Lind was having trouble with him."

"Where is Lind now?" she snapped. "And what about the girl? We were supposed to bring her back alive."

"I didn't see her. She may still be trapped inside."

Amanda moaned. "They are not going to be happy about that." She cursed under her breath. 'Frankly,' she thought, 'I'm not happy about that.'

"Keep an eye on him. I'm going back for Lind. I'll be right back."

"Hurry," Amanda said. "This fire has been reported. It won't be long before the fire department arrives."

Gillis shut the door. He walked back two hundred feet to the front gate of the estate and stepped onto the sprawling grounds. He jogged at an even pace through the grass. Up ahead, he could see Lind still lying in the yard. A moment later, he was standing over him. 'He's in bad shape,' Gillis remarked to himself silently. He contemplated leaving Lind behind. Gillis was certain that Lind and Valverdi were there to 'take him out' after the assignment was completed. He had no proof except the feeling in his gut. That was good enough for Gillis. Valverdi never came out of the house. Gillis felt it was safe to assume that he was dead. If Gillis left Lind behind, his problem might be solved. Then again, should Lind be captured by the authorities, new problems could arise. Gillis weighed options quickly. Then, he made a decision.

"Dammit," he cursed. He knelt by Lind's side and smacked the side of his face lightly. Lind didn't stir. Gillis smacked him again, this time, considerably harder. Still, Lind did not come around. Gillis placed his fingers against Lind's carotid artery. He felt a pulse. "Damn," Gillis exhaled in frustration. Without another sound, he pulled Lind to a sitting position. He positioned himself behind the unconscious man and hoisted him up into a standing position. He turned Lind around and let him fall over his shoulder. Gillis stood erect. He looked up at the burning fortress in front of him. He shook his head, "What a waste." He turned and headed back to the truck. The sooner they left the area, the better.

☙❧

Kelli dodged several falling light fixtures as she ran through the kitchen. The majority of the room had gone up in flames. The strands of hair that were on Kelli's manly arms had been singed by the fire, and the heat threatened to make her pass out. She had only a few feet to go before she would reach the side door that led to the porch and then to the backyard.

The ceiling in front of her began to collapse. Kelli, with James in her arms, hurled herself through the flaming doorway and onto the porch as the ceiling in the kitchen gave way.

Kelli twisted in the air to protect James from their landing. She hit the porch floor hard. She underestimated her strength, and the momentum of both bodies carried her through the burning porch railing and out onto the grass. Kelli's body took the blunt of the impact. Still, she feared that James may not have survived.

Kelli rolled James over. His eyes were opened. He blinked. Kelli wrapped her arms around him again. James protested again, "Kelli, no. Leave me."

"I can't," she said.

James coughed up blood. It landed on his chin. His breathing was shallow and his body was weak. "Please," he managed to say. Suddenly, he began to convulse.

Kelli watched as a tremor rippled through James' body. She burst into tears. James trembled for what seemed like forever, then all of a sudden, stopped. Kelli peered at his face. His eyes rolled in her direction. His mouth began to move, but the sound was almost inaudible.

"What?" Kelli moved her ear close to his mouth. She felt his warm breath against her cheek.

"Kelli," he whispered, his voice sounding at peace. He squeezed out another breath. "Platt . . . find Jeremy Platt."

"Jeremy Platt? Who is that? James—don't die, please— not you, too. James . . ."

"What he has . . . can save . . . everyone . . ."

"Who is that? How do I find him?" she cried. "James?" The warm breath was no longer there. Kelli pulled back and looked into James' eyes. The light was gone.

Kelli sat back and stared. She was hypnotized by the sight of James' dead body. What was she going to tell Nicholas? And Calliope and the children? How could she tell them that their father was dead?

Kelli didn't have time to think. She passed her hands over James's eyes and closed them. 'That actually works,' she thought to herself, surprised. She wanted to do more for James, but there was no time. She didn't know what had transpired with Agent West. For all she knew, the men from the Agency would be coming back to finish the job. Kelli stood. She wiped her tears as she raced towards the back of the house. She hit the paved walkway at a full sprint and bolted towards the garage at the end of the stone path. Suddenly, a white BMW appeared out of nowhere. It stopped dead in front of her. Kelli's heart leapt into her throat. She looked into the car. At the wheel, sat Bling.

"Get in!" he yelled.

Kelli didn't waste one second. She circled the car and hopped into the passenger seat. As soon as she closed the door, Bling pressed the accelerator to the floor and directed the car towards the driveway.

Kelli looked in the back seat. It was empty. "Where are Nicholas and the kids?"

"I told them to go," Bling explained. "They took another car."

"To where?"

"I don't know. Nicholas said he knew somewhere safe," Bling said as he maneuvered the car onto the concrete. "I hot-wired this one."

Kelli looked at Bling. "You came back for me."

"What was I going to do, just ditch you? That's not my style," he said nonchalantly. "What happened to James?"

"He's dead."

Bling hit the driveway and maneuvered the car around the burning house. Kelli touched his arm. He looked at her.

"He told me to find someone named Jeremy Platt," Kelli said.

"The news guy?" Bling questioned, confused.

"You know who that is?" she asked, amazed.

"I'm not completely stupid, you know!" he snapped at her. Bling turned the wheel sharply. The BMW swerved around the Lincoln Town Car that sat at the front of the house. Bling gunned the engine. The BMW raced down the tree-lined driveway and approached the large metal gate.

అంది

Gillis hopped into the front seat behind the wheel. Amanda regarded him with disgust and frustration. Lind, in the back seat, had finally regained consciousness.

"Took you long enough," Amanda said snidely. "Don't draw any attention to us when you drive out of here. The fire department should be cruising along any second."

Lind sat up. He looked in the back of the truck at West. He turned to Gillis. "Where's the girl?" Gillis caught Lind's reflection in the rear-view mirror. "They told me you had taken the girl," Lind said.

"We never saw her," Gillis said. "It was like she wasn't even there."

Amanda turned and looked at them. Though most operatives were kept in the dark about the particulars concerning their targets, Amanda was not one of them. She knew that Kelli was in the house. She also knew why it appeared as if she wasn't among the people there.

"She was there," Amanda spat at them. "She was camouflaged."

"No way," Lind said. "I left them all in that safe room. Our target was not in there. I know it."

"You don't know crap," Amanda retorted. "Did you see a young, teenage boy, an African-American boy?"

"There were two of them," Lind said.

"At least tell me you killed them," Amanda said.

"I left them in a burning house," Lind yelled. "Did you see anyone else come out?"

"Not through the front. No," answered Gillis.

Amanda shook her head in disbelief. "You guys are *supposed* to be professionals."

The sound of a revving engine caught their attention. They all turned back towards the large gate. A white BMW rushed onto the street, made a sharp right turn and then bolted by them.

Amanda turned and eyed Lind. "Two African-American boys?"

Lind nodded. Amanda turned to Gillis. Gillis started the engine and shifted the car into gear. The SUV reached the end of the long street, and then turned left in distant pursuit of the BMW.

A grey sedan that had been parked, unnoticed, at the end of the street shifted into gear, as well. As stealthily as possible, Special Agent Towers pursued the pursuers.

ॐ◦ई

The white BMW pulled up to a security gate in a gated community in Woodland Hills. Leaving the headlights on, Bling and Kelli hopped out of the car and went to the digital directory. Bling scanned the names quickly. He stopped at Platt.

"I can't believe this guy was in the phone book," Kelli said.

"Most people still are," Bling stated. "Everyone is so caught up in electronics and wireless everything, they forget that the phone book can still be used for a lot of things."

"I guess you're right," Kelli admitted.

"Yeah," Bling chuckled. "Back in the Bronx, when we wanted to steal some big-timer's ride, we'd look in the white pages to see where he lived—and just go take it."

"I'm glad that your street skills are applicable to other things," Kelli said sarcastically.

"Let's hope this is the right guy," Bling said as he dialed the code under Platt's name. The speaker clicked open. The phone began to ring. Surprisingly to Bling and Kelli, the phone rang only three times before it was answered.

"Hello?" a deep, wary voice said.

Kelli took a deep breath. She closed her eyes and concentrated for a brief moment. Though she was still in her male form, when she spoke, her voice was clearly female. "Mr. Jeremy Platt?"

"Yes," Platt responded. "Who is this?"

Kelli took another breath. It was physically taxing to maintain her female voice while in her male form. "You don't know me, but—my name is Kelli Freeman. I—"

"Do you have any idea what time it is?" Platt asked, annoyed.

"Yes, sir, I do," she answered. With all the excitement of the evening, Kelli had no clue as to what time it was. "But it's important that we speak to you."

"Why?" Platt asked. "Who did you say you are?"

"Kelli Freeman," she replied. "I'm a friend of James Connelly."

There was silence on the line. Then, "Dr. James Connelly?"

"Yes, sir," Kelli answered.

More silence on the line, this time, longer than before. Finally, the buzzer sounded and the security gate began to swing open. Kelli and Bling hopped into the car.

Bling turned to Kelli. "By the way, that thing you just did with your voice—yeah, weird shit right there."

Kelli smirked. They drove inside.

∂∾∽

Kelli and Bling entered Platt's townhouse. Kelli had reverted into her female form. It had been almost two hours since she had shifted into 'boy mode' in the hallway back at the mansion. To date, that was the longest she'd ever spent as a male. It felt a little strange being female again after that amount of time. Strange, yet comfortable.

Kelli looked back at the door nervously as Platt closed it behind them. She noticed a shotgun propped up against the door frame. Platt grabbed it and moved it quickly into a corner out of sight.

Platt led them into the living room. Most of the lights in the townhome were burning bright. The furnishings were contemporary, much like the architecture. A thick, plush rug lined the entire floor and felt like a soft cloud with every step taken. Celebrity photos, old and new, lined the walls. Platt himself was present in most of them.

Time had been kind to Jeremy Platt. A few wrinkles sat on either side of his lips and the crow's feet around his eyes were just starting to become prevalent. Still, his hair had not begun to go gray, and he seemed to be in good physical health. Age had mellowed him out and done away with the easily excited, drama-hunting reporter. Though Platt was once on the fast track to his own syndicated telecast, it never happened. Platt strived to be the best reporter he could be. 'Platt, Here with the Truth,' was the slogan that had been popularized alongside his name. Unfortunately, Platt had become so blinded by his own ambition that he slandered and committed libel against a young, female politician seven years ago. The politician, Betty Royce, had been rumored to have made her way to the top by sleeping with a multitude of powerful, married men. These men, listed in Platt's shocking exposé, were governors, senators, chief justices and presidential cabinet members. Royce had allegedly lured these men into intimate relationships and then used photos and recorded evidence to blackmail them into pushing her career along. Platt had seen some of the evidence himself, and then one day, the evidence disappeared. Betty Royce was revealed to be the beneficiary of nepotism, her father having ties to the federal court, and Platt was discredited. His fast track to 'Barbara Walters' status was instantly derailed. The story made national headlines, and Platt's corner office at the newspaper became the permanent residence of a career going nowhere. Luckily, Platt had made some profitable financial investments through the years which allowed him to live comfortably despite a mediocre salary.

Platt put on a pair of glasses. He regarded their appearance and took a step back. Both Kelli and Bling smelled of smoke and had blood stains on their clothing. Whatever reason these two strangers had for showing up at his door, Platt knew that it wasn't good.

Kelli noticed Platt's reaction. She spoke up immediately. "We can explain how we look."

"That won't be necessary," Platt responded. "The only thing I want to know is why you showed up at my door. You said you're friends of James Connelly?"

"Yes," Kelli said. "He told me to find you. He said you have information that can save us."

"He told you that, did he?" Platt said, shaking his head in disbelief. Suddenly, he paused. He turned to Kelli slowly. "He's dead, isn't he? Why else would you be here?"

Kelli nodded.

"Is that his blood?" he asked, pointing to their clothes.

"On me, yes," Kelli answered. "Look, Mr. Platt, we haven't got much time. James said that you can help us."

Platt's mind wandered twenty years into the past. He thought of the night that James gave him the key, and of the promise he made to James should anything happen to him. After so many years had gone by, Platt assumed that the danger to James' life had passed and that this moment would never come. And yet, the moment had arrived in the form of two, blood soaked strangers.

Platt gestured towards his living room. "Come. Sit."

Kelli and Bling followed him into the large living room that sat adjacent to the kitchen. Much of the plush furniture was sitting, disorganized, in the center of room. They sat on the sofa that was pushed up against a matching love seat.

"Are you moving?" Bling asked.

"Uh, no," Platt answered. "I'd heard the news story the other day about the man in the Bronx who claimed to have seen a girl turn into a boy. At first, I disregarded it as nonsense, tabloid fodder. Then I started thinking about what Dr. Connelly had given me. The documents, the key. Whenever I get nervous, I have trouble sleeping. When I can't sleep, I rearrange my furniture." Platt remained strangely quiet for a moment. Then, he turned to them. "How did you know Dr. Connelly?"

Kelli didn't know how to answer that question without sounding completely crazy. But then again, this entire situation was bizarre. This man knew James. For all Kelli knew, he was accustomed to the unusual, the weird, and the dangerous. Kelli attempted the best answer she could come up with. "He was friends with my father. My father lives in the Bronx."

Platt looked into Kelli's eyes. He interpreted her unspoken message loud and clear.

"Please, Mr. Platt," Kelli began, "people have died because of what I am. If you have information that can put an end to it, I beg of you to give it to me."

Platt nodded. "Yes. Yes, of course." He stood. He took a few steps then stopped and faced Kelli. "You know, there were many times in the last twenty years when I was in conflict with myself over this. I thought, 'this is nonsense, the stuff of children's fantasy.' Then, at other times, I thought,' what if? What if this is for real? I could revive my career, reclaim my credibility', but then I always remember how frightened James Connelly was that night."

"Mr. Platt, please," Kelli implored him.

He nodded. "Yes. Okay." Platt turned and exited the living room. Kelli and Bling could hear him rustling around in one of the rooms on the second floor. Then, after a few more minutes of silence, Platt reappeared. He carried a key in his right hand, and a small safety deposit box in the other. He handed them both to Kelli.

"You kept it here?" Bling asked.

"Not at first," Platt responded defensively. "But after so many years, I grew tired of having to pay to keep it hidden away. About seven years ago, I just brought it here and stuck it in my safe."

Kelli pushed the key into the keyhole. She gave it a quick turn. The top of the box popped open. Kelli lifted the top and peered inside. There, she found a stack of documents, a vial filled with an ounce of fluid, a vial with a strand of hair inside, several small cassette tapes, a pad of paper with what appeared to be dried blood on it, and an envelope. Kelli lifted the stack of documents and began sifting through them.

"Is that it?" Bling asked after a moment.

Kelli nodded. "It's all of James' and Marcus June's research—formulas, procedures, dates of experiments, the location." She looked up at Platt. "What's Rocketdyne?"

"It's an old nuclear test site on the northeast side of Simi Valley, not too far from here. They used to build rocket engines for NASA and the Defense Department up there. Most of that facility was torn down due to the effects of a meltdown back in 1959."

Kelli nodded at Bling. "This is everything we need as leverage against the Agency. These tapes, they have dates written on them."

"What do you think is on them?" Bling inquired.

"I would guess that they're recordings of the actual experiments."

"The FBI couldn't sweep that type of evidence under the rug, could they?" Bling asked. "I mean, can the government keep ignoring this stuff?"

Kelli looked at him. "Let's hope not." Kelli pulled out the notepad with the dried blood on it. She showed it to Platt. "Any idea what this is?"

"Looks like a set of fingerprints," Platt answered. "Dr. Connelly brought that to me about a month after he gave me the other stuff. He said that he found it in Dr. June's car the night he died. He claimed it was more evidence of *their* existence. I still wasn't sure if I believed him. I just tossed it in with the other things."

Kelli placed the pad back into the box. She opened up the envelope to reveal five photographs. The first two photos were of people Kelli recognized. James was in one photo, Dr. June was in the next. A beautiful black woman was standing next to Marcus June. Kelli turned the photo over. There was writing on the back. It read: 'Marcus and Serena'. Kelli assumed it was June's wife.

The next photo held an image of Harmony June. She was standing between Dr. June and Dr. Connelly. Harmony's arms were wrapped around Marcus June's waist and a big smile graced her face. There was also a Caucasian woman in the photograph with whom Kelli was unfamiliar. The writing identified her as Dr. Amanda Simons.

The next photograph was one of Christopher June. The inscription on the back placed him at nine months of age at the time the picture was taken.

The final photograph was of a man Kelli didn't recognize. He was a tall, lean Caucasian man. He was wearing a robe, the kind worn by judges. Kelli turned the photo over and read the name silently to herself.

"Now that I've trusted you with this information," Platt said. "I was wondering if you could do something for me." Kelli nodded. Platt swallowed hard. "Can I see it—the 'shifting'—will you do it for me?"

Kelli had grown more comfortable being in her male form. It made her feel strong, and relevant. However, the thought of transforming on cue made her uneasy, as if she was an attraction at a carnival or circus. Still, Jeremy Platt gave them the information they were seeking. She knew what a risk it was for him to have held on to it all these years. The least she could do was satisfy his curiosity.

"Okay," Kelli agreed. Just as she did, all the lights in the house went out.

Everyone was startled. Bling cocked his gun in the darkness. "What the hell?" he said aloud.

"They found us," Kelli whispered.

"What?" Platt asked in alarm. "Who's found you?"

"No time," Kelli said to him. "We've got to go. We've put you in danger." Kelli closed the box and pulled out the key. She stepped closer to Platt. "Is there another way out of here?"

"There's a ladder upstairs in the closet that leads to the roof," he answered her. "You can jump to the next building and hide there."

Bling nodded to Kelli. "Good enough for now," he said. "Lead the way."

Platt exited the living room. Bling and Kelli dogged his heels. Platt reached the stairs and ascended rapidly. At the top of the stairs, Platt turned to them. "At the end of the hallway there is a closet. Open the door. You'll see a string attached to the ceiling that will pull the stairs down."

The floor behind Platt creaked loudly as if weight had just been applied to the wooden floor boards. Platt turned around. A figure shadowed in darkness stood a few feet away from him. There was a gunshot accompanied by a quick spark of light. Platt's body recoiled. Blood splattered onto Bling's face. Jeremy Platt dropped to the floor.

"No," Bling yelled. He raised his weapon and began firing into the darkness. One shot, two shots, three shots, click. Bling cursed. The clip was empty.

Kelli's eyes widened. Chuckling was heard as footsteps moved closer. The intruder stepped into a stream of moonlight that managed to dance its way through the skylight. It was Gillis. He grinned smugly. Bling mustered every bit of energy he had and charged Gillis at full speed.

Gillis braced himself against Bling's physical attack. The impact of Bling's body moved Gillis back a few inches, but it didn't produce the result that Bling had desired. Gillis struggled with Bling in the hallway. Gillis threw a knee into Bling's stomach. Bling's grip on Gillis weakened. Kelli watched as Bling lost control. Immediately, Kelli lunged at Gillis, as well. Gillis swung with his free hand and caught Kelli squarely in the jaw. Kelli fell against the wall and slid to the floor.

Bling regained his footing. He pulled away from Gillis and swung his fist at Gillis' face. Gillis ducked the punch and retaliated in kind. Gillis' fist struck Bling in the right eye. Bling stumbled back and tripped over Kelli as she tried to stand. Gillis aimed his weapon at Bling. Kelli sprang at Gillis and knocked him off balance. The gun discharged and sent a bullet screaming past Bling's head into the floor. Gillis grabbed Kelli by the hair and yanked her to one side. He drew back his fist and punched her squarely in the nose. Kelli collapsed in front of him. Gillis turned to face Bling. Bling was already on him.

Bling thrust his weight into Gillis' body. Gillis back-pedaled slightly. He raised the butt of his weapon and slammed Bling in the center of his back. Bling crumbled to his knees. Gillis pointed his gun at Bling's head and pulled the trigger. Click!

"Damn!" Gillis exclaimed.

Bling looked up as Gillis smacked him with the barrel of the gun. Bling fell against the wall next to Kelli. Gillis pulled Bling to his feet. He launched an uppercut into Bling's torso. Bling tried unsuccessfully to defend him-self. Gillis pulled Bling to his feet once more. He punched Bling across the face. Bling backpedaled towards the top of the stairs. Gillis stayed with him. He launched a left hook that sent Bling careening into the banister. Gillis holstered his empty gun quickly. He grabbed Bling by the seat of his pants with one hand, and by the back of his shirt with the other. In one swift and powerful motion, Gillis hurled Bling at the banister. The banister broke apart and gave way to Bling's weight. Bling crashed through the banister, sailed through the air and fell into the darkness on the first floor.

Gillis listened for a moment. He heard nothing. There was no noise to indicate that Bling had survived the fall. 'Good,' Gillis thought. 'Annoying little bastard.' He turned and peered into the darkness down the hall. The moonlight that poured in from above allowed Gillis to see Kelli, now shifted into her male form, as she pulled herself to her feet.

Gillis reached into his pocket. He pulled out a taser gun. "Use this on the boy with the long hair," Amanda had said before he entered Platt's residence. "Once he's down, use the tranquilizer." Gillis didn't quite understand then, and he didn't really understand now. The only thing he understood was that he needed to take the boy down and fast.

Kelli sprinted towards Gillis. Gillis had barely enough time to point the taser gun and pull the trigger. Two dart-shaped electrodes, attached to a thin wire, erupted from the device and struck Kelli in the chest. Kelli lost control of her legs and fell to the floor in front of Gillis. Her body convulsed as low level currents of electricity surged through her body. With his free hand, Gillis pulled a tranquilizer gun from his other jacket pocket. He aimed the gun at Kelli's back and fired. The dart penetrated Kelli's skin, releasing the sedative into her bloodstream.

Gillis kept the electrical current flowing for a few moments longer. Then, he released the lever of the taser. Kelli's body ceased convulsing. Gillis knelt down next to Kelli's motionless form. He turned her over. Kelli was unconscious.

A light, gasping sound caught Gillis' attention. His head whipped around. It was Platt. Gillis looked closer. He could see that Platt's eyes were opened. "Still alive, I see," Gillis whispered.

Platt was mumbling to himself at a level that was barely audible. "I saw it. It's true—truly remarkable—I. . . I saw it."

Gillis stood. He pulled out his weapon and stepped in front of Platt. Gillis pulled a full clip from his holster. He ejected the old cartridge and inserted the new. He pointed the gun at Platt's chest and pumped two shots into him.

Gillis stood in the darkness. He listened carefully. Not a sound. Complete silence. He smiled.

Gillis retrieved the safe-deposit box from the steps. He hoisted Kelli's unconscious frame over his shoulder. 'Funny,' he thought. 'I expected him to be heavier.' Under the veil of darkness, Gillis hadn't noticed that the body he was now carrying was that of a female. Gillis slipped through the back door and stepped out in the moonlit night. Within moments, Kelli was stuffed into the back of the truck alongside West, and driven away.

11

Pain surged through his battered body. His head throbbed, his stomach ached and his groin was numb. Still, Bling couldn't complain. In fact, he was grateful that Jeremy Platt decided to rearrange his furniture this evening. If he hadn't, the sofa might not have been in the perfect position to break Bling's fall after he was thrown from the stairwell above.

Bling managed to pull himself up into a seated position. He touched his face and winced in pain. His face was swollen, and he felt warm blood trickling out of cuts and bruises along his cheeks, his lips and nose. Bling squinted in the darkness. Though he wasn't completely coherent at the time, he was certain that he had heard two gunshots. Bling trembled at the thought. He was afraid to walk up the stairs. He didn't want to face the fact that Kelli was dead. Not now. Not after everything that they had experienced over the last few days. No. Bling wasn't sure if he could handle it.

He pulled himself from the couch. He held his stomach as he limped across the living room. The base of the stairs was in front of him. Bling tried to resist the urge to climb the stairs, but he couldn't. If Kelli was lying dead up there, he had to know.

He lumbered up the stairs slowly. At the top, he saw a body slumped against what was left of the banister. Bling moved closer. He realized that it was Jeremy Platt. Seeing Platt lying there instead of Kelli didn't make him feel any better. Being a kid who spent much of his time running with the local street thugs, Bling thought he'd be better at handling death. He was quickly learning otherwise.

Bling turned and moved slowly down the hallway. He crossed into the beams of moonlight that fell into the corridor. Again, he squinted into the darkness, trying to make out any shapes he could. Nothing. He looked at the floor. No blood. He continued to the end of the hallway. Still nothing. Finally, Bling came to the only conclusion that made sense. Kelli was gone. Gillis had taken her away.

Bling panicked. He ran down the hallway and headed straight for the front door. His street sense kicked in and he became very cautious not to touch anything. He wrapped his hand in the bottom of his shirt and opened the front door. He slipped out into the night air and took a quick moment to compose himself. He looked out into the street. The white BMW was still there. Bling walked quickly to the car. He opened the door and jumped into the driver's seat. He paused as he collected his thoughts. 'Kelli's gone, West is gone. I don't know where Nicholas ran off to—I don't know where Kelli is . . . they're gonna kill her—if only I knew where they took her.' Bling shoved those thoughts out of his mind. He switched into survival mode and decided his first order of business was to put some distance between himself and Jeremy Platt's townhouse. Bling reached under the steering column, reconnected the ignition wires and started the engine. He put the car in gear and drove towards the security gate.

Bling slowed the car as it neared the gate. The sensors detected his car and the chain that operated the gate activated automatically. Bling was still breathing heavily as he waited impatiently for the gate to open. He glanced into the rear view mirror and inspected his battered face. It wasn't pretty. Blood dripped from his nose. There was a large gash on his cheek from where Gillis had slapped him with the gun barrel. The other cheek was swollen and badly bruised. Black and blue discoloration was already setting in around his left eye. Oh, yes. Bling had definitely looked better.

Bling's eyes dropped slightly and focused on a series of buttons that ran horizontally along the bottom of the mirror. Bling had been inside plenty of top-of-the-line vehicles in his travels, and knew exactly what purpose each button served. His eyes settled on the blue button labeled 'On'. The small 'On' was encased in a circle and a little star sat on top of the letter 'n'. Bling pressed the button. The car speakers emitted the sound of a ringing phone.

The gate was completely opened. Bling pressed the accelerator and cruised out onto the street beyond the gated community.

The phone line clicked open. A pleasant, female voice came through the speakers. "OnStar Services. This is Angela, Operator 555. How may I help you, Mr.Woods?"

"I need directions," he blurted out.

"I can help you with that," Angela said politely. "What is your destination?"

Bling's initial instinct was to ask for directions to the airport. He wanted to get back to New York and as far away from Los Angeles as quickly as he could. Then, an upsetting realization hit him. No money. There was no way he'd be able to purchase an airline ticket with no money. His bruised up face and blood-soaked garments would definitely result in a visit from the LAPD. That was attention Bling didn't need. He opened his mouth. Bling, himself, was surprised at the word that fell out. "Rocketdyne."

❧❦

The first sense that returned was that of sound. Strange, indiscernible noises that had no origin, no destination, or no logic, seeped into her brain, arousing her from the catatonic-like state into which she had been cast. The sounds morphed into frequencies and decibels, then, finally, into comprehensible language with syntax and meaning. The sense of smell returned next. An old, dingy odor, much like one found in the locker room at school, overwhelmed her. Her tactile senses alerted her to the fact that her wrists and ankles were restrained. Her returning sense of taste told her that blood was the last thing to have graced her tongue. Finally, her sight came into focus, allowing her to take in what appeared to be a laboratory. Kelli recognized the markings on the walls from the pictures in the safe-deposit box. It only took a moment for Kelli to realize that this was the same laboratory used by Dr. Connelly and Dr. June when they developed the Harmony Project. Kelli's journey had come full circle. The clone of Harmony June had come home.

Kelli's attention was drawn to the voices in the room. The operative from the panic room was there. He was sitting at a table. A woman, whose back was turned to Kelli, was sitting in front of him. 'What is she doing?' Kelli wondered. Kelli tilted her head slightly in an attempt to get a better view. The woman was applying a bandage to the man's wrist where Nicholas had shot him earlier.

"That's all I can do for you here," the woman said. "I've already made a call. They're sending someone to tend to you."

The man nodded. A coughing sound to Kelli's right drew her attention again. She turned. There, hanging from a chain that was suspended from the ceiling, was West. Both of his arms were handcuffed to the chain and his body dangled helplessly in the air. Kelli gasped loudly. The woman at the table turned around in response. She rose and approached Kelli.

"Good morning, Miss Freeman," she said to her. "I didn't expect you awake so soon."

As the woman moved closer, Kelli began to recognize her. 'No,' Kelli thought to herself. 'It can't be. She's dead.' Then, Kelli came to her senses. If there was one thing she had learned over the past few days, it was that things that were, at one time, impossible, were now, very possible.

"You're Dr. Simons," Kelli said to her. "How are you alive?"

"It seems that James might have gotten his story a little confused over the years," Amanda said smugly. "He had that same confused look on his face when I saw him earlier this evening."

A flash of memory struck Kelli. She remembered standing in the panic room looking at the image of Gillis and a woman on the monitors. That woman was Amanda Simons. "Why were you there?" Kelli asked and then paused before answering her own question. "You killed him."

Amanda nodded. "Guilty."

Tears welled up in Kelli's eyes.

"Don't cry for him," Amanda said. "He's the one who got you into this mess. If James had just crawled under a rock and disappeared like he was supposed to, you wouldn't even be here. You wouldn't even be alive."

Kelli looked over at West. His face was battered and bloodied. "What did you do to him?" Kelli asked.

"Agent Lind was interrogating him," Amanda said. "We needed to find out if he's told anyone else about the Agency. We can't have any loose ends."

"He hasn't told anyone," Kelli said in West's defense.

Amanda released a short, nasty, little giggle. "That's what he said, even after we tortured him. But just to make sure he's telling the truth, we're going to let him watch us torture *you*."

Kelli's heart threatened to jump through her chest. She tugged at her restraints forcefully. The bindings on her wrists did not give in.

Amanda smirked. She turned and picked up a long needle that was attached to an empty syringe. She walked towards Kelli. "But first, I need a blood sample."

"What are you doing?" Kelli said fearfully.

"Completing my work," Amanda replied. "Normally I would clean and sterilize the area, you know, for bacteria and contamination, but–," she stuck the needle into Kelli's neck. "-you don't need it." Amanda pulled on the other end of the syringe, extracting a sample of Kelli's blood. When she had the amount she wanted, she pulled the needle out. "I'm going to get things ready." She winked at Kelli. "Be right back. Oh, and don't bother trying to shift into the stronger version of yourself. While you were unconscious, I injected you with a hormonal blocker. It'll wear off eventually, but for now, you're stuck as you are." Amanda turned and walked across the lab and began preparing her instruments for Kelli's forthcoming interrogation.

Kelli turned to West. He didn't look good, but he was alive, at least.

"West," she called to him, trying to remain as quiet as possible. "West."

West lifted his head. He looked at Kelli through a bruised eye that had almost swollen shut. "I'm sorry, Kelli," he said. "I thought I could protect you. I let you down."

"No, you didn't," Kelli assured him. "You're the only person who's had my back from the beginning."

Though he was suspended in the air, West managed to shrug. He was in bad shape and Kelli knew it. She decided to keep him talking. Perhaps they could find a way out of this predicament.

"How did they find us?" Kelli asked.

West shook his head. "My fault," he answered. "I should have checked my coat when I was in the police station in the Bronx—my partner brought me my coat—tracking device—I should have checked the pocket."

"They were tracking us the whole time," Kelli surmised.

"Not while we were in the air," West said, "but once we landed, all they needed was to zero in."

"She told you all this?" Kelli said.

"No," West answered and gestured towards Lind with his chin. "He did. He said we were never supposed to make it out of the Bronx. When Gillis ambushed us at the stop sign, we were supposed to die then. The Agency had arranged for Markham's release so they could pin your murder on him."

"But Nicholas interfered," Kelli deduced. West nodded.

"What happened to them?" West asked.

"Nicholas took Blanca and the kids somewhere safe, and Bling—" Kelli paused as she struggled to say the words. "Bling's dead. Gillis killed him."

"Dammit!" West cursed.

"Where is Gillis?" Kelli asked.

"Outside, standing guard, probably," West guessed.

Kelli sobbed as she thought about Bling. Though they were at odds the whole time, she realized that Bling had her back, as well. She looked at West. "We need to figure a way out of here."

West managed a smile. "I'm all ears, Genius."

❧

Towers sat quietly behind the wheel of his rental. It had been almost an hour since he watched as West and the Freeman girl were carried into the building that towered in the distance before him. He could only imagine what was happening to them in there. Towers wanted to do something but he wasn't sure exactly how he should proceed. Towers knew, and understood, that the Agency employed extreme measures and tactics. He had felt completely honored when the Agency approached him so many years ago and asked him to be their eyes and ears in the field. He could still hear the words as if they were spoken yesterday. "We need someone on the ground floor to make sure that we remain invisible," the voice of One had said to him over the phone, "someone to alert us when our intervention is needed, or in danger of being detected. Mind you, not everyone agrees with our methods, but know that we are necessary for the safety of this country. The Agency takes care of its own." Towers had taken those words to heart. So far, the Agency had kept its word. Towers had received numerous commendations from the Bureau for his performance in the field. The outcomes of many of his cases were manipulated by the Agency. Towers loved the United States and he loved working for the Bureau. In his eyes, the Agency had helped him do a better job. He owed them much. Still, he felt bad that his young partner had gotten mixed up in this whole fiasco. It was his hope that he could go in there and save West's life, perhaps get him to see all the good that the Agency had done for this country and the rest of the world. Maybe, just maybe, West would agree and join him in his work with the Agency. It was a long shot, but Towers knew of stronger men than West who had re-evaluated their principles in order to stay alive. Towers hoped that West would see reason. If not, Towers knew he would have to do the unthinkable. Towers didn't want it to come to that.

What he needed now was a plan. He didn't want to just walk in there and end up getting killed. No. His next move required a little finesse. A tap on the driver's window startled Towers. He had been so distracted by his own thoughts that he hadn't seen Gillis approach his car from the rear. He looked up only to be staring down the barrel of Gillis' gun. Towers swallowed hard. Apparently, finesse had just gone out the window.

჻

Kelli continued to tug at her restraints. Despite how strong her genetic engineering had made her, she couldn't generate enough force to break free from the belted, canvas straps that held her down. She knew if she could just shift into her male form, she would have sufficient strength to free herself.

Kelli concentrated. The warm sensation began to flow throughout her body, then ebbed suddenly and subsided. Her heart raced and she began to perspire uncontrollably. Still, Kelli couldn't shift.

Amanda stood only a few feet in front of her. She was preparing several electrical devices to be used in Kelli's interrogation. She looked up as Kelli continued to struggle. She took notice of the sweat and of the accelerated breathing. Amanda regarded her smugly. "If you keep that up, you're going to rupture an artery and kill yourself."

"Isn't that what you're going to do to me anyway?" Kelli snapped ferociously.

"Not me personally," Amanda answered.

Kelli looked over at Lind. The Agency operative waited patiently by the door. He glanced at Kelli and grinned.

"If you're going to kill me, why did you need my blood?" Kelli asked. She was stalling for time, hoping a plan of defense would occur to her before it was too late.

Amanda held a small rubber rod. Protruding from the end of the rod was a small, cylindrical-shaped gathering of metal links. A wire extended from the opposite end of the rubber rod and was attached to a box that resembled a car battery in size and shape. A single red button sat atop the box. Amanda pressed the button. Electrical currents traveled from link to link along the cylindrical-shaped device, cracking and burning the air. Amanda pressed the button again. The electrical current ceased. She turned to Kelli.

"I'm going to complete the super soldier project for the government," Amanda answered.

"You mean for the Agency," Kelli corrected. Amanda smiled but she didn't deny Kelli's claim. Kelli continued,

"I thought the work was already completed," Kelli said. "I'm living proof."

"Precisely why I needed your blood," Amanda offered. "As many times as I tried over the last twenty years to duplicate James and Marcus' work, I couldn't do it. There was always some equation I was missing, some formula I was overlooking. But now, I have this." Amanda pointed to the safe-deposit box. "It contains a complete record of our previous work. Your blood and these documents will ensure that I get it right this time."

"Get it right?" Kelli said as she tugged at her restraints once more.

"Yes," Amanda replied. "We need to create a super soldier without the added ability of gender shifting. Don't get me wrong. I think it's fascinating. But the Agency is enlightened about these things. They recognize the dangers."

Kelli looked directly into Amanda's eyes. If she could not appeal to her sense of mercy, perhaps she could appeal to her sense of humanity. "You're a doctor. Doesn't it bother you that the cure for all diseases is about to be destroyed?"

Amanda paused. She didn't expect those words to come out of the mouth of someone so young. Amanda gave herself a mental check. 'What am I thinking? This girl is potentially the most intelligent person alive. I should never underestimate her mental faculties.' "Of course it bothers me," Amanda answered honestly. "That isn't the Agency's only concern."

Kelli became confused. What other concern could outshine the possibility of eradicating all sickness? "What do you mean?"

Amanda looked at Kelli. She could tell that her question was genuine. "Leave it to James to leave holes in his story," she said as she placed the electrical device on the table. She turned to Kelli. "The dormant gene we discovered, the June gene, it wasn't formed as a result of our genetic tampering. Further research revealed that this gene is a normal part of the human genome."

Kelli flinched. "That's impossible. That would mean everyone on Earth would have the ability to shift genders at will."

Amanda nodded. "If that gene was normally active, yes. Luckily, it isn't. Human evolution had somehow deemed this gene as unnecessary, probably because it would complicate successful procreation of the species."

Kelli shook her head. "I don't understand. If the gene is normally dormant, why is it an issue worth killing over?"

Amanda smiled. "You're a smart young lady, so I'm pretty sure you'll understand what I'm about to tell you." She gestured to West. "You, on the other hand, might get a little lost, so listen carefully." Amanda stepped closer. "Although that gene is dormant in humans, there was some vivid speculation about the influence it may still have on the lifestyles of everyday human beings."

"Lifestyles?"

Amanda took a step back. "Genius or not, maybe this is a little over your head."

"No," Kelli said immediately. "I'm about to die over this. I want to know everything."

Amanda considered Kelli's words. She stepped closer again. "Back in the ancient Roman and Greek times, politicians, heads of state and wealthy landowners would throw lavish, elaborate parties. It was at these parties, once certain people became intoxicated, they would lose their inhibitions and show their hidden penchants for–alternative sexual habits and lifestyles."

"Go on," Kelli urged.

"Through the years, even in Biblical text, these types of desires have been frowned upon," Amanda explained.

"If a man lies with mankind, as he lies with a woman, it is an abomination- Leviticus 20:13," Kelli quoted.

"I'm impressed," Amanda said.

"My parents take us to church every Sunday," Kelli said. "I've managed to read a few scriptures here and there. What does this have to do with me?"

"Keep in mind, none of what I'm about to say has been proven. But it weighed heavily in the Agency's decision to scrap the Harmony Project once Harmony began shifting."

Kelli could tell that Amanda was enjoying this conversation. On some level, it gave Amanda pleasure to be able to reveal things that she's had to keep bottled up for the last twenty-five years. Kelli was going to take full advantage of it. "I'm listening."

"These tendencies towards homosexuality and alternative lifestyles are still relevant issues in today's society. What an uproar it would be if gay-rights activists knew about the June gene. Though dormant, it could still have some influence on why people feel attracted to the same sex, or why some people feel that they were born as the wrong gender. Knowledge of the June gene would give these people a biological leg to stand on. Proven or not, it would be enough to start a major revolution that this country isn't ready for. And let's not forget the debates over same-sex marriage in the last few years. Most states still do not recognize them as legal. The June gene would be a powerful platform on which to base the argument that their lifestyles are natural, biologically driven, and deserving of legal, governmental recognition and acceptance."

"And the Agency gets to decide what the country can and can not handle?" West asked.

Amanda turned to him. "Somebody has to." Amanda moved back to her table and picked up the electrical device. "Enough of your questions. Now, I have some questions of my own." The doctor turned to Lind and nodded to him. Lind crossed the room and circled the table upon which Kelli was laid. He tugged her sweatpants, pulling them down around her hips. Kelli screamed out in horror.

"What are you doing?" she yelled hysterically.

"Leave her alone!" West screamed.

"Relax," Amanda shouted back. "This little device of mine works best with direct skin contact." She turned to Lind. He continued to yank at Kelli's sweatpants until he had pulled them down past her thighs, just above the knee. Amanda retrieved a pair of scissors from the silver tray and began cutting Kelli's shirt open. Kelli struggled relentlessly to free herself. She pulled at her restraints again and again, to no avail. Seconds later, Kelli lay on the table with her shirt pulled to her sides. Her underwear and bra were exposed, as well as a fair amount of flesh.

"Now, Kelli," Amanda began, "who else have you and Agent West told about the Agency and the Harmony Project?"

"We haven't told anyone!" she screamed defiantly.

Amanda exhaled sharply. "We'll see." She turned and pressed the button on the battery box. The electrical current jumped to life.

"No! Don't!" Kelli begged as Amanda brought the device closer. Tears gushed from Kelli's eyes as she watched the hot device get closer.

"Don't you do it!" West yelled at Amanda. "She's just a kid!"

Amanda ignored them both. She placed the sparking metal links against Kelli's right thigh. Kelli screamed in agony as the electricity burned her skin, sending waves of energy throughout her body.

West struggled to pull himself from the chains that held him suspended in the air.

"Kelli!" He called to her. Kelli continued to cry out in excruciating pain. Amanda removed the device. The smell of seared flesh wafted into the air. Kelli cried uncontrollably.

Amanda looked into Kelli's eyes. "I don't like doing this, but we can't afford to have this information get out. It's too dangerous. It could cause anarchy on a national level."

Kelli's temperature was rising. Her brown skin glistened as her entire body became covered in sweat. She screamed at the top of her lungs. Her voice reached an almost glass-shattering decibel. "I haven't told anyone. I swear."

"What about Agent West?"

"I haven't spoken a word to anyone," West screamed.

Amanda paused for a moment. Then, she pressed the button again. The blue sparks of energy danced around the metal linked coils once again. "I'm not sure that I'm convinced," Amanda said. "Let's try this again."

Amanda pressed the device against Kelli's thigh once more. Kelli's scream sent chills up Amanda's spine. Still, Amanda held the device firmly for a second longer.

Kelli jerked violently on the table. She had never experienced this level of pain in her entire life. She cried as never before. She knew things were going to get a lot worse before it was all over.

≈∽≈

Towers and Gillis had walked over one hundred fifty yards. The entrance where they had unloaded West and Kelli Freeman was just ahead. Towers turned to Gillis.

"If you'd just listen to me," he said to him. "I work for the Agency, too. Just call your Designate and confirm. I'm Special Agent Towers. I know that you've heard of me."

Up until this point, Gillis had been completely silent. Gillis did recognize the name, but after his recent failures to kill West and the girl, he wasn't taking any chances now that he had come through and captured them. Gillis kept his weapon trained on Towers. He had relieved Towers of his firearm as soon as he discovered him and extracted him from his vehicle.

"What are you doing here?" Gillis asked stoically. "If you weren't summoned to be here, then your presence will put your life, as well as our lives, in danger."

"I understand that," Towers said to him. "I don't mean to complicate matters. I'm here to help."

"No one asked for your help," Gillis stated bluntly. "You should have remained in Washington, minding your own business."

Towers stopped walking and turned to Gillis. "Listen to me. I'm trying to correct a mistake here. I think I can benefit the Agency and help minimize the loose ends if you'd just let me talk to—"

"Keep moving," Gillis ordered and leveled his weapon at Towers' head. "We'll figure out what to do with you once we get inside." Towers took a step towards the door. Then, his attention was drawn to something in the distance. Gillis followed his gaze and saw a car moving slowly under the shadow of the night. Its headlights were off as it pulled over to avoid cruising into the moonlight.

"What the hell?" Gillis said. He placed the gun against Towers' head. "What's going on?"

Towers threw up his hands in submission. "Hey, whoever that is, they are not with me."

Gillis thought for a moment. "Don't move," he ordered Towers. Gillis reached for the walkie-talkie that was clipped to his belt. He pulled it off and spoke into it. "Hey, it's me. I've got a situation. I need you to come out."

There was radio silence for a brief period. Then, the frequency cleared. A horrendous scream accompanied by shouting came through the speaker, followed by Lind's voice. "Be right there." The speaker went silent.

Towers cringed slightly. The cry he heard was blood curdling. Whoever was screaming, Towers could tell they were in agonizing pain. He hoped that he wasn't already too late to save West. If he was, he knew it was already too late to save himself, as well.

∽∽

Kelli sobbed in agony. Lind had received a call over the walkie-talkie and was leaving the laboratory to tend to a situation outside. Amanda had pulled the electrical device away for a moment. For now, Kelli had a chance to think. While the device was pressed against her body, her muscles contracted involuntarily and she had no control over her movements. Despite the torture, Kelli had come up with a plan. She had not yet grown accustomed to her new ability to shift genders, but she was hoping that she understood it enough for a gamble. She didn't know if it would work, but she had no choice. With Lind leaving the room, the best opportunity to play her hand had presented itself. Kelli had to make it count.

Amanda looked at Kelli. The girl was crying incessantly. Her spirit was long broken. She surmised that if Kelli did have anything to tell, she would have divulged it by now. In truth, she felt bad about inflicting that type of torture on such a young soul. But Amanda Simons knew of what the Agency was capable. The last thing she wanted to do was defy their orders and put herself in their crosshairs. Still, she couldn't bring herself to torture the girl any longer. The only thing to do now was to put her out of her misery. When Lind and Gillis returned, that's exactly what she would have them do.

Amanda placed the electrical device on the tray. She stepped closer to Kelli and leaned over her. "For what it's worth, I am truly sorry."

Kelli felt an uncontainable anger towards Amanda. The torture to which she was just subjected was barbaric and inhumane. Her skin was still hot from the device that sent currents into her body. Kelli was sure that she was scarred for life. She hated Amanda. For the first time since all of this started, she felt that she was capable of taking a life. Still, she managed to look Amanda in the eye. When she did, Kelli saw that Amanda had placed the device on the tray. She knew that Amanda's job was done, and the mercenary's job was about to begin. It was now or never.

"Go screw yourself," Kelli sneered at her and spat in her face. "You think that you've won? You haven't. After we're dead, the Agency will be coming for you."

Amanda wiped her face of Kelli's saliva. She took a deep breath and retained her composure.

"Kelli, stop!" West advised fearfully.

Kelli lifted her head and pushed her voice through the tears. "No, West. She has to know."

"I understand that you're afraid," Amanda said. "I promise I'll make sure that it is quick and painless for both of you."

"You don't get it, do you, Dr. Simons?" Kelli asked, antagonizing her. "I saw the name on the back of the photo."

Amanda took a step closer to her. "What photo? What are you talking about?"

"The photo in the safe-deposit box that was given to me by Jeremy Platt," Kelli said. "It's in the envelope. Look for yourself."

Amanda's eyes widened. 'Surely, this girl was lying. A fully grown man would have found it difficult to withstand that type of torture. How could this young girl—this *super soldier*?' Amanda whipped around and made a beeline for the box that sat on a lab table across the room.

When Amanda was out of earshot, West whispered to her. "Kelli, are you crazy? What are you doing?"

"I think I can get us out of here," she said.

"You think? Kelli, she's going to torture you again. She's going to end up killing you."

"Maybe," Kelli said. She looked across the room. Amanda was rifling through the photos that were inside the envelope, tossing each one aside after another. Then, she stopped. She held a photo in her hand. Amanda stared at it much longer than she had at the others. She had found it. The photo of the robed man, and on the back, his true identity was written. Kelli could tell that Amanda was contemplating the danger of possessing such knowledge. Amanda hesitated. Kelli could see her wheels turning. Finally, Amanda's curiosity got the better of her. She turned the photo over and read the name on the back silently to herself. After a few seconds, she turned and walked towards Kelli.

Amanda was strangely quiet. She stopped in front of her metal tray. She ripped the photo in two. She pulled a lighter from her pocket and set each piece on fire. She turned to Kelli. "Clever girl," Amanda said. "Unfortunately, that secret will die with you."

Kelli's heart began to race. She shook her head. "No," she said, "it won't."

With two long strides, Amanda's face was only inches away from Kelli's. "Who did you tell?"

"Figure it out yourself," Kelli said. "So when the Agency comes knocking at your door, you'll know why."

"Kelli! No!" West yelled to her.

Amanda began to panic. She gripped a piece of Kelli's ripped, blood-stained shirt. "Tell me, dammit!"

Kelli gritted her teeth. "Go to hell!" She spat in Amanda's face again to send the message home. Amanda slapped Kelli across the face with the back of her hand.

Amanda turned and grabbed the rubber rod. She pressed the button on the battery box and the electrical coil links sparked to life once again. "You will tell me what I want to know."

Kelli braced herself as the sparking device was brought near her flesh once again. Amanda pushed the device against Kelli's stomach and pressed hard. Kelli released an agonizing scream.

West began yelling at Amanda. "Stop it. Leave her alone! Please!" Amanda ignored West's plea.

"She's going to tell me what I want to know if we have to do this all night," Amanda yelled.

Kelli continued to cry out in pain. Her body jerked about uncontrollably as the electricity stimulated all of her muscles simultaneously. Amanda held the device against her body longer than she had before. She screamed at Kelli again.

"Tell me!"

"Stop!" West continued to yell at Amanda.

Finally, Amanda pulled the device away from Kelli's body. She screamed at Kelli, "Now talk!"

With the electrical currents gone, Kelli regained control over her movements. She breathed heavily and her body sweated profusely. Her heart raced out of control and she could feel the massive amount of adrenaline that was now coursing through her veins. This time, Kelli knew it was enough. She knew that the amount of adrenaline her body was producing was enough to do what Amanda claimed was impossible just a few moments before. Kelli focused as quickly as she could. The familiar warmth swelled within her body and expanded into her limbs. Her skin tingled. In one instant, Kelli shifted into her male form.

Amanda's eyes widened. She couldn't believe it. 'How on Earth?' she thought. "That's not possible." Though Amanda couldn't explain it, Kelli had somehow managed to overcome the hormonal inhibitor and shift into her male form. 'If she breaks free . . .' Amanda knew she didn't have time to complete that thought. She had to act, and she had to act now. She thrust the electrical device at Kelli once again.

Kelli, now stronger, yanked at her wrist restraints, ripping them from the fabric of the bed that held her. She blocked Amanda's assault with a wrist block. Kelli rotated her wrist and grabbed Amanda's, twisting as hard as she could. Amanda screamed in pain as Kelli applied the wrist lock. Amanda dropped the metal device on the floor. Kelli ripped through her other wrist restraint. She sat up and grabbed Amanda by the back of the head. Forcefully, she shoved Amanda's forehead into the metal frame of her bed. Amanda collapsed to the floor, disoriented.

Kelli loosened the belts that held her feet. She hopped off the table and darted towards West.

"The table," West yelled to her. "The keys are on the table."

Kelli ran across the room to the lab table. She spied a small, silver key and retrieved it quickly. She sprinted across the room towards West and set herself to the task of opening West's handcuffs. Within seconds, West fell to the floor, free of his restraints.

Kelli knelt beside him. "Are you okay?"

"I think so," he answered. "Yeah."

Across the room, Amanda's voice was heard saying, "Get back in here. They've broken free."

Kelli looked in Amanda's direction. Amanda was pulling herself to her feet. In her hand, she held a walkie-talkie. Kelli turned back to West.

"They're coming back in," she said.

West stumbled to his feet. "Just great," he managed to say. "I don't have a gun."

౿౽

Lind exited the building. He was surprised to see that Gillis was not alone in the darkness. He took his time crossing the short distance between the door and where Gillis and the other man stood.

"Who the hell is this?" Lind asked when he moved closer.

"I'm Special Agent Towers," he offered quickly. "I work for the Bureau but I do ground work for the Agency."

"So what are you doing here?" Lind asked. He placed a hand on the butt of his firearm. "Nobody told me you were coming."

Gillis chuckled. "We can figure that out later," he interrupted. He gestured towards the car that sat in the distance. "We've got company."

Lind looked at Towers. "Don't look at me," Towers said quickly. "I have no idea who that is. Look, just call Mr. One. He can verify who I am and my involvement in this whole matter."

"Oh, don't worry," Lind told him smugly. "I'm gonna call." He turned to Gillis. "You took his piece?" Gillis pulled his jacket aside, revealing Towers' appropriated gun that he shoved into the top of his pants. Lind nodded and

then began walking across the distance towards the mysterious vehicle. "Let's check this out."

Suddenly, the speakers on the walkie-talkies came to
life. It was Amanda. "Get back in here. They've broken
free."

"Holy shit!" Gillis exclaimed. Lind pulled out his gun.
"What about him?" Gillis asked, referring to Towers.

"Take him with you. Use him as a shield," Lind said.
He turned and began moving towards the uninvited car
again. "I'll be right back."

Gillis grabbed Towers forcefully by the collar and positioned the FBI agent in front of him. "Let's move. Make
it quick."

Towers stepped at an accelerated pace towards the door.
Gillis stayed on his heels with his weapon drawn. Gillis
had had several run-ins with West over the last few days.
As he rushed into the building, he made a promise to himself that this would be the last.

≈◦≈

Bling drove the car up the long, dark road as it twisted
and curved through the Santa Susana hills. Without the
aid of the OnStar route guidance system, he would have
had very little hope of finding Rocketdyne. The absence
of streetlights, coupled with the abundance of large, bare
rocks and wooded trees, made the area seem more remote
and deserted. Bling cruised up the isolated road no more
than two hundred feet before he decided that he might be
on a wild goose chase. It wasn't until he came to what used

to serve as a gate, or security barrier, that he realized that something might, indeed, be further up the dark street.

Bling continued to steer the car up the road. He ignored several signs that he managed to read in the darkness, signs that warned "Private road, no trespassing," or "For your own safety, no bicyclists or joggers beyond this point." To the right, he passed what appeared to be an old fire station. An old fire engine sat outside the structure, alone and unattended to. Bling pushed on. In the distance, he saw a car parked on the side of the road. Further beyond the car, he spied several large metal constructs that, to Bling, resembled an old oil refinery or some other type of industrial machination. Then, walking out of the shadows, two men appeared. Bling's heart jumped. Luckily, the men were headed in the opposite direction. There was a series of buildings clustered together that sat adjacent to the metal goliaths. Bling could tell that the front building was their destination. Bling pulled the car over, careful to avoid the moonlight and remain in the shadows.

He watched the two men. Bling recognized one of them. It was Gillis. Jackpot! Any thoughts of being on a wild goose chase were instantly washed away. Bling didn't recognize the man with him. He guessed that he was an Agency operative as well, except, this man sported a shoulder sling that held his left arm. 'Wait a minute. Is that the guy from the police station in the Bronx? The one with the cane?' It didn't matter. Though Bling arrived with good intentions, he was smart enough to realize when he was outnumbered and outgunned. The gun he had taken when West was hauled out of the panic room had run of out bullets during his encounter at Platt's townhouse. Bling handed the other gun he had, Nicholas' .38, to Blanca before Nicholas drove off with her and the children. So there Bling sat, without a plan, without a weapon, and suddenly, without time. The two men looked in Bling's direction. He ducked behind the steering wheel. 'There's no way they can see me,' he told himself. He was certain of it. 'It's too dark.' Still, Bling didn't want to take any chances. He'd already had enough confrontations with this group to know that they will not hesitate to kill him.

Bling continued to watch the men. They stopped walking towards the building, and now they stood there, waiting. 'Waiting for what?' Bling wondered. He remained diligent and kept his eyes trained on the men. One minute passed, two minutes. Then, a third man exited the building and joined them. Bling recognized him as the operative from the panic room. This didn't look good. All the bad guys were present with no sign of Kelli or Agent West. Bling contemplated leaving. With no weapon, what good could he do for Kelli or for anyone? Bling watched the three men. Two of them raised their walkie-talkies simultaneously. Then, Gillis and the man with the sling moved towards the building's entrance. The other man, the one from the panic room, headed directly towards Bling.

Bling panicked as the man moved closer and closer by the second. His head ordered him to throw the car in reverse and get out of there as fast as the car would allow. His gut told him to come up with a better plan. Bling surveyed the area. The car was mostly shadowed in darkness. Bling pressed the automatic locking mechanism and unlocked all the doors. Then, he made a fist and punched the overhead light with everything he had. The light fixture cracked, and the bulb shattered. He ducked behind the steering wheel and scurried into the backseat. He risked a quick glance through the front windshield. The man was still over fifty yards away. Bling reached up and opened the back door just wide enough for him to slip out and fall into the darkness beside the car. He peered to his right. The large rocks and the cluster of trees offered dark refuge. The only foreseeable problem about which Bling worried was, 'Can I get to those trees without being seen?' The man drew closer. Sooner or later, the man would be near enough to see him no matter how dark it might be. Bling knew he had to risk it. If he didn't, he was dead.

෪෴

Lind drew nearer to the car. As more of the car was revealed to him, he recognized it. 'That's the Beamer we followed from the fire,' he realized. Lind pointed his weapon at the car. 'Gillis told me the other kid was dead. If he is, then who the hell is in the car?' Lind slowed his pace. He had to be cautious since he didn't know if the driver was armed. He kept his gun trained on the driver's door as he stepped within thirty feet of the car. He saw no one behind the wheel. That meant nothing to Lind. The driver could be hiding in the backseat waiting for Lind to get close enough to ambush him with a blaze of gunfire. 'Maybe I watch too many movies,' Lind thought briefly, 'but maybe, just maybe, I've been doing this long enough not to underestimate my adversaries.'

Lind inched within mere feet of the driver's door. In one swift motion, he sprang to the door and pressed his gun against the window. He peered inside the car. He saw no one. He stepped cautiously to the rear door and looked inside.

Still, he saw no one. Lind opened the rear door of the Beamer. There was no one in the car. Then, something caught his eye. The rear passenger door was slightly ajar. He circled the car quickly. His initial thoughts were confirmed. Whoever was in the car had managed to slip out without being seen. Lind turned and looked towards the growth of trees that sat covered in darkness to his right. Instantly, he knew that was where this person had gone for cover. Lind took a step towards the trees. He turned his attention back towards the building where the laboratory was housed. There, emerging from the darkness, Lind saw the teenage boy from the house in Pasadena. "Damn!" Lind cursed. Somehow this kid slipped by him using the trees and rocks to mask his movements.

Lind bolted after him at full speed. The kid had quite a head start on him. There was no way Lind was going to catch the boy before he reached the building. Lind pulled out his walkie-talkie and screamed into it. "Gillis, we've got another uninvited guest who's about to enter the building! Be advised!" Lind listened for a response as he ran. He heard nothing. "Gillis!" Still no response. "What the hell is going on in there?" Lind picked up his pace. He was still a little tired and weakened from the gunshot he sustained earlier, but he pushed as hard as he could. This was the strangest assignment he'd ever been on. There were just too many unforeseen variables for his liking. Lind decided that, 'One way or another, this ends now!'

᠅

"Grab her!" West yelled to Kelli. Kelli turned and sprinted towards Amanda. The doctor had circled the far lab table and was doing her best to avoid Kelli until Lind and Gillis returned.

"They'll be back in a minute," Amanda warned her. "You'll never make it out of here alive."

Kelli stood on the other side of the table. From where she stood, she could see the entrance to the laboratory. She knew that it wouldn't be long before Gillis and his partner would be bursting through that door. "We should run!" she yelled to West.

West ignored Kelli's words. He was tired of running. It was time to make a last stand. He and Kelli were going to fight their way out of this or die trying. West moved towards the entrance door. He picked up a piece of old metal piping from the floor along the way. He stood off to the side of the door, ready to pounce on the first man who stuck his head inside. He turned to Kelli. "Get ready to take cover."

Kelli bit her bottom lip. She heard rustling on the other side of the entrance door. The moment had come. There was no turning back now. The door opened.

Towers was forced through the doors of the laboratory. Gillis slipped through the doors behind him with his gun pressed into Towers' spine. Gillis looked across the room. There, he saw the Specialist standing on one side of the lab table, and the teenage boy he captured in Woodland Hills poised and ready for action on the other. Gillis shoved Towers hard, causing him to fall to the ground. Towers howled in pain as he landed on his left shoulder, aggravating the gunshot wound he sustained a few days prior in Brooklyn. Gillis swung his weapon in Kelli's direction. Then, a second too late, it dawned on him that West was nowhere to be seen. Gillis looked to his left as West swung the metal pipe and brought it down hard on Gillis' hands. Gillis yelled in painful response as his gun was knocked from his grasp and bounced near Towers. West did not relent. He lunged at Gillis and tackled him to the floor. There the fight began.

Kelli's heart began to beat rapidly. She took a step towards the two struggling men. In that instant, Amanda took advantage of Kelli's lack of attention and ran across the laboratory. She grabbed the safe-deposit box and darted towards the back entrance. Kelli turned and saw Amanda escaping. She was torn. Part of her wanted to remain and assist West, but part of her wanted to catch up to Amanda and make her pay for the heinous and horrendous torture that she put her through. Kelli decided that the information in the deposit box was too important for Amanda to get away with it. Kelli sprinted after her in hot pursuit.

West rolled on top of Gillis. He drew back and punched Gillis in the face. He drew his fist back again. He launched another blow, but this time Gillis blocked his punch and countered with a shot to West's ribs. West, already having been beaten and battered just an hour before, screamed out in pain. Gillis struck him in the ribs again. West grunted. Gillis threw a fist into West's swollen eye. West was momentarily dazed. Gillis pushed West off of him and rolled onto his side. Gillis reached for Towers' gun which he had shoved into his pants. The gun wasn't there. He looked to his far right. The gun rested on the floor. Somehow during his tussle with West, the gun had fallen free.

Gillis looked back at West quickly. West had already initiated another attack. He struck Gillis' face with a right cross. Gillis reeled back. West followed the right cross with an uppercut to Gillis' floating rib cage. Gillis doubled over slightly. West delivered a swift kick to Gillis' abdomen. Unfortunately for West, Gillis caught his leg. Gillis raised his arm and brought his elbow down into West's knee as hard as he could. West yelled out. Gillis grabbed West by the torso and swung the young FBI agent into the wall. West tried to recover but found he could no longer support his weight due to Gillis' brutal assault on his knee. West fell to the floor. Gillis turned and moved for the gun near Towers who continued to writhe in pain. West reached out and grabbed Gillis' ankle. Gillis stumbled clumsily and hit his head on the floor.

West spied the other gun to the right. He pushed off the wall with his good leg and dove for the gun. He landed on top of the weapon, rolled over onto his good knee and came up with the gun. He pointed it in Gillis' direction. Gillis was within an inch of grabbing the other gun. Through blurred vision, West fired a shot. The bullet sailed through the air and missed Gillis' hand by a millimeter. Gillis picked up the weapon with one hand and pulled Towers into the line of fire with the other. Gillis positioned himself behind Towers, using the elder FBI agent as a shield. West leveled his weapon at Gillis.

Gillis smiled. "What are you going to do now? I've got your partner here. Now, maybe you're a good shot when both of your eyes are wide open, but, look at you–you can barely stand."

West's vision had cleared slightly. For the first time since they entered the room, he realized the other man was his partner, Special Agent Towers. "What are you doing here, Jimmy?"

"I came here for you, Donald."

"Why do I find that so hard to believe?" West questioned.

"Aw, look at this. A lover's quarrel," Gillis mocked.

Suddenly, the laboratory door swung open. Bling slipped through the door. He surveyed the situation and cursed, "Oh, shit!"

"Bryan?" West asked in surprise.

"Now we have a party," Gillis said sarcastically.

"This party's about to end," West countered. He kept his eyes and gun trained on Gillis. "Bryan, Kelli went after the doctor. Go help her."

"What doctor?"

"Long story. Go out the back door, and be careful," West advised.

"Got it," Bling moved around West and ran across the lab towards the back door. As he rounded the corner, he shouted back to West, "This time, kill him!" Then, Bling disappeared down the hall.

"Let me tell you what's going to happen," Gillis shouted. "You're going to let me out of here, and maybe then I'll decide not to kill your partner."

"Not what I had planned," West responded sharply.

"Donald," Towers spoke up. "It doesn't have to be this way. We can work this out and we can all walk out of here alive."

"Like I said," West snapped back, "not what I planned."

Gillis' temper flared. "Who cares what you planned? Look at you. You've been lucky up until now, but you're an amateur. No matter what happens, the Agency will get you. It's only a matter of time, Agent West. You're a dead man."

West's palms were sweaty. Just a few days ago, he was in the same position, only then, the perp was Keith Waters, and West could see clearly out of both eyes. Now, his face was battered and his left eye was almost swollen shut. His body was racked with fatigue. At this point, he didn't care about the Agency, or what they may or may not do to him in the future. All Special Agent West cared about right now was putting an end to this ordeal and ridding the world of unscrupulous murderers like Gillis. West inhaled slowly. He didn't want to shoot his partner accidentally, but after all that had transpired because of Towers' betrayal, West was willing to take the risk. He exhaled and squeezed the trigger. A bullet penetrated Gillis' right eye. Gillis' head jerked back and he fell to the ground, pulling Towers down with him. Towers turned and stared at Gillis' lifeless form.

West lowered his weapon. His arms ached and his head throbbed. He killed Gillis. If nothing else, he knew that Bling would be proud. He lowered his head and attempted to catch his breath. It only took a moment for him to realize that he'd just made a fatal mistake. The sound of Towers pulling himself to his feet confirmed it. West looked up at his partner. Towers had retrieved his weapon. It was pointed at West.

"So what now, Jimmy?" West asked.

"That's up to you," Towers answered. "I know you don't believe this, but I came out to save you."

"You set me up," West sneered. "You were supposed to be the one man that I could trust with my life. How could you do it, Jimmy? How could you inform for the Agency knowing the kinds of things that they do?"

"They do a lot of good for this country," Towers responded.

"By killing teenaged girls? Was murdering Francine Rodriguez good for this country, Jimmy?"

Towers narrowed his gaze at West. He could tell that he wasn't getting through to his partner. That bothered Towers. If West wouldn't see reason, then there was only one course of action to follow. West would have to die. Towers decided to give him one last chance. "I won't pretend to understand why that happened, nor have I figured out why the Freeman girl is considered a threat, but, Donald—the Agency, you, me—we all want the same thing. We want to protect the country we love."

West shook his head. "I don't know, Jimmy. Their methods, their tactics—"

"The same methods and tactics are used when they're dealing with a terrorist cell or any other threat to the security of the United States of America. These are the same people that protect us even when we don't know we need protection. I can talk to my contact, Donald. You're a good agent. I know I can get you in. Don't throw away an opportunity to do something really worthwhile for your country."

West stood silently. He tried to pretend that he was contemplating Towers' words, that he was considering his offer. But he couldn't. He couldn't bear to look at his partner. He was a man who had sold his soul to the devil, and now he wanted to drag West along for the ride. "I can't do it. Whatever good these people might do for our country, it can't possibly justify what has happened over the last few days. I'm sorry, Jimmy."

Towers choked back a surge of emotion. It pained him to hear West say those words, but it hurt him even more to do what he had to do next. "I'm sorry, too, Donald." Towers raised his weapon, pointed it at West's head, and squeezed off one shot.

The noise echoed throughout the entire laboratory. West's head spun around, jerking his body into the air before collapsing onto the floor in a twisted heap.

The door to the lab opened again. Lind entered the laboratory. He spied Gillis' dead body on the floor. He looked to his left and saw West lying there. A small puddle of blood collected under his head. Lind turned to Towers.

"He wouldn't see reason," Towers said sadly. "He didn't understand what the Agency is trying to do. I . . . I had to do it."

"I understand," Lind responded flatly. Then, he raised his weapon and put a bullet through Towers' neck. Towers slumped over onto Gillis' body. Lind scanned the laboratory quickly. He noticed that the Specialist, the girl and kid from the Beamer were still unaccounted for. Lind stepped over Towers' body. He walked across the lab and headed for the back entrance. There were only two more loose ends to tie up, and Lind was the man for the job.

12

Amanda arrived at her car. She reached into her lab coat and pulled out her keys. She knew she had to get out of there and fast. Things had not gone as planned. Kelli, the shifter, had somehow broken free of her restraints and was now pursuing her. Amanda decided the best course of action would be to take the safe-deposit box and leave while she still could.

Amanda pressed the lock button. The sound of the levers sliding to one side told her that the doors to her Jaguar were unlocked. Amanda opened the door and slid in behind the steering wheel. Just as she did, Kelli appeared out of nowhere.

Kelli grabbed Amanda by the left arm and pulled her forcefully from the car with ease. Amanda sailed through the air and landed fifteen feet from her car. Kelli turned and approached. Amanda pulled herself to her knees. There was one overhead streetlight on that side of the lab building. Amanda could see Kelli's rage as the male form approached. Amanda reached into her lab coat again. This time, she produced a .22 caliber handgun. She raised the weapon. Kelli didn't flinch. Instead, Kelli slapped the pistol out of Amanda's hand. The gun disappeared into the shadows.

Kelli seized Amanda. She wrapped her hands around the doctor's neck and began to squeeze. Kelli's mind traveled back to the torture in the laboratory. Her skin was burned and her body was still in pain. Uncontrollable images of the last few days flashed through Kelli's mind as she tightened her grip around Amanda's neck, cutting off her airway. Kelli saw James Connelly, the one responsible for creating her; she saw the Agency operatives who had been trying to kill her; finally, she saw her parents, Arthur and Diane, who kept the true nature of her origin a secret her entire life. Kelli felt used, betrayed and discarded. She was full of fury and hatred to such an extreme that she was surprised that she was capable of it.

Amanda's face turned red, and her eyes began to water. She struggled to push the trapped air out of her lungs to no avail. Amanda attempted to pull Kelli's hands away from her neck. Kelli was too strong. Amanda surmised that Kelli would be too strong for her to fight off even if she were in her female form. She, James and Marcus had done an exemplary job in creating the super soldier. Amanda knew it would be merely seconds before she lost consciousness, and then her life.

Kelli heard footsteps approach. She looked up. Bling bounded into view.

"Bryan?" she called out in disbelief. Suddenly, Kelli snapped back to reality. She looked down at Amanda. Though she wanted to squeeze the life out of the doctor, something inside of her begged her to stop. Kelli knew of what this woman was capable. She couldn't allow this woman to live and hurt another human being. Still, Kelli knew better. Arthur, her father, had taught her better. Being a New York City police officer, Arthur had come across many bad seeds in his time. Regardless of what his personal feelings might have been, Arthur had told Kelli that he was on the streets to serve the greater good, to draw the line between those who do wrong and those who do right. Kelli heard those words echo in her head.

Amanda's eyes rolled back in her head as she slipped into unconsciousness. Kelli released the woman and let her fall face first onto the pavement. Kelli looked up at Bling once again. Overjoyed to see that he was alive, Kelli ran to Bling and threw her arms around him.

"Oh, God! I thought you were dead," she said.

"Naw, girl. The couch broke my fall," he responded.

Kelli hugged him tighter. "Thank Goodness."

Bling stood motionless as Kelli embraced him. Though he knew that Kelli was a girl on the inside, he was, none-theless, 'creeped out' by her show of affection while in her male form. "Uh, Kelli. This is freakin' me out—you know—the whole guy thing."

Kelli released Bling and took a step back. She real-ized how strange Bling must feel. Despite the fact that he'd been there as she learned of her true origin, she didn't want to thrust her situation on anyone who wasn't ready to handle it. Kelli had made that mistake with Francine and it ended up costing Francine her life. "Sorry—uh—man," Kelli said.

"No problem," Bling shrugged.

Kelli looked past Bling and into the darkness. For a brief instant, she thought she saw someone approaching. Suddenly, Lind stepped into the moonlight. Kelli's eyes widened and her heartbeat increased. "Oh, God!" She exclaimed. Kelli grabbed Bling by the wrist. "Run!" She turned and ran, pulling Bling alongside of her.

As they ran, Bling glanced back. He saw Lind raise his weapon and point it in their direction. Bling threw his weight at Kelli, forcing her to stumble and stagger clum-sily. They ran in between Amanda's Jaguar and the black SUV.

Lind fired two shots. The bullets shot past them and smashed into the black truck. Lind ran after them at full speed. They had quite a jump on him, but he was familiar with the area. It would only be a matter of time before he cornered them and ended the pursuit.

Kelli and Bling made it to the corner of the building and rounded it without looking back. Kelli dashed several strides ahead of Bling before she slowed and turned to him. "Where do we go?" She asked, trying to catch her breath.

Bling looked around quickly. The area surrounding this side of the building was well lit. He knew that they couldn't stay out in the open or they would be sitting ducks. He gestured ahead. They sprinted around the building and headed for the large iron behemoths that Bling had passed earlier. "In there," Bling said.

The large, towering metal constructs stretched endlessly into the night sky. The lighting was minimal, and the path beneath their feet was difficult to see. Bling stopped and ducked behind a large piping system that extended out from the ground. Kelli crouched down and took cover by his side.

"Do you see him?" Kelli asked.

"I can't see much of anything," Bling confessed.

"Where's West?" she wondered aloud.

"I saw him inside. He's the one who told me to find you," Bling explained. "He seemed to have a handle on things."

"So what do we do?"

Bling thought for a minute. In all his years of running the streets and being a self-proclaimed thug, he never once developed a strategy if, by chance, he should become the prey. None of his fantasies about gangster life presented him as being the one without a gun. Unfortunately, life rarely imitated fantasy. In life, you can't always choose to be the one with the advantage. Still, Bling felt he had enough street smarts to figure out almost anything. Now, his street acumen was being put to the test.

He turned to Kelli. "We need to split up."

"What!?" Kelli exclaimed. That wasn't what she had in mind.

"Listen to me," Bling whispered as he grabbed her by the shoulders. "It's you he's really after. Me? I'm expendable."

"No, you're not, Bryan, you—"

"Kelli, listen," he interrupted. "I'm gonna draw his fire. You got to get to a car and get outta here."

"What? I can't hotwire a car. How am I supposed to start it?"

Bling thought quickly. "What about that Jag back there? The door was opened when I ran up. Where are the keys?"

Kelli frowned. "The doctor has them."

"You've got to get back there. I'm gonna—"

"No, Bryan. I can't do this without you. I know what I said to you back at the house, but I didn't mean it."

"That's not important," Bling countered. "I'm just an ordinary kid, but you, you're—"

"No more important than you are," Kelli retorted. "You've saved my neck a couple times already. Don't give up on me now. Don't give up on yourself."

Bling looked over his shoulder towards the adjacent building. He knew that the operative would be along any minute. There was no time to argue. For once, he felt important. He felt as if he could actually make a difference to someone. He nodded.

"Okay. If we can reach the Beamer—it's down the road—but we have to move fast. There's a lot of open space between us and the car."

"Let's try it," she agreed.

Bling motioned ahead. He stood and started in the direction of the road. As he did, he saw their pursuer moving towards them. Lind raised his weapon. He fired several shots. Bling turned and dove onto Kelli. Bullets sparked as they ricocheted off of the large metal pipes and iron gratings.

Kelli and Bling jumped to their feet and ran back the way they came. Lind turned and ran in the opposite direction in an attempt to cut them off. He circled around the front of the iron giant. He stepped onto the grass and pointed his gun at the open space that lay between him and the building that housed the lab. There, he waited. His finger stroked the trigger in anticipation of the two teenagers sprinting out into the open before him. Still, he waited. They did not appear. Lind took a couple steps forward. He tilted his head and listened carefully. In the distance, he heard their footsteps as they raced quickly across paved ground. "Damn!" Lind cursed. He had underestimated the speed of his prey. They had managed to cross this open space before he could arrive and pick them off. He dashed for the lot behind the laboratory once again.

He approached the corner of the building. He stopped and placed his back to the wall. He hadn't seen a weapon in either of their hands, but he'd underestimated them once. Lind didn't want to make that mistake again. He listened again. He heard a car engine spring to life, followed by a strange sound of clapping metal. Lind peered around the corner. He saw the taillights of the Jaguar flash as the car was shifted into drive. Lind rushed into the open. The car began to move away. Lind stopped and aimed his weapon. He fired several shots into the rear window. The window shattered as the car burned rubber and screeched away. Lind continued to unload his clip at the Jaguar. The car sped out of the lot and continued down the road into the night.

Lind crossed the distance to the SUV. He pulled the door ajar. He was on the verge of stepping inside when he took a second and looked around. The Specialist, whom he had seen lying there unconscious a few moments before, was now gone. Lind holstered his weapon. He turned slowly and walked back to the rear entrance to the lab. It was there that he saw it. Attached to the back of the building was a flight of metal stairs that ascended to the roof of the structure. It was then that Lind knew what had made the strange, metal clapping sound. He grabbed his weapon again and ascended the stairs slowly and quietly.

Lind stepped onto the roof of the building. From there, the northeast side of Simi Valley came into view before him. The lights of the city against the black landscape accentuated the fact that Lind had climbed quite a ways before reaching the top step. He scanned the roof quickly. A small shed sat in the far corner at the edge of the building. A group of boxes were piled up to his right. Lind could see another large, bulky object to his left but even with the aid of the unobstructed moonlight, the darkness prevented him from discerning what it was. His weapon was extended in front of him, raised at eye level. He decided that neither of the teenagers had a weapon. If they had, he surmised they would have returned fire, or at the very least, had it in their hands as they ran. No. They were defenseless. Lind was certain that, at least, one of them was here on the roof. His guess was that it was the strange girl, or boy, that was held captive in the lab earlier. Lind had overheard bits and pieces of the Specialist's conversation with her prisoners. Much of it sounded like scientific mumbo jumbo, nothing in which Lind was especially interested. Still, Lind knew that the initial assignment was to acquire the Freeman girl. Back at the mansion in Pasadena, the girl vanished mysteriously, only to reappear on the lab table after Gillis returned to the truck in Woodland Hills with a teenaged boy. Lind wasn't aware of the details, but he was beginning to understand why the Agency might have taken such an interest in this person. With that in mind, Lind made sure to keep his eyes peeled.

Lind maneuvered himself closer to the pile of boxes. He moved around it slowly. He listened for any movement that would alert him to someone else's presence. He cleared the other side of the boxes and found no one. He walked towards the large object that stood to his left. As he inched closer, a pile of metal pipes of different lengths came into focus. He circled the pile. No one was there. Lind eyed the small shed. He moved to the door of the shed and inspected the padlock and chain that secured it. The lock and chain were still intact, unbothered. Lind stepped to the corner of the shed. He peered around the corner cautiously. He saw no one. Lind turned back to search the other side of the shed. As he did, he heard a faint whistling sound followed by a metal pipe slamming down on his already wounded wrist.

Lind howled in pain. He dropped his gun onto the roof of the building. He turned toward his attacker.

Kelli swung the metal pipe again. This time she aimed for Lind's head. He ducked the assault. The pipe bounced against the shed. Lind launched his body at the strange-looking boy who stood in front of him. Kelli fell onto her back under Lind's weight, releasing the metal pipe. Lind shoved his left hand into Kelli's throat and grabbed firmly. He slammed the back of her head against the roof repeatedly. He tightened his grip on her neck and squeezed with all the strength he had.

Kelli, calling on her ju-jitsu training, raised her legs behind Lind's back and held them at ninety degrees. She threw her legs down forcefully while, simultaneously, arching her back and lifting her buttocks off the ground. Lind, unsuspecting, was bucked off of her. He landed on his butt as Kelli rolled to her knees.

Lind attempted to scrape the ground for dirt. His plan was to throw dirt in Kelli's eyes; therefore, compromising her vision, but there was no dirt to throw. Kelli lunged at Lind. She threw an elbow strike at his jaw. She connected barely, which caused a shift in her balance. Lind countered with a backhanded fist across Kelli's cheek. Kelli fell to the ground.

Lind reached for his gun which rested two feet in front of him. He scooped it up with his left hand and brought the weapon around towards Kelli. Kelli grabbed his forearm and pushed as hard as she could. Lind resisted. He struggled against her strength in an effort to bring the gun in line with her head. Once he did, he could end the fight. Lind found this to be a difficult task. 'This kid is strong,' Lind remarked to himself. He continued to push. The gun began to inch in Kelli's direction. Kelli managed a quick breath as she refocused her strength and kept the gun away from pointing at her skull.

Lind knew he had one chance of defeating his opponent. Unfortunately, it was going to be painful. He raised his right arm into the air. Blood saturated the bandage after the wound was reopened as a result of Kelli's attack. Lind brought his forearm down across Kelli's nose. Kelli's head slammed back against the roof. Her resistance weakened. Lind pushed the gun towards her head another inch, then another. He heard a violent yell break the silence of the night. Lind looked up. Bling, already airborne, had launched himself at Lind. Bling collided with Lind's body. Lind was pushed back forcefully. The impact caused Lind to roll backwards and over the side of the building. Bling slid across the roof's surface and tumbled over the side as well. Kelli jumped to her feet.

"Bryan!" She yelled, her voice cracking the air.

Kelli ran to the edge of the building and peered over the side. There, hanging on for dear life, was Bling.

"Help me!" he pleaded.

Kelli reached down with both arms. She took a firm grasp of Bling's arms and yanked him on to the roof to safety. Bling fell onto the roof next to Kelli. He struggled to catch his breath, as he realized how close he had just come to losing his life.

"You okay?" Kelli asked. Bling said nothing. He nodded his head vigorously. Kelli inched to the edge of the building once again and looked over the side. Lind's crumbled body lay motionless in the grass.

Kelli returned to Bling's side. She allowed herself to relax enough to shift back into her female form. Bling looked over at her.

"I'll never get used to that. You know that, right?"

Kelli smiled in the moonlight. "Tell me about it."

❧

Kelli and Bling entered the rear entrance of the laboratory. Kelli carried the safe-deposit box. They crossed the room and moved towards the front door. Kelli gasped. Gillis' lifeless form was sprawled out on the floor. Blood poured from his missing eye and an exit wound in the back of his head. Another man, whom Kelli didn't recognize, lay next to Gillis. A fountain of blood covered his neck. Kelli looked to her far right. There, on the ground, lay West.

"No!" Kelli ran to West and knelt by his side. She placed the box on the floor. A small puddle of blood dripped from West's head. "Oh, God! No." She looked up at Bling. "I thought you said he was okay."

Bling was confused. "He was. Maybe our roof diver shot him," Bling said. He knelt down on the other side of West. Kelli hung her head and began to cry. Bling looked at West. West's eyes opened. "Kelli. His eyes are open."

"What?" Kelli lifted her head and looked at West. His eyes were, indeed, open. Kelli leaned forward. "Agent West, can you hear me? Are you okay?"

West's expression was blank. His eyes rolled to the side, and he looked at Bling. West brought a hand to the wound on his head. "I've got a headache."

Kelli smiled at him. "How is this possible?"

Bling repositioned himself behind West and looked at the wound. He placed a hand on Kelli's shoulder. "It looks like he was only grazed. I think he's going to be okay."

West looked up at Kelli. "The doctor, did you get her?"

Kelli nodded. "Yeah. We tossed her in the trunk of her Jag out back."

The door to the laboratory flew open. Several men and women brandishing firearms charged into the room. Printed in bold white letters across their vests were three letters: FBI.

They pointed their weapons at Kelli and Bling. "Don't move. Hands in the air!" one agent ordered.

Blings hands went up. Still, after all that had transpired, he couldn't resist asking, "Are you the real FBI?"

"Of course we are, kid," the agent responded.

West tried to lift his head. Kelli held him down gently. "Don't move. I think everything's going to be okay. It's over." She turned to the agent. "This man's an FBI agent. He needs help."

The agent turned and began barking orders to the other agents in the room. Several of them swarmed around the two dead bodies that lay near.

Kelli put her hands in the air. She turned to Bling. "I don't believe it. We did it."

Bling nodded. One of the FBI agents grabbed Bling by the arms and helped him to his feet. Another pulled Kelli upright. She could hear them commenting on their appearance.

"You still need an English tutor?" she joked.

"Told you, I got that covered," he said as they were led outside. Kelli and Bling were helped into the back seat of a dark-colored SUV. Bling and Kelli exchanged a quick, worried look. A male agent slid into the front seat and turned to them.

"Miss Freeman. Mr. Ling. I'm Special Agent Landau. We're from the Los Angeles Field Office. We've been in contact with our office in New York in an effort to track you and make sure that you're brought back safely."

Bling sneered, "Well you guys sure took your sweet time."

Kelli leaned forward. "Is Agent West going to be okay?"

Landau smiled. "We're going to take good care of him."

Kelli nodded. She hoped Bling's assessment of West's wound was an accurate one. It was amazing to her that the three of them made it through the ordeal alive. With that in mind, she turned to Bling. "I really couldn't have gotten through this without you."

"You saved my ass in the end," Bling said, grinning modestly.

Kelli shook her head. "Only after you saved mine, more than once, in fact. You didn't have to intervene in the park, but you did. You've had my back ever since. I can't thank you enough."

Bling looked at Kelli. A serious look crossed his face. "Actually, you can." Bling leaned closer and spoke to Kelli quietly. The FBI agents summoned an ambulance for West as they continued to survey the area and gather information. Almost an hour passed before Kelli and Bling joined West at the hospital for observation. Soon after, the questions began. Agent West requested the presence of Assistant Director Marsh from the D.C. office. He arrived early the next day.

Kelli didn't know what to expect from her life from this point forward. One thing she knew for certain. Her life had been affected forever. When you're carrying an earth-shattering secret, nothing could ever be the same.

13

FBI Field Office,
Washington, D.C.

Two months had passed. Special Agent West walked into
Marsh's office. It was his first official day back at work.
In the time since the events took place at the Rocketdyne
laboratory, many things had transpired.

Ballistic evidence tied Gillis to the gun used in the
killing of young Francine Rodriguez. Gillis had also
been posthumously linked to the arson of the home of one
Professor Hiram Woods in Pasadena and the murders of
Franco Pineda of Pasadena and Jeremy Platt of Woodland
Hills. Dr. Amanda Simons was awaiting trial for the kid-
napping and torture of Kelli Freeman, as well as the murder
of Professor Hiram Woods, aka Dr. James Connelly. Lind's
posthumous charges included arson, and the murder of Kelli
Freeman. In the interest of her safety, the Bureau declared
Kelli Freeman officially dead the day after the Rocketdyne
incident. She had since been placed in a Federal Witness
Protection Program. Only West, Assistant Director Marsh,
and Special Agent Monica Davies knew that Kelli was still
alive. Davies had been assigned as Kelli's sole contact while
she remained in witness protection. Marsh felt that allowing West to be her liaison would only serve to blow her
cover. West did not like it, but he agreed that it was best
for Kelli.

West greeted Marsh as he crossed the threshold to the Assistant Director's office. Davies sat in a chair in front of the desk. She nodded to him as he sat next to her.

"Welcome back, Agent West," Marsh greeted him.

"Thank you, sir," West responded.

Davies smiled at him. "It looks like all that time off did you some good." West was placed on medical leave after his close call with death in California. After his medical leave was over, West used his vacation days and took some additional time off. While away, West contemplated his place and purpose at the Bureau. He decided that not everyone had been influenced by the Agency. He knew there were still some honest law enforcement agents and officials who still believed in doing the right thing, no matter what the cost. Although he knew that some of the rules had now changed, West returned to work, ready to continue the fight.

"It's good to be back," West said.

Marsh closed the office door. He crossed to his desk and sat before the two young agents. He picked up three files and handed them to West. West opened the file on top. It was the file of Lt. Colonel Samuel Edwards, better known as Agent Raymond Gillis. Lt. Colonel Edwards was an ex-marine who had been declared dead more than twenty years prior. West looked up at Marsh in surprise.

"Is this for real?" West asked.

Marsh nodded. "It seems that the military's National Personnel Records Center out of Missouri fixed an information glitch they've been having the last few months. All of a sudden Gillis' old military record appeared out of the blue. Finch's and Lind's files are there, too."

"Imagine that," West said sarcastically.

"It would seem that it's easier for the Agency to give them up than to continue keeping their files inaccessible," Davies surmised.

"Two months after the fact?" West questioned skeptically.

"That's probably how long it took the Agency to erase their connection to them," Marsh said. "Officially, the Agency's existence is still in question."

"Well, I know they are out there," West said firmly.

"And so do we," Marsh assured him, "which is probably why they haven't attempted to kill you. If you showed up dead suddenly, it would draw more attention to the question of their existence. Right now, it's still only water-cooler speculation."

"That's just wrong," West stated.

"I agree," Marsh said. "But we can't run out there waving any flags. For now, I need you to keep your eyes open. You can bet the Agency will have their eyes on you."

"Is that why you've assigned me to a desk?" West asked.

"That desk assignment is on paper only, Agent West. Since we're the only three people with confirmed knowledge of the Agency, this will be our private pet project—private being the operative word."

"Understood," Davies nodded.

"So," West began, "the family of Francine Rodriguez and the media are pacified by Gillis being handed over, and the Agency has no reason to pursue Kelli anymore because they think she's dead. Where do we go from here?"

"We continue to do our jobs," Marsh said. "The Agency will rear their ugly head again, and when they do, hopefully, we can drag them out into the open. Just be prepared, both of you. We'll probably be biting off more than we can chew."

West leaned slightly forward in his chair. "Any word on the contents of that safe-deposit box?"

Davies turned to him. "None. One day we had it, the next day the box was empty. No one saw or heard anything."

"I hope the Agency didn't find a way to get to it," West said.

"If they did, there's nothing we can do about it now," Marsh replied. "Until then, we have to return to business as usual." Marsh stood. West and Davies followed suit. Marsh and West shook hands. "Again, welcome back, Agent West."

"Thank you, sir."

West and Davies exited Marsh's office. West went to the small office that he had occupied with Towers, and he sat. He began organizing paperwork. He glanced over at Towers' desk. West still couldn't believe that someone with whom he worked so closely for three years was involved in activities that fell outside the boundaries of ordinary law. West had imagined that there were people masquerading as law-abiding officials; he just couldn't believe he didn't see it coming. His ability to trust had been severely compromised. He chuckled to himself. It didn't matter. West realized that it was, most likely, a good thing. He reached into his pocket and pulled out an airline ticket. West smiled to himself. There was one more thing he had to do.

❧◦❧

Boston, Massachusetts

Twelve days had passed. The huge crowd swarmed the entrance to Fenway Park. West pushed his way through the hoard of excited fans. An ocean of Red Sox caps spread out as far as the eye could see. West wore one, as well. Finally, he managed to find his way to Gate Ten. Kelli stood by the entrance. She wore a pair of overly-baggy jeans, a large blue tank top and an oversized hooded sweatshirt. Atop her head she wore a New York Yankees baseball cap. West gestured to her hat as he greeted her.

"You're a lot braver than I thought," West commented. "Wearing that hat out here is pretty dangerous."

Kelli smiled. "I'll take my chances. Besides, my father would be proud," she said. They hugged.

"How have you been?" West asked.

"You mean since we lived an episode of the X-Files? I can't say it's been easy," she answered honestly. "The family I'm living with is nice. Boston is a great city. I love studying at BU. Summer term just started–I tested in as a sophomore, but . . . I miss my family."

"They miss you, too," West said. "They send their love."

Kelli choked back her emotions as a tear welled up in her eye. She wiped it away immediately. "How long do I have to stay in the program?"

"Until the Agency is publicly exposed and you're no longer in danger," West answered. "I know it's hard, but right now it's necessary. You have to hang in there."

"I know, but my family–"

"Will be safer if they go along with the charade that you're dead," West said. "It's too soon to have any contact with them or anyone else from your old life. When the time is right, I'll make sure it happens. Okay?"

Kelli nodded.

West placed a reassuring hand on her shoulder. "I'm sorry I missed your birthday."

"That's okay. I understand." Kelli said. "It's just that it was the first birthday I've ever spent without my family."

"I know. I'm sorry. Did you get my present?"

"Yes," Kelli replied. "Agent Davies delivered it. My new identity is officially official."

West smiled. "My boss helped to get the paperwork processed quickly."

"Thanks," Kelli said, then grinned coyly. "She's pretty."

West raised an eyebrow.

"Agent Davies," Kelli clarified.

"Oh. Yes, she is, but—no, we're just colleagues."

Kelli laughed. "Maybe to *you*. I think she likes you."

West waved a dismissive hand at her. "No." A slight pause, then, "Why? Did she say something?"

"No," Kelli answered. "But a girl can tell these things."

West had always thought Davies was an attractive woman, but he'd never thought of her in a romantic light. Until now. He laughed nervously. "Whatever you say."

"Any luck finding those documents from the safe-deposit box?"

West shook his head.

"They have them, don't they? The Agency has them."

"We don't know that for sure," West countered. Kelli remained silent and glared at him. "Okay," West conceded. "Probably."

"That's not good," she said.

"It's not your problem anymore, okay? Let us worry about that now."

Kelli shrugged. "Yeah. Okay. How's Bling?" Kelli asked.

"He's good," West answered. "And since when did you start calling him that?"

"Since I had an identity crisis of my own," she answered. "Two months ago I discovered I was the clone of Harmony June. The Agency was trying to kill me because of what I am with no regard for who I am. During that whole ordeal, I struggled to understand it all–am I really Kelli Freeman . . . or just Harmony's clone?"

"I think you know the answer to that," West said.

"I do now," Kelli responded. "But for a minute there, I was fighting to stay alive simply out of innate survival instinct. Then Calliope said something to me that made me realize that, regardless of how I came to be, I had value. Imagine that. A twelve year old girl made me realize who I am." She grinned. "I didn't know it at the time, but Bryan was struggling with his identity, as well. He didn't have a father so he couldn't identify with being a man's son. His mother was in and out of the hospital so, quite often, he was left to his own devices, trying to fit in somewhere, anywhere. I think he felt most comfortable on the streets. Bryan didn't fit in to the street scene, but Bling had a place there. It's where he could identify with himself, where he felt important. And if he's comfortable with being Bling, then, I guess I can respect that."

West nodded. "I guess we all found some new revelation from all of this. Bryan, uh, *Bling* has enrolled in summer school. He's trying to catch up on some of the work he missed this year. He says that he wants to stay on the right path."

"I'm glad to hear it," Kelli said happily. "And what about his mother?"

West smiled. "Alive and well. Nicholas, under the alias of Dr. William Woods, paid Ms. Ling a visit at the hospital. He was able to use the blood sample you gave to Bryan and manufacture a vaccine. Her cancer went in to full remission. The doctors were completely baffled."

"It felt good being able to help," she said. Kelli looked at her watch. A pang of sadness filled her heart. "I've got to go. I came with the family that I'm staying with. They think I'm grabbing a soda."

"I understand," West grinned.

Kelli added, "Are you sure you don't want to stay for the game? It's going to be a good one. The Yankees are going to slaughter the Sox today."

"No, thank you," West declined. "You go have fun."

"Okay," Kelli said. She took a few steps back. "See you around."

West nodded. Then, he took a quick step forward. "Hey. I've got a question."

Kelli stepped forward eagerly. "Yeah?"

"When we were being held prisoner, you told Dr. Simons that you knew the name of the man in a photo, that you read it on the back."

"I remember," Kelli said.

"Was that true? Do you know Mr. One's real name?"

Kelli smiled at him. "No," she lied. "I saw that there was a name on the back but I didn't get a chance to read it."

West wasn't buying it. He knew that Kelli had a photographic memory. Nevertheless, West didn't push the issue. If Kelli didn't want to divulge that information to him, he was certain she had a good reason. "Oh. Okay," he said. "That's good. If you do happen to remember something, don't do anything crazy. Promise?"

Kelli smiled innocently. "Come on, Agent West. I may be a genius, but I'm only fifteen."

"Yeah," West nodded. "Okay. See you around."

Kelli flipped the hood of her sweatshirt on to her head. She turned and walked towards Gate Ten. West could see the slight changes occur in her body; the growth in height and the broadness of her shoulders. Her clothes, which were baggy just a moment before, now fit perfectly.

Kelli turned around. Her male form waved to West. Then, she turned around again and disappeared into the park.

West inhaled deeply. The smell of popcorn and Fenway Franks inundated his senses. He smiled. West hoped that Kelli would find some serenity in her new surroundings. If anyone deserved a normal life with peace and security, it was Kelli Freeman. West turned and walked away.

৵৽৽

Washington, D.C.

Twelve men in suits gathered in a small, secluded office. They sat quietly and waited for Mr. One to start the meeting. Finally, Mr. One spoke.

"As you all know, we allowed access to three of our operatives' files last week," he said. "The media frenzy covering the death of young Miss Rodriguez is over."

"And what of Dr. Simons?" a designate asked.

"Amanda Simons will be standing trial and will, most definitely, be sentenced to several years in prison, if not for life."

"Do you think she's going to talk?" Three asked.

"She's been advised of the consequences," Four answered.

"And we did manage to recover the Harmony Project documents," another designate stated.

"Yes, we did," One said calmly. "With the Freeman girl dead, we can consider our mission accomplished. Another win for America."

The men looked at each other and nodded their approval.

One produced a photo from his pocket. "Moving on," he started. He passed the photo around the room as the other eleven listened to the plan for handling their next dilemma. Once again, it was business as usual for the Agency. Protecting the United States against all threats, at any cost.

Thank you for coming on this writing journey with me. My hope is to build a fun and adventurous relationship with my readers. I will be sending out occasional newsletters with details about new and upcoming releases, any special offers, and other bits of news relating to the Harmony Project Series and future upcoming series.

Sign up to my mailing list and you will receive:

1. A **FREE** copy of "The Enemy Clone", book 2 of The Harmony Project series.

.

To redeem your FREE copy, type the following link into your browser:

https://BookHip.com/TGNASXN

Thanks so much for reading The Harmony Project. I hope you enjoyed the story. If so, I would be grateful if you would please leave a rating and review on the site where you purchased the book. Reviews can make a huge and impactful difference in the quest to reach new readers.

BIBLIOGRAPHY

Books page at http://randyvdanielsauthor.com/books-2/

Universal Book Link (UBL) https://books2read.com/u/bOjxRQ

About Randy V. Daniels

A passionate fan of science fiction, Randy V. Daniels began writing at a young age. His other interests include martial arts, fitness and travel. He has completed the follow up to "The Harmony Project" and is currently working on the next installment of the series, as well as several other literary projects. Daniels has three children and lives with his wife in Simi Valley, California.

Daniels' online home can found at www.randyvdanielsauthor.com

https://www.facebook.com/MenascusBooks/
https://twitter.com/RandyVDaniels
instagram@randyvdanielsauthor